THE WASP EATER

THE WASP EATER

William Lychack

HOUGHTON MIFFLIN COMPANY BOSTON NEW YORK 2004

For information about permission to reproduce selections from
this book, write to Permissions, Houghton Mifflin Company,
215 Park Avenue South, New York, New York 10003.

Visit our Web site: www.houghtonmifflinbooks.com.

Library of Congress Cataloging-in-Publication Data

Lychack, William.
The wasp eater / William Lychack.
p. cm.
ISBN 0-618-30244-1
1. Boys—Fiction.   2. New England—Fiction.
3. Fathers and sons—Fiction.   4. Loss (Psychology)—Fiction.
5. Separated people—Fiction.   6. Adultery—Fiction.   I. Title.

PS3612.Y34W37 2004
813'.6—dc22   2004042728

Book design by Anne Chalmers
Typefaces: Janson Text and Trade Gothic Condensed

A version of this book won the Major Hopwood Award at the
University of Michigan in 1991, and portions have appeared
in *Quarterly West*, *The Sun*, *TriQuarterly*, and *Witness*.

Printed in the United States of America

MP 10 9 8 7 6 5 4 3 2 1

For my mother
and for Betty

History has given
And taken away; murders become memories,
And memories become the beautiful obligations:
As with a dream interpreted by one still sleeping,
The interpretation is only the next room of the dream.

—Howard Nemerov

PART ONE

CHAPTER ONE She became a widow well before his father died. It was how she managed—the grief made her strong, the man dead before he died, and the boy still just a boy, a little wisp of a kid, ten years old, an only child, end of story. End of story, except she stood in his bedroom doorway that afternoon and said, "Your father's not going to be home for dinner tonight."

And Daniel turned to her. "So?"

"So," she said, "I just thought you should know." She stepped across the room and pushed closed the dresser drawers until they all lay even. The house seemed to hold its breath as she turned with her mouth pinched down and her chin trembling so fast she could not have been control-ling it. The boy watched her and felt as if he'd swallowed a bit of metal—a washer or a coin—and someone was bring-ing it back up along his spine with a magnet.

Anna clicked her tongue and walked away, head up, out of the room. He listened to her run the water in the kitchen sink and imagined her looking out the window at the line of trees in the backyard, the bulbs already up with flowers, it being springtime and rainy and warm again now, the days growing longer. She crossed the hallway to the bathroom, and Daniel waited for the toilet to flush and refill, for her footsteps to pass his doorway and climb the stairs to the bedroom above. Daniel stood still and uneasy and waited below her, with nothing but his own breathing and swallowing.

The mantel clock in the living room ticked louder, then softer, then louder again. It chimed six and she returned to the kitchen, where he found her staring at the cuckoo clock on the wall. The pendulum—a maple leaf—hurried back and forth, and he caught her chin starting to tremble again. It was awful, and she turned away, and the clock struck and played "Edelweiss" as the pinecone weights inched down the flowered wallpaper.

For dinner they drove across town to the old train station, a pizza parlor now. At one time this town had been big with factories and mills, textiles and lumber. It was the county seat, and its rail yards once ranked third in all New England for the volume of freight handled. The trains still pounded through at night, but no passenger trains stopped in Cargill Falls, Connecticut, any longer.

On the way home, Daniel sat quietly and held the pizza box on his lap and watched the cars, the department and grocery stores pass, the drugstore, the post office, the bank. There wasn't a window he hadn't helped his father clean, and Daniel caught glimpses of his mother's Chevelle in the glass of the shop fronts as she drove home. The town looked dusty and grainy in the half light. On past the church, the cemetery, the brickwork mills along the river, the memorial bridge, his mother saying to smell the water, all chokeweed and carp.

He didn't know what to say to this broken edge in her voice. She told him that she hated this place and their lives here and had half a mind to just pick up and leave, to never so much as look back. It made the hair on his arms go electric to hear her like this.

"Hello?" she said. "Am I talking to myself over here?"

"What do you want me to say, Mom?"

He kept his eyes on the familiar turns of their neighborhood, everything prim and trim, their house like any of the others, a square of lawn, the trees ripe with birds. Inside the front door, the walls and furniture seemed to hold their breath. Daniel and his mother sat on the couch in front of the television news—this was 1979, and the news was gas lines in California, Skylab falling, and then ads with gorillas and suitcases and *plop-plop, fizz-fizz*—Anna just staring at the picture window, at the curtains hanging in long folds. She moved a slice of pizza around in the box.

"Mom," he said, "aren't you hungry?"

She shrugged and shook her head slightly.

"So where'd you say Dad was so late again?"

"I don't remember saying anyplace," she said. "Did I?"

He couldn't help but laugh a little—a nervous bubble in his throat—and he looked away at the carpet and the phone and the television and tried to chew the smile from his face.

She stood to leave.

"What's the matter?" he asked.

"What d'you mean, 'What's the matter?'"

"I don't know—it's just you're acting like a statue."

"And what, pray tell, does a statue act like?"

"You're just staring, I guess—it's creepy."

He followed the sound of her that night as she paced the floorboards over him. Back and forth, the scuff of slippers almost endless over his ceiling. Her pacing became, eventually, a kind of patrol, and only the phone stopped her. It rang in the living room and she appeared in his doorway, her shadow bent large and long across the wall.

"We're not home tonight," she told him.

The phone kept ringing behind her—ten, fifteen, and then twenty rings made it eternal. The bells hummed in his ears when they did end, at last. And from the hallway she told him to sleep, though he knew he'd never be able to fall asleep now. He lay in bed cold and afraid and still as a stone, his breathing shallow as he listened to her move upstairs. Her voice sank down through the ceiling as she talked or sang to herself. Rain began to blow against the windows like sand, and he must have fallen in and out of sleep, because he'd sit up in bed in the dark and believe the front door had just flown open and that his father's car waited idling in the drive.

In the morning the rain continued. Half asleep, Daniel rolled onto his back and stared at the ceiling and the light fixture. The water stain was a map of the Great Lakes. Or it was the Indian on a nickel. Or a dinosaur fossil. In the ashy light he could either blur his eyes and fall back to sleep or else he could turn and watch the evergreen branches sway against the window.

He never woke all at once like his father did. His father could wake up like a shot, or so he said, but the boy woke slowly, layer by layer, like his mother. He would step out of bed and find himself in the bathroom and then at the end of the hall. Now he heard the faint sound of the shower upstairs and went up to their bedroom, where the bed had been stripped, the blankets and sheets piled on the floor, a pair of suitcases open on the dressers.

"He's not here," she said from behind him.

She wore a robe and had a towel on her head like a turban, her face scoured and red. "You're not going to miss your bus now," she said, "are you?"

Anna called in sick to the department store where she worked. She stayed home all morning, changed the locks, and packed her husband's things into boxes and bags. She took everything out into the rain, hung his pants and shirts on the low branches of the trees out front, dragged trash bags over the grass, cartons of paper and files to the curb. Let the whole town drive by and see, she thought. What did she care? It wasn't the waitress in bed with him; it was the shit-eating grin that made her insane, the way he couldn't seem to wipe that smirk from his face.

Had they still lived in the saltbox by the river, she would have dropped everything into that slow brown water.

But here she could only put him out on the street for the garbage men to remove the next day. This was better, she told herself, a public decision was more real, more decisive. A river would've just carried it all away. That was what rivers did—they forgave.

Just another day at school for the boy, but the house he came home to seemed like a pocket turned inside out, more like the empty skin of an animal than the place he lived in and had left that morning. He felt ashamed by the clothes draped over the bushes, by the shoes in the grass, the boxes at the end of the drive, everything dark and soft with rain. If he could only have kept walking past this house, past this whole display of theirs, but he didn't know where else he could go.

Daniel went around to the backyard and saw her through the storm door in the kitchen. She was never home at this time, but there she was, lifting the mop into the sink. She seemed somehow undone—her duster half opened, her hair uncurled, her hands pressing the braids of the mop under the running water. He opened the door and stepped slowly inside, his mother wiping her hands on her hips. "And why aren't you at school?" she asked. She stood there and didn't turn to him, just looked up at the ceiling until he answered.

"It's three-thirty, Mom."

"So, you should be outside playing," she said, "shouldn't you?"

She took the mop from the sink and faced him, a black

smudge across her nose. "Well," she said, "you usually go play or something, don't you?"

"It's raining," he told her.

"So? Babe Ruth would've played through a little rain."

"Babe Ruth?"

"Whoever," she said.

He stared at her, and she swiped the mop around his shoes and told him to go away. He went to his room, closed his bedroom door behind him, and sat on the edge of the bed and waited and hoped that her shadow would come to the stripe of light under his door. But she never came to explain any of this to him.

Out through his side window he could see his father's shirts and pants hanging in the trees. Daniel looked at the papers blown over the yard, at the other houses on the street, and then back at the shirts and pants, all of them like versions of the same man—one hanging out there green, one brown, one blue. Daniel lifted open the window and screen and curled himself over the sill to the grass outside. He tore the clothes from the branches and brought the cold bundles up into his room, where he hung them in the closet to dry.

Closer to night, Daniel heard the growl of his father's car on the street in front of the house. His mother shut off the television and checked the new locks and then hurried the boy upstairs to the attic. "Pretend no one's home," she whispered, her breath so close he felt the words like cobwebs across his face. And downstairs, his father began to knock at the door, his car still idling at the curb.

"C'mon, Anna," he called, "open up already—it's me."

She stood with the boy behind the gauze curtains of the attic window and listened as the man pounded and yelled himself hoarse. "I could break this fricken place down," he hollered. "Goddammit, Anna!" He kicked the door and stepped into the yard, to the limp boxes near the street, where he was visible to them.

Anna stared down at Bob as though he was some trespasser, his foot on the hydrant as he lit a cigarette and rested, the car exhaust rising faint red around the taillights behind him. Daniel stared too and began to shiver from the damp and the chill and the way his father waited as lean as a ghost through the curtains. The rain paused and the other houses on the street began to darken. His father drew his jacket tight. "Hey, Daniel," he called and looked up at the house. "I know you're in there."

The boy reached his hand slowly to the glass, as if under a spell.

And she hissed to him, "Don't you dare."

Daniel dropped his hand and crouched by the window. He gathered the husks of wasps and flies from the floor and held them in his fist and looked down and saw his father picking through the piles of letters and magazines outside. Bob took the rest of his clothes from the sidewalk and laid them over the front seat of the car. He lifted garbage bags into the trunk, carried luggage and boxes to the back seat, took the buckets and window tools, the extension ladder, the paper bag full of things from his medicine cabinet, and between each trip he glanced up to the windows of the house.

Soon the man and his car disappeared into the long wash of streetlights and rain. Anna and Daniel started downstairs in the dark, the boy's mother holding his hand and telling him to be careful as they went. They felt their way down the steps, and Daniel crushed the wasps in his hand and scattered the pieces behind him.

The storm picked up that night. At least he could blame the rain and thunder for his sleeplessness. In his mind his father kicked at the front door every time Daniel closed his eyes. He first appeared to the boy like branches scratching at the screen of his bedroom window, but late in the night the man grew more and more insistent, until he actually stood under the eaves and tapped at the metal frame of the window, his face close to try to see inside the darkened room.

Out of bed, the boy lifted open the window to the sound of the rain, his father's hand to the loose mesh of the screen. The man was soaked and shrunken down as he leaned up toward the boy. "Hey there, bud," he said, his voice sore. "How's it going?"

The rain gusted through the screen, and Daniel didn't move, the cold spray on the tops of his feet like sparks. Lightning flickered in the clouds and the storm groaned over the house, the town, the trees and hills beyond. "C'mon now," said the man, "just gimme a hand with the screen."

Bob wiped the rain from his face and looked up at Daniel for a moment, and then he cocked his arm and hit the screen with the heel of his hand. He pulled back and punched the frame again, harder, jimmied it sideways out of the window and dropped it to the grass. He put his forearms on the sill and started to lift himself into the house, but Daniel pulled the window down on him, leaned his weight on the sash, and then locked it.

Bob fell back, his face contorted through the wet glass. He stood there and blinked the rain out of his eyes, his head tilting to one side slightly, as if he—Robert S. Cussler, forty-seven years old, this former marine, this self-made, self-commanding, self-*everything* sort of man—as if he couldn't believe what was happening either.

He raised his face to the wind and rain and bent to get the screen from the ground behind him. He tapped the grass cuttings from it and replaced the frame in the window as best he could, and then he just turned and disappeared into the woods that bordered the yard.

Daniel never told anyone that his father stood there that night in the rain. He never said how the man came back and kept coming back, how Bob would pull up to the house in broad daylight, how he'd waltz through the rooms when she was at work.

Mom, he wanted to say, *I did like we did.*

I hid.

I didn't move, he almost told her. *I didn't dare. I just kept hiding.*

That much of the story had words, and Daniel pictured the words crawling from his throat, half sprung from his mouth with clicking wings. But if he never talked about it, if he never opened his mouth, then maybe none of it had to have happened: his run to the attic, the quiet of the boxes and the dusty heat upstairs, his father's footsteps in the kitchen, the man's voice singing into the house for the boy.

"Ding-dong," he'd say through the rooms. "Avon calling."

He'd go heavy and hard and deliberate, room to room to room, his legs as straight and sharp as scissors until he found the stairway to the attic.

"What's this?" said Bob. "Not even a hello for your old man?"

Daniel sat on a paint can at the window, his back curved, his chin on his knees, a line of broken wasps and beetles at his feet.

The man shook his head and came over to the window. His dress boots had bronze zippers up the inside ankles and creases in the leather, dust in the creases, and he squatted next to Daniel and reached to open the curtain. The light wavered as the cloth moved.

"C'mon now," said the man, "it's not *that* bad, is it?" He looked at the side of the boy's face and put his arm around his shoulder, Daniel hunching his back so that his father's hand would slip off. Bob touched the floor to catch his balance and went to one knee, waited for his son to say something. But Daniel didn't say a word.

His father stood and laughed and looked up at the peak of the roof, the dark beams that crossed like the ribs of a ship. He brushed the dust from his knee and said he was hungry and thinking about a little spin for some lunch or something. He tapped the keys in his pocket and watched the boy, but Daniel kept his eyes down and didn't offer anything in return to the man.

"Well," said Bob, finally, "you'd make a mean card player, that's for sure."

CHAPTER TWO Anna knew all about loss and the nature of making do. Her sister, Jean, had passed five years ago, an aneurysm on Easter weekend. Her mother had gone in her sleep two years before that. And her father had been only forty-two when he died — a snowstorm, a heart attack. Anna was six, Jean was eight, and that had been Bayside, Queens, another world entire.

Anna remembered rubbing lemon oil into the arms and legs of the furniture, all of it made by her father. And she remembered Orchard Avenue and his wood shop, the milky glass of skylights, the drumroll of lathes, the racecar whine of saws. She could go on and on like this — the rifle stocks for the army, the smell of lumber, the glue pot of horse hooves, the adding machine in her father's office, its accordion buttons, its sidearm, its cheerful bell inside. This all seemed like a life she'd heard about or read about somewhere, a happiness against which she could measure her own life now.

Soon after her father died, her mother lost the wood shop and sold the little brick house in Bayside with everything in it. Ellen took the girls back down in the world to

Greenpoint, a basement apartment with bars over the windows. Nothing remained of Bayside but a pair of blue china swans and a piece or two of furniture, a family ring, some old photographs.

Her sister, her mother, her father, and Bayside—all these losses felt like so many thefts to Anna. And with Bob all but gone now too, who was left for her, besides the boy? Who would listen to her now? Or care? Or worry? Her friend Rosemary in Petaluma? Her niece Joelyn in Staten Island? The girls from work? She used to be a person surrounded by friends, but she got married and moved away and that list of Christmas cards began to slowly disappear. The potlucks, the card games—she wondered how she could have been so careless and let so many friends fall away, let herself become the type of woman who had no one in her life to get a cup of coffee with.

She came home from work to an empty house and the sense that the boy had gone with Bob. She called Daniel's name and held still and listened. She could almost smell the man's cologne. She locked the front door behind her, knowing that waiting never brought anyone home sooner. She remembered how her whole childhood was spent inside the cool, soft linings of the coats on the wall, how she always waited in the foyer for her sister's face in the beveled glass of the door.

Even now, with her back against the door, she felt afraid to go into the house, afraid to stay out of the house. She had to physically turn herself from the mail slot and the scatter rug and go to the boy's room, stand there with his stray shoes and books, the solar system tacked to the wall, the poster of Evel Knievel above his desk— THERE'S A LITTLE EVEL IN ALL OF US. She picked up one of his school shirts from the floor and turned to open the closet, surprised but not shocked to find Bob's clothes hanging there already, neat and smooth, as if they had taken a place here and started to return home.

Bob drove the boy the long way, so as not to pass the front of the house and let her see them together. They had eaten at a dairy stand on the way out of town and had driven on past farms and stretches of land and roads that looped back to the opposite side of town. They took their time and pulled over a few streets from the house and sat with the car idling. Bob straightened his legs to get the wallet from his pocket. He counted out three twenty-dollar bills and pressed them into Daniel's hand.

"Just leave this somewhere that she'll find it," he said. "And make her think it's hers, okay?"

Bob glanced in the rearview mirror and touched his fingers to his tongue and took another bill from his wallet. "And how about keeping this for you?" he said. "Don't make any trouble for her or anything."

Daniel closed his hand on the money and looked at the ashtray, at the plastic Saint Christopher, at the afternoon light draped like lace on the street and trees. Sometimes he wondered how his father always managed to have a wallet full of money like this, though it often seemed the man carried his whole life around with him in that wallet.

"You should probably get going now," said the man. "She's gonna have a conniption as it is."

Daniel glanced at his father, made his mouth into a line, and opened the door. He crossed the street and walked away with the money in his fist.

Bob watched until the boy turned the corner and was gone. Only then did he put the car in gear and roll slowly from the curb. He knew every street for miles and had that urge to drive street by street through town, past all the houses and cars and yards, past all the lives that people came home to at night.

It grew dark and Bob drove the empty back roads out of town. Tree trunks flared past in the headlights, and there were dips and hollows and pockets of fog to fly through blind. Half a tank in one direction, half a tank back, and Bob kept both windows down as he made his way past farms and hills back to Cargill Falls again. He went slow and lawful into town, came to complete stops, used his blinkers. He'd once told Anna he'd never get a tattoo in case he ever turned to a life of crime. "Oh, you and your life of crime," she'd said. "Why don't you just go rob a gas station already?"

Bob had made a face across the dinner table to her and the boy. "Will you visit me in jail, Anna?"

"Of course," she'd said. "Just to remind you of how stupid you are."

"See?" he'd said to Daniel. "That's one thing I just love about your mother—she'd get the last word on an echo, wouldn't she?"

. . .

When Daniel unlocked the door and walked into the house that afternoon, neither he nor his mother mentioned the man. One look and the boy felt she needed loyalty from him, so he swallowed away the attic and roads and everything else. He found himself in a tunnel of talk about friends and teachers and Little League this year, the meat of the Boston batting order—Lynn, Fisk, Yaz, Rice, and Dewey Evans. Even at dinner that night, Daniel chattered and wished she'd just reach her hand out to stop him. Instead she mentioned that the lawn needed cutting and that she had to work late tomorrow. They talked just normal enough to make him feel crazy, as if he'd dreamed up everything, as if his father were asleep on the couch in front of the television, as if everything were just fine.

Later, he lay in bed as his mother became that constant scrape of slippers across his ceiling again. She was each creak and scuff, back and forth, all hours of the night. If afternoons were his father, then nights like this would have to be his mother. She was the bedroom and the living room and the L-shape of kitchen, its sink and stove and cans of food. She was every pillow and piece of furniture in the house, every curtain and book and lock and door, but his father would have to be the desk upstairs. And he'd be the stairs themselves. And the crawlspace under the porch, as well as the windows, the screens, the electric sockets, the wires in the walls. Bob was the car in the street, just as he was the street itself, the back roads, the towns beyond. If Anna was the world within, then Bob was the world without.

And Daniel took whatever was left—the attic and

basement. He was the sweaty pipes, the fuse box, the blue of pilot lights under the furnace and water heater. He was the moldy damp and the underdog corners of the house, the slant of roof, the mortar and brick and sharp tips of nails through the shingles, his vents clotted with leaves. He was what no one else wanted to be — the dust, the dirt, the tindery heat upstairs, the dead wasps at the screens.

A week after his father had gone, everything still had the air of a prelude to it. Normal life was school and the department store, groceries and math homework, though it seemed he was watching his whole world in the mirror of a spoon now — everything recognizable but upside down and warped. He often glimpsed the Bonneville on the street after school, and he always looked for it. At night, darkness led to Bob at the boy's window for the length of a cigarette, just long enough to say hello and tell him not to silly-sally in school, the sky clear and plush, the stars close enough to stir with a finger. Bob would spit into the grass and ask for a couple of spare blankets, say it got cold at night in that drab little room where he slept in town with his buckets and ladders and cleaning supplies. And because he had to do something, Daniel handed his father blankets from his bed and clothes from his closet and anything else that he thought the man could use.

Long evenings with his mother came peppered with sitcoms and phone calls — *Happy Days*, *Laverne and Shirley*, a wrong number, a call from someone for Bob. Another would be Daniel's Little League coach with a practice schedule. And then it'd be Rosemary from Petaluma. She and Anna were each other's oldest friends, and they went all the way back to Greenpoint together. Rosemary had a husband and twins now, a pretty house with a pool, all the specifics of a life that was charmed. Even the weather in California was sunny and warm. It all made Anna plead a headache and beg off the phone. It was the last thing she wanted — this luck of hers to rub off on anyone, especially someone like Rosemary.

But when a call from her niece in Staten Island came, that was different. Anna moved away from the living room with the receiver, and the cord clicked around the door frame as she stretched to the kitchen counter. She kept quiet for the most part, just listening to the girl's latest dramas, her niece always with a flair for the dramatic. Everything was fine, said Anna, except Bob was gone. She'd caught him with someone, she said, and thrown him out with all of his things. She knew Daniel could hear her from the next room, and she talked in that happy, good-witch voice of hers. "Yes, Joelyn," she said, her voice calm. "I found them here in my own house."

"But what did you *say?*" said the girl. "What did you *do?* I mean, I'm sure you didn't just stand there — you must've screamed or thrown things at the bastard, didn't you?"

"No, I didn't," said Anna, "that would have been you. I did just stand there, actually, like an idiot."

"I didn't say that, Aunt Anna. All I said was you've got to get it *out.* You've got to *emote.* Put one of Grandma's salt curses on him or something."

Anna heard the girl swallow on the other end of the

line, and she said, "Let's not run up your bill, Joelyn. I've got to get Daniel off to bed."

"And how's he with this?"

"He's fine," said Anna. "We're both just fine— thanks."

She returned the receiver to its cradle and Daniel was gone from the living room. He was in bed, the lights off already, the boy lying with his back to the door. "Daniel," she whispered. "You're not asleep yet," she said, "are you?"

She approached and drew the blankets to his neck, tucked them around his body. When he was little and tired and couldn't sleep, she'd mummify him in the covers like this, brush his bangs from his face, tuck his hair behind his ears with her fingers. She sat and he rolled toward her weight on the edge of the bed.

She touched his hair and looked at him. "So," she said, "where'd you two go today anyway?"

He looked up at her.

"Tell me," she said.

"Where'd who go, Mom?"

She put her hand on his shoulder. "Just tell me," she said, "it's okay."

"But I don't know what you mean," he said. "I didn't go anywhere."

"I could slap you when you lie like that," she said, and stopped short. She pushed herself up from him and left the room. The hours grew small before she came back down the stairs, the boy feigning sleep as she pulled the blankets over him again. Slowly, so as not to wake him, she lay on top of the covers.

He kept his breathing steady and watched the window and the trees at the back of the yard, anxious for a face in the glass, a hand cupped to the screen, the orange point of a cigarette. The shrubs and shadows waved against the glass, but a branch was still only a branch, the wind just wind, the shadows shadows. The next thing he knew, morning had come and a twenty and a ten lay curled between the screen and window.

CHAPTER THREE She had her presentiments from the beginning, but when Bob asked her she said yes and pulled him close and felt as buoyant as a cork. Anna fit his head under her chin and held him there and watched the street, his breath in the scoop of her shirt. This was Meserole Avenue, 1959—the year of Castro, of *Ben-Hur,* of "Put Your Head on My Shoulder"—and Anna wasn't yet eighteen years old, had scarcely started her senior year at Saint Angela Hall. And yes meant goodbye to Greenpoint and Brooklyn and every piss-sour street and avenue from here to Flushing and Coney Island. It meant goodbye to the bricks and the pigeons and the dog-shit sidewalks, to the stink of the brewery and the buses, the trucks, the braying car horns, goodbye to the catcalls from the corner, to the fights in the park, to her mother exhausted by swing shifts at the sugar factory, and to her sister living up on Steinway now with her cheating husband, her daughter walking and talking already.

It'd been nearly three years since Anna first met Bob on the church steps at her sister's wedding. He'd been a friend of the groom's, someone she secretly admired from afar. At the reception he'd caught her looking at him and came over and asked her to dance, her face blushing, Bob smiling. She'd smelled his aftershave and cigarettes as they moved to the dance floor. She'd touched the star on his chest as they danced, and Bob told her that all marines were at least marksmen.

And now, standing on the empty stoop, she drew him still closer. Girls from the neighborhood had chalked boxes for hopscotch on the middle of the street, and Anna stepped with her eyes through the squares and breathed deep the clean smell of his hair. The sun laid columns along the street and on the cream-colored brick apartment buildings. She felt him whisper into her collar. "It's not every day you get a sweepstakes ticket like me, you know."

She loosened her arms and leaned back to smile at him and his crooked grin. He was older than she, more worldly and strong and cocky, and he should have swept aside her sudden fears of leaving and eloping with him. She wished he would just lead like in a dance and say what they'd do and where'd they go and how they'd make each other so happy.

"You're not gonna cry or anything," he said, "are you?"

She shook her head no.

"So what's the matter, then?"

It was the first time she'd seen him nervous, and she felt almost relieved to see him like this, almost grateful to get some glimpse of his real feelings. If he couldn't be strong, she thought, at least he could be emotional for her.

"Something wrong?" he asked.

"No," she told him. "Everything's just fine."

"We can have a big wedding if you want—is that it?"

"No," she said, and smiled. "I don't need the spoiling."

"So I was thinking I'd get my brother's car and we could just go—go down to this place in Maryland, stay at the shore for a few days, and then start our new lives together. What d'you think?"

She didn't want to *think*—that was the problem—she wanted to *feel* for once. She wanted him to make a stand, to look her straight in the eye and say he wanted to be with her forever. "Ask me again," she said. "Just ask, like they do in love stories—you know, Bob, propose to me."

That simple string of words—*Mom, Bob and I are going to get married*—seemed to freeze her mother and sister, their faces horrified. Ellen disappeared into the bathroom, and Jean asked when this would happen, this wedding of hers, to which Anna just burst into tears.

She'd always hoped for a day like her sister's—a princess dress, flowers, rice tossed. She'd always wanted to be a bride, to be the girl waiting for her soldier, to have a touch of poetry in her life. And when his first letter arrived from Camp Lejeune, North Carolina, she carried it in the pocket of her school uniform, taking it out so often that the paper became as soft as cloth. She studied the combination eagle, globe, and anchor in one corner, the purple Jefferson stamp in another, the seismogram of his handwriting: *Miss Anna Opiela, 55 Meserole Avenue, Bklyn 22, New York*. She'd returned four to him by the time his next letter found her.

In page after page of beautiful Palmer script, Anna described her counter job at Park Deli, her visits to Jean on the weekends, how she'd ride an extra stop on the subway just so she could walk along Driggs and see the steps of Saint Stanislaw's, where she first saw him, the marine in those deep-clean blues. She wrote how miserable it was to live alone with her mother now, how her mother's lipstick touched every coffee cup and cigarette end, how the woman seemed to always need flowers and bracelets and attention from men. Anna connected this need to the Depression and Greenpoint, to the sugar packets and butter rolls that Ellen slipped into her pocketbook from restaurants. Anna traced this back to her father's dying and the house they lost in Bayside, their windowsills clean to the touch, whereas everything in Greenpoint left your fingers so black they never seemed to come clean.

Anna hoped to be irresistible to him, asked if he was left- or right-handed. Did he have any tattoos? If so, where? Of what? What about his life, she asked, and his family? And the farm he grew up on? What about the service? How was the food? How was the weather? And how long did he have to go? Would he re-up?

She'd wince the instant she dropped the envelope in the box and wish she'd never written a word of it. An eternity would pass while she waited for his answer to arrive, and she would agonize—had she even signed her name? Had she gotten his address right? Or had she scared him away already? Who'd write back to all this girl gush, anyway?

Jean scoffed at her and the way she talked all dreamy, as if she suddenly lived some kind of movie-star life. "Sometimes," said Jean, "I should just drop a brick on your head and put some sense into you."

"Don't squelch me," said Anna. "People are supposed to glow when they're in love."

"Must you?" said Jean. "Do you really have to say these kinds of things?"

"Well, it's true," said Anna. "And I want to glow."

"Oh, you glow all right—you're a regular light bulb, Anna."

"Shut up, Jean."

"No, I'm serious," said Jean. "I swear—come over here so I can read by you."

In one letter he sent a small photograph of himself smiling, his hat pushed off his face as if he'd just won a thousand dollars. *Your Loving Bob*, he'd written on the back, and she could recite whole stretches of the words he wrote:

> *So everyone wants to know who's this girl who keeps writing all these letters to me. My new best friend is the mail captain and he says that if I don't make an honest woman of you, then he's going to Brooklyn to look you up himself. He says he knows where you live and I believe him.*

She smiled every time she read his letters, and she read and thought of them endlessly to take herself away from the soot and tenements and egg-smell gas of the kitchen stove, her mother's preening for boyfriends, her sister married to her own unhappiness.

Until Bob, Anna's dreams had always brought her back to the little brick house off Horace Harding Boulevard in Bayside, in Queens. When they were younger, much younger, she and her sister would sometimes go to their old house instead of school. They would stand on the front sidewalk in the middle of the day and recall to one another each shelf and carpet and picture on wall, the louvered windows in back, the fireplace made of fieldstone in the parlor. She and Jean would then walk the neighborhood and notice a nicely kept lawn, a fancy car, a school, a park, a particular patch of sky so exaggerated and beautiful it belonged on a church ceiling. Jean bought penny candy for the bus ride back down to Greenpoint. They rationed the pieces, one for every stop until the doors opened onto Nassau Avenue again.

Greenpoint might have been who they were now, but Anna knew Bayside was who they were supposed to be. It was the end of every good-night story their father ever told; the herringbone brick of the house; the wedding ring on their mother's finger, the stone and gold so precious to them it seemed the last relic of a saint.

Once upon a time, the stories went, a young man left his village in the Ukraine to join his brother in America. There was a train ride and days of land spread wide with light, the mountains like the moon, always with him when he looked up. Passage on the steamer took two weeks, the seas rough, the steerage so cramped and sour with people that he took straw from his mattress and slept with the crates between decks. He was seasick and lonely, and he made room beside him for a woman with a baby.

The woman's face had the sea in it—cold, gray, unstable—and she smiled without showing her teeth when he brought her meals. Below deck, they ate together from mess kits: potatoes and soup and eggs, salted fish and hard bread, water that tasted like old pennies and screws. He'd say he spent most of the voyage topside, alone with the wind and the sun and the watchful rows of rivets along the side of the ship, a scent of burning coal, icebergs in the distance, people talking nearby about the buffalo, about birds, about the custom of handshakes in America.

He had twenty-two dollars, a suit of dress clothes, and a family ring when he reached New York—the stone perfect and set in white gold. It was the pole star, this ring, and he'd tell the girls how he carried it in his pocket to remind himself to work and make a life worth leaving home and family for.

Their mother never forgave him for dying. On Sunday mornings, Ellen would walk the mile to Calvary Cemetery and fit twigs into his name on the stone to mark her visits. She'd weave her way among the many crosses and crypts and trees, her trail behind her in the wet, silvery grass. A chapel by the gate sold flowers and vigil candles, the money always untended, and Ellen would kneel in the vaulted quiet. She'd finger the ring on her hand and then go wandering again over the graves and hills.

On the way home she'd cross a drawbridge over the Newtown Creek—Brooklyn on one side, Queens on the other. She'd glance down at the water below, all mother-of-pearl with oil, the gulls crying at a barge of garbage upstream. Ellen would rest at the rail, Jean and Anna sometimes there beside her, each of them staring into the whorls of sludge and sewage, each of them trying not to love their past more than their future.

As the wedding day approached, Anna bought a suitcase and a new dress and shoes. Her sister let her borrow a string of pearls, bought her champagne and flowers, and did her hair for her that afternoon. Her mother got off work early and set up tables beside the stoop—platters of deli food, sandwiches, buckets of beer, paper streamers. All their friends and neighbors, a whole party, they all waited in front of the apartment for Bob.

What a relief to hear the horn and see that ruby-red Clipper easing up the avenue, Bob and his brother, Danny, in their Everly Brothers coats, their ties already loosened at the neck. The car edged up to the curb like a small motorboat. Bob found her on the steps and everyone cheered and imitated the clink of silverware and glass. He and Anna kissed, and he dipped her, her leg kicking high. A real brush with happiness.

Bob took her by the hand to ask her mother's consent, and Ellen's mascara blurred around her eyes. Jean opened the champagne, boys fought for the corks in the gutter, a bouquet of roses appeared in Anna's arms. Danny stood on the top step and made a toast, and then Jean announced that her sister looked as bright as brass, as bright as Broadway, as bright as bright could be. "Shade your eyes, everybody— it's the bride and she's all aglow!"

Flashbulbs popped in the dark, and hands slapped the hood and fenders as Bob and Anna set off, cans strung behind the Clipper. Even eloping had a scripted feel, but it was good to drive with the windows down and the air cool and the streets nearly empty of cars. They sailed over loud patches of cobblestone, past factory warehouses and darkened lots and tenements and bars, the neon slurring across the windshield. He clicked on the radio and steered with his arms straight and wrists flexed over the wheel. At the bridge anchorage, they stopped and waited for a break in the traffic. Anna leaned over the flowers to kiss him.

She slid close and the bridge lifted them high with its wires and mint green lights. The radio echoed under each crossbeam as the bridge lifted and then tipped them slowly toward the city and the avenues, the glare and glass and lights. He drove with his arm around her, and they circled into the tunnel, the traffic roaring as they ran like a cord under the river and were shot into the night again, the lighted prow of the city behind them now, the smooth hum of turnpike and flats of Jersey before them, the sky chalky and gray.

They stopped for gas and coffee and watched a refinery fire close to the road. They rode on through the dark and the pockets of factory smells—a half mile of cake mix, a mile of fresh paint, an exit's worth of bleach. Bob told her she should sleep if she was tired, but Anna wanted to keep him company. She said she'd never been out of New York before, and Bob smiled and told her she was beautiful. Almost all night they drove through Jersey and Pennsylvania, and he nudged her awake in the morning to see the ocean and the billboard on the side of the road—WELCOME TO ELKTON, MARYLAND.

He steered them onto a main strip of chapels and bars, bowling alleys and restaurants, garland strung over the street. They read their vows in a tiny cinder-block chapel, and the marriage license from Cecil County doubled as a coupon for the Blue Haven Motor Lodge with AC & Perfect Sleepers. The jeweler across Bridge Street was open, and they bought matching gold bands and went to the motel. Lightheaded, Anna signed her new name in the ledger and felt her hand shake.

He carried her over the threshold and placed her on the bed, which was so wide and soft that she could only laugh and bounce. The headboard knocked against the wall, so Bob pulled the bed toward him with her on it. He lifted open the windows and closed the blinds, and she watched out of the side of her eye as he took off his shoes and socks and climbed onto the bed next to her. He touched his lips to her neck, to her earrings, to her temples and hairline and eyes and lips, her mouth open and dry and cool. She took quick half breaths and lifted herself to his touch, pressed herself against him and felt his voice in her ear as they made love for the first time. He was strong and beautiful to her, and she tried to be the same for him, not clumsy or bashful or shy or afraid or anything but generous and wild and alive.

When it was over, they slid beneath the covers and he slept. She could still feel him inside her as they lay together, and she moved with his breathing, his nose whistling quietly as he slept. Daylight filtered in through the blinds, and she circled her fingertips around her mouth and chin, her skin irritated and red. She listened to the cars outside, listened to heels clicking quickly down the hallway. She could not find an emotion to fit any of this—it was all more than she'd hoped for but still less than she'd dreamed.

She closed her eyes and pictured all the places they would wake up together: on the pull-out couch in her mother's apartment on Meserole Avenue; in front of a woodstove on his family's farm; a sunny bedroom of their own somewhere. One day, she hoped, they'd have a house by a river and fix it up nice, fill it with children and dogs and cats, have a big lawn to mow, leaves to rake, all the clichés of happiness. That was the dream, to have him polishing his car on the weekends and teaching her to drive and to fish and to shoot a rifle. They'd stay up half the night, sometimes, drinking and talking and playing cards with friends. He'd remember her birthday and bring her flowers and chocolates and pieces of jewelry. If unhappiness had felt as solid and permanent as a stone to her, then she imagined happiness would run through her fingers like sand.

CHAPTER FOUR Daniel skipped the bus and walked to school by way of the railroad tracks and truss bridge. He met up with friends and passed the empty wool works and silk mills, the old boxcars up to their axles in weeds. For the week after his father had gone, he and his friends covered their mouths every morning and poked a dog lying dead near the waterline of the slough. With sticks they opened the matted fur and grease where the train must have caught her, and Daniel could barely look, her teeth bared, her eye blackened. And if a train approached, Daniel hollered at the sound and they all chucked stones at the tankers and the heavy flats of lumber, chains dragging from the last car.

School started with morning announcements, the Pledge of Allegiance, and then Math, Music, and all the odd-folded notes from Marsha before lunch. They were just her way of saying hello, but still she doodled hearts and flowers in the margins, and Daniel kept them to himself, as if they were love notes.

In Social Studies, Mr. Falzarano started every class with finger flexes to get the kids' blood moving. He had lumberjack muscles and the wadded-up build of a third baseman, and he always tried to make them laugh by *how* he said things—the man always a bit highhanded and out of tune. He quoted songs and movies and books and cracked his yardstick across desks to bring daydreamers back—back to the orphanages of London, back to Johnny Tremain's hand, back to John Brown's trial.

The red arrow swept around the clock over the door— past the ladylike finger for minutes, the fat-man thumb for hours. Daniel's mind would wander out the windows or become lost as he stared at Marsha in front of him, that *click, click, click* of chalk against Falzarano's wedding band. He rolled his hands back and forth and waited with the whole room for Daniel to answer him. "Oh, pardon us, young Cussler," he said, all surprise-eyed. "We didn't mean to disturb your philosophizing back there—did we, class?"

Everyone had turned in his or her chair, and Daniel's heart became a drum. Falzarano walked toward him with the yardstick and sniffed. "It's just we smelled something burning," he said, and smiled and turned to Marsha. "It seems he's lost his place, Miss Ingraham. Would you be so kind as to catch our young friend up to where we are now, so he can continue reading for us?"

She turned to him, her smile so calm, her teeth short and chipped. A flip of a page, a hint of spearmint, and she brought Daniel back to Ellis Island with the moon of her fingernail.

At night he sat at the table with his mother after supper and helped her lay out their bills, helped her perform a sort of triage on who got paid and who could hold out a little longer. The phone company could wait, but the bank mortgage couldn't. The car payment could wait another week, just like the oil company and the water department, but the light and power bill had been typed in red ink and capital letters and had to be postmarked in tomorrow's mail. He licked the envelopes and stamps, and she wrote the checks and smiled with quiet triumph. "It's only money," she said. "Just remember that."

She had a way of looking at him that left his heart in the notch of his throat. She began to ramble on about work and weather and chores, as if the chatter would help. And Daniel never knew how to help her to say whatever it was she couldn't seem to say directly. He could never do enough, he thought, could always have done more. He could have given her the money he had from his father, could have been more loyal to her, could have done so much better for her, if he only knew how.

In the meantime, his friend Brownie told him about the go-carts he built with his father and brother. And Marsha talked about filling the pool in her backyard and how she took piano lessons and traveled to England and France with her parents. Daniel thought of his father waiting out in the shrubs for him, his mother beginning, unexpectedly, to cry.

After school, he went to look for his father's Bonneville on the street, the man at one of the stores or offices that he cleaned in town. When he found him, Daniel sneaked close and watched him work. He hid and waited until his father stepped away for a moment, then Daniel ran and stole an extension pole and squeegee before the man could return.

And when his father came back, the man stood there on the sidewalk as if he'd lost his mind suddenly, looking up and down the sidewalk and street.

"Okay, Daniel," he said, finally. "You got me that time —good one."

Daniel crawled from between the cars, and he and his father laughed and went for a coffee break together. They stopped at the little storefront on Livery Street, where Bob slept at night with a steel desk and swivel chair, a daybed and five-gallon buckets of cleaning supplies. And as Daniel tried to tell the man how she seemed shattery, how she sat like a statue and confided all those haunted feelings, Bob scowled and asked what he meant, exactly, by *shattery*—was that even a word?

That night he stayed up late with his mother and watched the weather forecast and baseball scores on the news. She sent him to bed during Carson, and he woke, later, to her standing at the threshold of his room, as always. He rolled in his covers and heard his voice, thin and reedy: "What are you *doing*, Mom?"

"Nothing," she told him. "Just looking at you."

"Well, I'm trying to sleep."

She deflated a little and returned to her bedroom and that scrape of slippers over his ceiling. Daniel stayed awake with guilt, as if he'd hit a bird with a stone.

Bob tapped at the window on clear nights, but he never tried to climb inside again. He just leaned against the house and let long breaths of silence drift away in cigarette smoke.

Daniel knelt at the sill and glanced back over his shoulder, wary of the hallway and his mother somewhere in the house, his father's cigarette smoke carrying in from outside. Daniel started to tell the man about the bills on the table and the dreams she said she had, the nightmares that made her sleep with the lights on.

It was the last thing on earth he wanted to do, but Daniel found himself again and again handing his fears through the open screen to his father. He handed each one over the sill like an apple—one at a time—and the man seemed to take and kick them aside, saying that the lawn looked a little shaggy, that the garbage needed to go out in the morning. He always gave the boy money and said not to give her a hard time, not to slack off in school.

And in the morning, Daniel gathered all the cash that his father had given him over the week. He listened for his mother upstairs and his hands fluttered as he sorted and piled the bills. He followed the sounds of his mother in her room and began to count and stack the money again. He held it all to his face, the smell of oil and ink and dirty hair, two hundred dollars seeming like a fortune to him.

He had half a mind to go to his mother and hand everything to her—explain what he could in one great burst—but instead he started down the hall to the kitchen. Her pocketbook hung on the chair and he opened it. He looked down at the compacts and checkbook inside, the cellophanes from candies, her wallet. He was supposed to make it look like hers, the money, and he unclicked the pearls on the wallet and crumpled a ten, a five, and three ones, left the bills with her change, her photos, her green stamps.

He put everything back in its place—the wallet, the turn-catch, the strap over the arm of the chair—and then Daniel went outside and stood by the trash drums in back. His mother stayed up most nights and slept deep into the mornings now. He waited out here for her to wake, the sun bright across the yard and house.

It was late morning, a Saturday, and the birds were singing, rapid-fire, in the trees. He fought the urge to go back into the house and made himself circle around to check his window screen. He gathered his father's cigarette butts from the grass, his hands soon so full he couldn't close his fists on all the yellowed filters.

At the edge of the woods, he scattered them over the leaves and picked his way through the trees and vines at the back of their yard, constantly untangling himself from the branches and brushwood. And every bird whistle made him turn. Every little touch of wind made him shrink back, expecting his father to leap out with a snap of twigs or rustle of leaves—*Gotcha!*

Daniel bent down and rubbed his hands in the dirt until the smell of cigarettes and money was gone. He stayed in view of the house but walked through the scrap woods, the empty bottles and paint cans and twisted storm drains. He kept an eye on the back patio of the house, watched for his mother to step outside to hang laundry or call for him, and he ended up near the old abandoned car, which his father left out in the woods and used for parts.

Daniel stood at the front grill and tipped water from an oil pan onto the ground. He rolled a tire iron under his foot and picked it up, felt the metal cold and heavy in his hand, gritty with rust. He looked back at the house and the yard and then turned and touched the hammer end of the iron to the headlight, tapped it, and then tapped it again harder and then again until the headlight popped with a crash of glass. A couple of steps across to the other headlight, and he lined up and made the car go blind.

He looked back at the house, almost daring her to come out and stop him from going to the side of the car and swinging at the mirror, splashing more glass into the leaves. At the back of the car, the taillights went brittle and tinseled into tiny red shards of plastic. The slightest knock on the bumper would ring as serious and satisfying as a church bell. He pried the handle off the driver's door and threw it away into the woods. He stopped and looked at the clear glare of the windshield, the reflection of sky and trees, and he raised the iron and put a small star into the glass. He pressed spidery lines across the windshield's curve, the cracks racing away from the heel of his fist.

Just then a car pulled into the yard, and Daniel stood frozen in the woods. He traced the outline of money in his pocket and inched slowly backwards, keeping his eyes on the little Datsun and its opening door. A young woman stepped out and onto the grass. For a second he was afraid that the flash of blond was the woman that his father had been with — a person he'd never want or need to meet.

But it was Joelyn, and he felt the peculiar relief of family as she walked toward the house. She wore a sleeveless shirt and stood with her face to the sun, her arms reaching up as she turned and smiled to Daniel, more like a sister to him than a cousin.

"I see you over there," she called, her voice a seesaw.

The last time he'd seen her, her hair had been long and brown, not short and bleached like this. And as he stepped out of the woods he could see her face, still pretty and smooth as a leaf, and as he got closer the spritz of freckles across her nose and arms, the vaccination scar on her shoulder. She laughed so easily that he couldn't help but feel drawn to her.

"What's the matter with you?" she asked, and hugged him to her. "Don't you recognize me?"

He said, "Hi, Joelyn." He was nearly as tall as her collarbone, and she kissed the top of his head and told him how big he'd gotten, her breath like water over his scalp. "And so where's your mother — is she home?"

"Yes," he said, "but did she know you were coming?"

"I don't believe she did," said the girl, her voice strong and sunny. "I mean, that would've ruined the whole surprise, wouldn't it?" She laughed and then quickly stopped and turned to the house, as if she'd been touched on the shoulder. Anna stood there on the back steps, hugging herself, arm over arm.

"Aunt Anna," said the girl, her hands out. "*There* you are."

And Anna — or part of her — would always see her niece as a girl of seventeen, tanned and pretty and slightly inappropriate, half naked and asleep on the Hide-A-Bed in their den. Joelyn would be the girl of nervous, gangly energy, incessantly cleaning and straightening to relieve her tension. Anna would never forget the orange U-Haul in the yard, its engine still ticking itself cool, her sister's things inside the truck to be unloaded. And she'd never quite shake the feeling of being watched in her own house, as if Joelyn was somehow the thin end of the wedge between herself and Bob. This was almost six years ago, but still—Jean had died so unexpectedly, and Joelyn had had nowhere else to go but Cargill Falls. Her own father had disappeared years before, and Bob was actually good with her, the closest thing to a father she'd ever really have. Joelyn cooked and cleaned for them that summer, brought the boy to the park in the afternoons, and put a brave face on it, though at night her crying came like chanting through the bedroom wall.

Anna always associated the girl with those humid nights, just as she always remembered packing up Jean's apartment with Joelyn, the girl's unspoken promise—to give the ring to Anna—Joelyn sauntering into the living room with her hands all covered in flour. It was so brazen that it was hard to follow just what had happened: Joelyn taking the ring from the kitchen where Jean had hidden it, Anna with a look so angry it could have burned a hole in the girl's shirt. Bob stood and led Anna from the room by the elbow, took her outside to the street and sidewalk, everything sunny and busy and loud with life. He put his arm on Anna's shoulder as they walked.

"I don't think I should have to explain this to her," she told him. "Do you think I should have to?"

"No," said Bob, "of course not."

"It may have been her grandmother's ring," she said,

"but it was *my* father—it is the ring that *my* father gave to *my* mother."

"I know," said Bob, trying to calm her and keep her walking.

The years all passed since then like a landscape in Anna's mind—one natural feature giving way to the next, none of it turning out to be the end of the world. Anna would smile and watch for each visit or holiday that brought the girl into the yard again. She'd take her into her arms, welcome her sister's daughter home, and they would survive the weekend.

The girl always helped around the house as best she could, kept Anna company at the breakfast table, and stayed into the week this time. She saw the boy off for school in the mornings with Anna. She washed the dishes and counters and made a square of the towel on the oven handle. By Wednesday, Anna sat with the newspaper and the girl asked if she could see the classifieds, her voice almost flip. "I mean, when you're done, of course."

Anna looked at Joelyn and folded the paper and handed the whole thing over to her.

"I'm thinking I could be a help to you," said Joelyn. "Just be a support for a while—I'd have to get a job and an apartment first, so if you hear of anything."

"I thought you hated Cargill Falls."

"Oh," said Joelyn, "it's not so bad, is it?" She smiled and opened the paper in front of her.

"Who says we need any help, Joelyn?"

"No one."

"What about your things?"

"Everything I have," said the girl, "is here already."

Joelyn found an apartment by the following weekend and started to waitress breakfasts at Zip's—a little silver-sided diner a few exits north. Anna and Daniel would go see her or pick her up when her car was in the shop. If they stayed to eat, Joelyn would slide into the booth and complain that it was too busy or too slow or that the night cook had goosed her. One morning she leaned over the table with a smile she couldn't seem to pinch off her face. They'd just missed him, she said, and pointed to the uncleared plate and napkin at the counter, the dollar tucked under the knife. They watched one of the other waitresses take his cup and plate and wipe the counter clean with a rag.

"Well then," said Anna, turning to the boy, "how about a nice big breakfast for a change?"

They ordered the works—eggs, bacon, pancakes— and they ate without worrying whether the Bonneville would drive into the lot for once. They dialed songs on the jukebox consolette at their table and basked in the drowsy light from the window, watched Joelyn flirt shamelessly with the men at the counter. It was the first time that Daniel could remember not holding his breath, not waiting and watching for his father to suddenly appear. And in the absence of the man hovering over them, in the lack of that quicksand look in his mother's eyes, he began to sense just how much their lives had changed.

CHAPTER FIVE Past certain stretches of farm and river and Daniel could usually guess where he and his father were going. Certain bridges or barns, and Bob might say the bowling alley or Stop & Shop was next. Once they passed the state line, Daniel almost believed that everything was back to normal again, happy-go-lucky in a way it sometimes was before, the two of them riding after school from job to job.

The owner of the bowling alley let them fill their buckets in the bathroom, and Daniel carried the water outside and got the chamois and the brushes ready. A scoop of dishwashing powder, a splash of vinegar, and Bob rolled up his sleeves and swirled each window along the sidewalk. Everyone seemed to watch them work as if Bob and Daniel were mimes, the windows an illusion, the turning of a squeegee onto its handle all part of the show. Bob drew long, unbroken strokes down the glass and paused only to wipe the blade clean. He sent Daniel back to the car for coils of Mortite and putty knives, and the boy crumpled pieces of newspaper and dried the sills and caught the stray drips.

At the end of the job, the windows seemed so clean

that Daniel had to touch the glass to make sure it was still there. He dumped the dirty water onto the street and fit the buckets into the trunk of the car, and his father smoked a cigarette as he filled out the pay slip. His rate was a buck a window, twenty-five for the bowling alley, almost always cash, and almost always one more stop before home.

Back when she still had a sense of humor for his father, Anna would tilt her voice and tease Bob about his one last stop at the Elks or the VFW. She'd be the same about how he wasn't too handy around the house, or too clean or tidy, how he was really just a junk-swapper at heart. This was a running joke between them—the dead car in the woods, the oil barrels, all the half-broken things that ended up at the bottom of the driveway—and she tried to lure Daniel to her side.

"I don't know," said Daniel, "it's not like we're Jim's place or anything, Mom."

"That's my boy," said Bob, "right, Anna?"

"You're an evil man," she said and smiled at Bob. "Brainwashing my son like this."

But Jim the Swapper reminded Daniel of an older version of his father. The old junk dealer was like some hermit out of a storybook, the man's face made with pinches of clay like a mangy old Santa Claus. He'd been a friend of his father's father, and Bob always seemed to owe Jim a visit. On the way he'd stop for a case of beer or a bottle. Never arrive anywhere empty-handed, he told Daniel. It was a sign of respect.

Jim's property started at an old hay baler and a dump truck on the side of the road. A line of bathtubs stood as white as whale teeth in the pasture, and a fire smoldered in an oil drum near the gravel drive. Stones kicked up into the footwalls as they rumbled up to the house, dogs surrounding the car as it slowed. There were old soda machines and water heaters, toilet bowls and big wooden spools by the porch, and Jim was halfway across the yard as Bob and Daniel got out of the Bonneville.

They'd just come from cleaning the supermarket windows in the next town, and Daniel knew his mother would be home from work soon. She'd be starting dinner and looking out the windows for him on the street. But his father took his time across the driveway, as nonchalant as ever, and Jim hollered the dogs aside, his voice like a chainsaw. The old man shuffled to Bob and clapped him on the back like a son.

"Now you remember Daniel," said Bob, "don't you?"

"Sure I do," said the old man, "though it's been a while, hasn't it?"

It was bright, the air dusty, and Daniel handed a bottle of brandy to Jim and shook hands. "So how y'doing?" said Jim. "Keeping your old man out of trouble?"

Daniel raised his shoulders and smiled.

"It's a full-time job," said Bob, "isn't it?"

Jim ushered them into the house, through the front rooms all crammed with books and boxes, the dining room piled with bowls and baskets and pots and plates. In the kitchen, he cleared a little table and slid a chair toward Daniel, got him a can of ginger ale and a straw, some cashews and crackers. He got ice, poured a couple of drinks for Bob and himself, and said cheers.

He stood at the sink and peppered them with questions about Anna and work and whomever they'd seen around town lately. Bob shifted in his chair and said Anna was fine, his voice clipped and quiet. Jim never really sat at the table, but always seemed to stand a few steps away at the counter. Souvenir plates lined the wall behind him—from California, Montana, Michigan, Louisiana, Maine—and Daniel watched and sipped his soda and listened to the two men talk about people and places they knew in town.

"So, Daniel," Jim said, and turned to him. "How old are you, anyhow?"

"I'm ten," he said, "almost eleven."

"And what grade does that make somebody these days?"

"Fifth," said Daniel.

"And is that old enough to have a girlfriend yet? A good-looking guy like you—you must have a girl by now, right?"

Daniel squirmed in his seat and looked down at the table and the water stains on the wood. Bob picked up his drink and leaned back and smiled. He crunched a piece of ice and watched the boy.

"So what's her name?" said Jim.

"Marsha."

"And is she pretty?"

"I don't know. I guess so."

"Well, what color hair does she have?"

Daniel sighed and said yellow, and both men started to laugh.

"Yellow," said Bob, as if explaining a joke.

Jim laughed and coughed and took the bottle, refilled the two glasses once more and raised a drink to Anna and the yellow-haired girl. Daniel watched his father tip the glass to his lips and put it down empty again. The dogs barked outside, and Jim went to the window and started to say something but stopped and stood there.

The boy sensed something in the silence, in his father's impatient glance at Jim, and he pushed away from the table and asked if he could use the bathroom. He zigzagged through the parlor and sat like a girl on the toilet seat, closed his eyes and held his head in his hands, waited for them to say whatever they had to say to each other. And whatever it was, he felt himself on the edge of tears and pressed his knuckles into his eyes.

When he came back to the kitchen, the two men were leaning close and talking low. Jim looked gravely at Daniel and moved back from the table. There was something quiet and overly kind about the way they smiled with concern at the boy, as if it wasn't Anna or Bob they'd been talking about—but him.

Bob slid his glass forward, and the old man filled it once more. "Can I go outside?" Daniel asked his father.

"Don't ask me," said Bob. "It's not my house."

"It's fine with me," said Jim. "Go ahead, just watch for the goat—he's in one of his moods today."

Daniel stepped out to the porch and saw the goat standing on the hood of their car. The dogs crowded around as Daniel turned to the house and then back to the goat in disbelief. The animal just stood in the sun and stared at the boy and the dogs as if possessed. It looked like it had conquered the car, its bones and muscles under a tight suede of fur, and Daniel crossed the yard and waved his arms at it. "What d'you think you're doing?" he said, his voice more shrill than he'd expected it to be.

The goat didn't even blink.

"*Get off*," he yelled, and tried to push the animal from the hood. The goat turned and bared its teeth and stepped off the other side, mud from its hooves on the car. The dogs barked but kept their distance as the goat slowly walked around to the boy.

Daniel moved away across the pasture behind the house. He passed sinks and bathtubs and old stoves and refrigerators on the slope, and still the goat stalked him to a stone wall on the brow of the hill. And at the wall Daniel stumbled and almost fell, and the dogs started to bark and growl again as the goat closed in, its eyes and horns lowered toward the boy. Daniel climbed over the stones and turned and ran back down to the house, his father and Jim outside on the porch.

"You ready?" said Bob.

Daniel tried to catch his breath and tell them about the goat, but Bob raised his hand for quiet.

"C'mon," said Bob, "let's just go."

They said goodbye to Jim and drove the back roads home, the fields bright and contoured with the start of corn. Sunlight flashed in Morse code through the trees, and the boy closed his eyes and felt each dip and rise of the road.

He heard the switchblade of his father's lighter and held his breath against that first smell of cigarette. Daniel watched his father chew the smoke and let it out his nostrils as he drove in silence.

"He's nice," said Daniel, "isn't he?"

"Is he?" said Bob.

"I think he is," said Daniel.

"That scrubby old queer," said Bob. "What the hell's he know, anyway?"

Daniel looked at the side of his father's face and knew enough not to ask anything more of the man right now—though he couldn't help but hope that they were going home, that he could leave his father soon. And as they drove, Daniel thought how people bent forks and spoons with their minds, how they talked with dolphins and traveled in time—so why couldn't he make the steering wheel turn left at the light? Why couldn't he, by force of will, just urge his father home this once?

It was getting toward dusk, and the lights had come on over the streets and in the windows of houses, but still they pulled around to the Elks and started inside. There were always four or five men at the bar in the basement, all of them sitting on stools with belt-cut guts and rounded shoulders. Daniel stood at his father's side and watched him talk with the other men. The bartender poured his father a drink without even asking, and Bob gave the man a plastic token and got quarters for the boy, sent him off to the other side of the room with a handful of change. Daniel slipped coins into the pinball machine and pool table as fast as possible. The balls rolled into the tray, and he set them up and ran his hands over the velvet as he circled to the other end of the table for the cue ball, which he took like an egg from a birdhouse.

Daniel knew the difference between a couple and a few drinks at the bar, just as he understood his father's switch from salted peanuts to pickled eggs, what it meant to have Jim Reeves versus Patsy Cline on the jukebox. A fist of quarters lasted two or two and a half drinks, and Daniel went from anxious to angry to desperate, as if his father was doing this on purpose. A round of pinball and his hands were sweaty and sour as he waited for his father to notice him standing at his side once again. He knew he came as a shock to the man sometimes, like a strange dog nosing his hand. "So what d'you want from me now," said Bob, "a soda or something?"

"Not if we're going to go soon," said Daniel.

Bob touched the empty glass in front of him on the bar, turned it with his fingertips as if opening a safe. He asked the bartender to fix a cherry soda for the kid and got another handful of quarters for him. There'd be yet another round before Daniel could shy up to the man again, the boy standing there as Bob finished the drink in front of him and picked his keys up off the bar.

It was cool and dark outside, and Bob took the long way home, as always. He drove loose and fast and seemed to swagger over hills and curves, past farms and houses and trees. Daniel held his armrest and braced himself for the reckless corners and turns back into town. It was always hard to know what touched his father off, exactly, but Daniel had an instinct for nights like these.

He tried to stay clear of his father when the man was like this—Bob careless as he drove right up to the house and dropped him off in the driveway in silence. Anna stood framed in the light of the front door. She let Daniel into the house, and Bob tooted and pulled slowly away. She'd held dinner and didn't say a word as they ate in the kitchen. She would normally have been livid, would have tapped her foot and demanded an explanation, an apology—where did he and his father go all day? It scared him that she seemed so quiet and unsure now. He felt a chill in the house and caught the smell of cellar, he thought, and when he looked at her he saw the strain in her face. He saw the fear, the worry, as if she'd caught a ghost in the window.

They didn't need to say it, but they both knew that his father would be back. And when he barged through the sleeping house that night, it came as a relief to Daniel. He got up and followed his father along the darkened stairs and saw his mother on one side of the bed. She pulled on a shirt and stood brushing her fingers through her hair, her face trying to stay indifferent to him.

Bob squared himself in the room and seemed to take up more space and mass than his size. "I don't care what you say," he said. "You're gonna let me back in here, Anna."

"Okay," she said, "so you're back in, Bob—now what?"

"Now," he said, "I'm just gonna put myself down and sleep here, in my own bed, like a human being."

He turned to Daniel in the doorway. "And you," he said to the boy, "you can be the witness."

Daniel could smell the man from across the room, his stale cigarettes and salami and sour mash. Bob smiled and let himself fall onto the bed. His feet hung over the end of the mattress as he rested there, his eyes closed, his face almost peaceful.

"No, Bob," said Anna, "you're not staying in this bed like this—get out."

"Just lemme rest, woman," he said, his voice stilted and unfamiliar, the sound not quite connected to him.

Anna tried to roll him off the bed, and Bob let himself go dead and heavy. He lay still as she pulled him by the arms, and then he reached out to try to grab her, Anna stepping back and turning to Daniel. "Go put on some clothes and shoes," she told him. "And dress warm, okay?"

She took the boy outside, where the night was as cool and dark as a pond. They walked away across the grass, past the Bonneville, past the sleeping houses and streets and trees. Everything was quiet and still, and Anna led them down the center of the empty streets, Daniel afraid to ask where they were going. They crossed the bridge as they passed into town, the water black and polished like onyx.

It would be like describing a dream, he thought, to tell anyone about this—the man in the house while he and his mother went in silence through the middle of town, through the undersea streets of night. If someone came across them out here, what would that person be able to make of him and his mother? Would they need all the claustrophobic details, every hammertoe and bunion on his mother's feet? Because if someone wanted a sense of their life in Cargill Falls, Daniel knew his mother could give it to them, right between the eyes.

She walked him to the other end of town and waited on the doorstep of her friend Sylvia. It was cold, and Anna rang the bell and the lights went on in the window upstairs. They heard the ratscrabble of the chain on the door, and Sylvia took them inside. She wore a bathrobe and rollers and sat with Anna in the kitchen, the glide of their voices like a radio in the next room. Daniel tried to sleep on the strange couch in the strange house, and in the morning Sylvia drove them back home, the Bonneville still parked in front of the house, two of its wheels on the lawn.

Bob was asleep on the couch. They stood in the living room, the man lying there with his belt unbuckled, his stomach swollen, his mouth left open for dead. Anna chewed her lip and wavered, and Daniel caught in her face a glimpse of whatever she was trying not to feel anymore.

She took a deep breath and turned to the boy. "Either you get rid of him," she said, "or I call the police."

She looked at the man again and then went and climbed the stairs to her room, and Daniel approached the couch and leaned over his father. "Dad," he whispered, and he quietly shook the man by the arm. "C'mon, let's get up now," he said. "You have to go." Daniel took him by the shoulder and rocked him awake. "C'mon, Dad," he said. "It's time now."

Bob groaned and rolled toward the boy. "Hey," he said, "so what do we got for breakfast, kid?"

"You can't," said Daniel. "You have to leave—she's going to call the police."

"Okay," said Bob, "so we'll scratch breakfast, then— let her be that way." He sat up and swung his feet to the floor. Anna walked across the ceiling to the top of the stairs and threw his boots down to the hall.

"Dad," he said, "get *out* of here." Daniel hurried to get the man's shoes, and Bob stood and zipped his pants, tapped his pockets for his keys, for his pack of cigarettes. "I guess I gotta run," he said. "Tell her I was asking after her."

"Please," said Daniel, *"just go away."*

Bob smiled and reached for his wallet—but it was empty. "What's the chance I could borrow some cash?" he asked. "Don't worry, I'm good for it."

On the verge of tears, Daniel went to the front door and held it open, and Bob winced to see the car on the lawn. But the man somehow made his way outside and into the car. A turn at the corner and the street was empty and sunny, the other houses in the morning light, as if nothing had happened—just this mysterious rut in the grass, the sun bright on the trees, the broken door and nothing else. He missed his father and wished he could just come home. It was like a thread through everything, this feeling, and yet, in an odd way, he missed his mother even more, as if she were the one who needed to come back home.

He felt the air on his face and closed the door. He looked over the room and fixed the pillows on the couch and went upstairs to her. She'd already stripped the sheets and opened the windows to change the air in the room.

"Is he gone?" she asked.

Daniel nodded and watched her finish making the bed. And when he didn't leave from the doorway, she stopped and looked at him. "Are you okay?"

"I'm fine," he told her.

"You sure?"

"Yes," he said.

"So now what about school?"

"I'm gonna need a note," he said. "If that's okay."

CHAPTER SIX The afternoon before his game, Daniel put on his baseball uniform and went to look for his mother at work. She ran the personnel department and liked to parade him around the store to all her friends. He helped her water the birds and hamsters, and she told him to smile as they went to the offices in back. She found her boss, Mr. C. Berry Libby, and asked if she could leave a little early and bring the boy to his baseball game. The man unpuckered his face and reluctantly let them go.

Behind the wheel of the Chevelle, she turned the mirror and painted her lips, and Daniel sank down in his seat and watched. The open compact, the blush of powder on her cheeks, all of it seemed like armor to him. It felt like longer, but it had been only a couple of weeks since his father left, and now his mother pressed a tissue between her lips and combed her hair and readied herself against the man.

Daniel worried threads from the cuff of his jersey. He chewed the cotton until she turned the ignition at last and asked if he was ready to go, her voice bright and cheerful and all wrong to him. They rode to the park in silence, and Anna walked with him to the concession stand and field.

"You know, you don't have to walk with me all this way," he said. "I can go alone."

"I know," she said. "But I want to."

"Yeah, but *I* don't want you to, Mom."

"Oh, I know that," she said and smiled. "But still, I'm here—and I think you worry too much for a boy, anyway."

He was sick with her here, and he swallowed the last of the threads in his mouth and started to tell her that he didn't want her to be around him at all, where everyone could see, but she just raised her hand and smiled him silent, shooed him on toward the field. He turned and jogged down to his team and tried to forget her at the outfield fence, a paper cup of coffee in her hands.

Anna moved with a clutch of other parents to the stands when the game started, and Joelyn walked through the front gate as if on cue. She ambled over to the field and carried on with the men at the fences. And from the dugout, Daniel watched her laugh and then climb the bleachers to his mother. The sun was pale and low over the trees, and Joelyn smiled, her hand on her aunt's leg as if Anna might try to stand up and leave.

Another inning and then Bob appeared out of nowhere. He stood at the low fence near first base, his hair slicked neat. Daniel watched his mother go stiff and straight when she saw him. His own stomach rose to his throat, his world in the reflection of a spoon all over again. He half pretended to play second base and watched his father start down the first baseline. Anna stayed in the stands with Joelyn, who looked back and forth as though Bob and Anna were tossing something between them. The man disappeared behind the scoreboard and backstop, and Daniel held his breath and waited to see him walking on the other side to his mother.

It didn't take long for Bob to reach her, but it felt like a lifetime to Daniel, all the eyeball silence of the town on his mother and father. Joelyn sat with her sideways smile as Bob took the stairs toward them. Anna set her mouth strong as she stood and excused herself, stepping around him and down the stairs along the handrail. She looked small and sad and old, a woman afraid to fall, and Daniel watched her shuffle her way through the lot behind the stands.

Anna had gotten thirty, forty, maybe fifty yards across the lot, and Bob set off after her. He shadowed her across the length of the football field and track, past the swing sets and picnic tables. She walked toward the river, which bordered the park, and he followed a few yards behind her. They passed the last line of trees, and Anna had the strange sense of watching herself from some height. It felt like this had all happened before, right down to this final run of grass, the two of them here together, the slow crawl of water in front of them. She stopped at the edge of the river and waited for him to close the distance between them.

"You know things are bad," he said quietly, "when your own son tells you to get out of your house."

Anna steeled herself as he reached his arms around her and began to whisper all the things she expected and even hoped to hear—how he'd make it up to her, undo every-thing he'd done, find some way to set things right again. She felt the brush of his breath on her neck and listened to his voice and couldn't help but give way to him. It was awful to her and all the worse for being so common and empty and small in the end, her life no different, no better than anyone else's. And there in his arms, she watched herself from above and saw how she'd always hoped for better, how she'd always eluded true unhappiness, how she'd secretly believed that they'd be the ones who made it through. He could have been saying anything to her in the end, but she finally knew it didn't matter anymore—she didn't have any feelings left.

She closed her eyes and smoothed them with the cool of her fingertips. "Now," she said as she turned in his arms, "I don't look like I've been crying, do I?"

She leaned away from him, and he said, "No—you just look fragile."

"Is that all?" she said, smiling. "I think I can live with fragile."

He walked her to the car and watched her silhouette in the rear window as she drove away home, as if to hide from him. The wooden poles and electric lines sloped one to the next, and he waited on the empty edge of the road, on the sand and the crabgrass. He heard the cheers from the ball field in the distance, the sparkler sound of applause.

There were only one or two innings left, and Bob went to the concession booth and stood with some other men he knew from town. He bought a can of soda and took it to his car. He turned the key in the ignition and drove away, past the water tower.

He was alone with the quiet and the windshield's curve of sky and trees in front of him. He sat and watched the vacant bend of road out his window. It was such an Anna moment that he felt aligned with her — sitting here by himself, waiting for nothing, unable to will her life into what she'd wanted it to be.

He turned the car around and drove toward home and found them walking along the sidewalk, Joelyn and Daniel. He coasted up to them on the undertow of the engine, cleared the seat, and reached across to roll down the passenger window. "Say," he called to them, "who wants a ride?"

Bob sprang the door open, and with some hesitation they got in front and rode through town. It was a short ride, but it felt long and slow, the man's elbow brushing Daniel's shoulder as he steered and tried to chat about the ball game and the weather. One last corner and they saw the Chevelle in the driveway and eased over to the side of the road before he reached the house.

It was getting dark, and they stared at the empty street, the trees, the houses. Bob sucked his teeth, and Joelyn turned and grinned at him and the boy sitting there like henchmen. "Don't worry," she said and smiled. "This is close enough, I guess." She opened her door and slid out of the car and just stood there and waited, her hip against the door.

Bob tapped the dash and told Daniel he'd stop by and

see him later, but the boy didn't say anything. He gathered his glove and nodded and climbed out of the car. And as the boy began to walk away, Joelyn slid back into the front seat next to Bob.

"Hello again," she said and closed the door behind her. Bob turned from her to the boy walking in the gutter in front of them. The way he went so slow, it seemed Daniel didn't want to go home, didn't want to leave his father alone with her.

Bob turned to the girl. "What's up, Joelyn?"

"Oh, c'mon," she said. "Don't be so sour all the time. I mean, *really*, can't anyone be happy around here?"

"No," he told her. "Now what d'you want from me, a ride home?"

"That'd be swell," she said. She leaned so close he could hear the crackle of saliva in her smile. "I actually have something for you."

He looked at her again—at her eyes, her hair, her fingers playing with a necklace.

"You remember the ring," she said, "don't you?"

"Just cut to the chase, Joelyn."

"Fine," she said, "the chase—the chase is I'm thinking that you should get the ring for Anna and see if it changes her mind about things—what do you think?"

He stared at her, and she waved her hand for him to drive. She said go, but Bob just held the wheel and looked down the street at the boy lingering in front of the house.

"What do you think?" she said, and touched him on the arm.

He looked at her hand and tapped the horn for the boy,

as if to save himself from this, as if the boy might keep him somehow anchored to the world. Bob got out of the car and met Daniel on the sidewalk. They walked back to the car together, Bob with his hand on his son's shoulder as they approached.

"Go on," he said, opening the door to the back. "Just push all that shit aside."

Daniel climbed in over the newspapers and food wrappers on the seat. Empties clinked under his shoes and he sat and watched his father and Joelyn in front of him, as if they needed a chaperon. It was almost dark by now, and Bob pulled the car around hard, the buckets thumping in the trunk. Joelyn directed them through every turn and street in town, and Bob finally threw his hands up. "I know the fricken way, Joelyn."

"I'm just trying to help," she said. "And I don't need to be yelled at, either."

Bob looked up, catching the boy's eye in the mirror. "What d'you think back there? Is anybody yelling?"

Daniel pulled himself forward, and Bob rolled slowly through town. "Tell her," he said to the boy. "Somebody yelling here or not?"

"No," said Daniel. "Not yet."

They drove over the bridge and circled behind the shopping center, Joelyn pointing out one more street, her Datsun sitting out by the curb. Bob parked and turned to Daniel. "You sit tight a minute," he said. "I'll be right out."

He left the Bonneville running and followed Joelyn across the little courtyard to her apartment. She switched on the lights as Bob stepped into the living room—a shoebox of a room, no frills or furniture to speak of, just the two windows, the wallpaper textured like bamboo. He walked across the floor and looked into the kitchen and the hall to the bedroom and bathroom. "Real nice," he said. "Done a lot with the place, Joelyn."

"So glad you like it, Bob. Now can I get you anything? Water? Juice? Back rub?"

He shook his head and smiled. "No, thanks," he said. "Just the ring, please."

She sighed and moved lazily toward him. "Of course," she said, putting her hand on his arm. "One question, though, if I may—I just want to know why. I mean, why'd you do it, Bob?"

He shook his head and said, "No—I gotta go now, Joelyn." He turned from her and started to the door.

"Just hold on," she said. "I'll go get it. Just wait here."

She pushed away from him and turned on her toes and disappeared into the bedroom. He stood alone in the room and picked the calluses on his hand. In a moment she came running back in, laughing and loud. She had a slip of paper and shook it open at him, wagged it in front of his face.

He tried to swat her away, but she kept just out of reach, starting to laugh and dance around him, her voice all nonsense and singsong. She pushed the piece of paper at him, waved it like a cloth, laughing and saying that it was the receipt for the ring. She kept teasing him with it, almost mocking him, kept fluttering around until he caught her, finally, by the wrist and turned her arm down and said, "Stop."

She stopped and looked at him. "What are you going to do?" she said. "You going to break my arm, Bob?"

She leaned close, and he shook his head and said, "No, but I am gonna go now." He let her wrist loose and smiled and slowly turned toward the door.

She watched him walk across the room. "Aren't you forgetting something?" she asked. She held the receipt out to him with two hands, as if offering it up to him.

He stopped by the door. "So give it to me, then."

She smiled and hid her hands behind her back. "All right," she said, "but what's in it for me?"

He just stared at her.

"I mean, what do I get out of it, Bob?" She kept her arms behind her and swayed up close to him again.

"What did you do," he asked, "pawn it?"

She pursed her lips. "Don't be so mean," she said. "Here I am trying to help you out, Bob—talk about ingratitude."

"Save it, Goldilocks."

Her smile widened and she leaned against him. "By the way, Anna told me the whole sad story."

"You know," he said, "I doubt that very much, Joelyn—now what d'you want for your ring?"

"A kiss," she said and laughed. She pursed her lips and closed her eyes. He held himself back from her and didn't say anything. She opened her eyes and called him a coward. He was a coward about everything, she said, Bob stepping back from her as she tried to press herself against him.

"Just one kiss," she told him.

"You're crazy," he said, and kept stepping away, as if frightened of her. And then he stopped and put his arms around her and held her. She didn't struggle or move, as he grabbed behind her back for her hands, her body tightening against him. She felt like ropes and cords all tense in his arms. And then she raised her face to him and seemed to almost kiss him, and after a moment Bob let her go. He had the slip of paper in his hand and stepped away from her to look at it, the claim ticket for the ring. And when he turned from her to leave, there he was, Daniel, the boy standing at the door, watching them.

CHAPTER SEVEN School seemed such a comfort to Daniel—his friends, field trips, films in science class. Even a fight, the fact that he rubbed someone the wrong way, it all made a certain poetic sense to him, as if a bully like Scott Dixon could see the real Daniel underneath the mask he fit himself into each day.

Not especially strong or imposing, Scott Dixon was just sly and mean. His parents let him stay out at night, and he lurked near the pay phones and gas stations of town, his arms braided with scars, as if he'd been tied with twine. He simply hated Daniel and jumped him from the woods after school one day—a fist to the throat, another to the side of the face, a kick to the ribs as Daniel lay on the ground.

By the time Brownie and everyone else could get there, Scott was already gone. Everybody talked tough and milled around and helped Daniel to his feet, got his gym bag from the gutter, brushed off his shirt, but Brownie had to bring his brother home, and only Marsha stayed to make sure he was all right. She walked with him past the armory, away from school, past the long row of snowplows, the mounds of road sand, the culvert that ran under the street.

Past the brook and the railing, they stopped and stood in the light between the trees. They set down their book bags, and Marsha wet the corner of her sleeve with her mouth and cleaned the scratches and dirt around his eye and cheek. Daniel winced as she brushed the grass from his collar. "What's your mother going to say?" she asked.

"I don't know," said Daniel. "Maybe she won't notice."

Marsha looked at him and smiled and said that she'd notice, if she were his mother. He shrugged and pressed the bone under his cheek with his fingertips, the pain somehow satisfying. An airplane unzippered the sky, left to right across the line of trees, and Marsha asked if he could walk her home, before her parents started to worry.

They went through the cemetery and she slipped her hand into his as they reached her street and moved under the spread of trees. It was the first time he'd held hands with anyone. Her house sat before them with its curtains open and lawn freshly mowed, the window boxes full of flowers. It was a house he wanted to take home with him.

"Anyway," she said, "I guess I'll see you tomorrow." She kissed him quickly on the side of his mouth and hurried away to the porch, turning for one last glance back at him. She waved and disappeared inside the house, and Daniel just stood on the sidewalk and stared at the windows and smiled. Though it hurt, he couldn't stop smiling, and he ran the whole way home, ran the railroad tracks like a high wire, ran along in the air over everything.

At home, his father's Bonneville sat tucked beside his mother's Chevelle in the drive — it felt like a blow to the body to see it there. He ran his hand along the hood of the man's car, still warm to the touch. The Chevelle was cool, his mother's paint sandy under his hand. He waited outside and stretched himself over the back of her car, half hidden from the house.

In the fading light, he leaned against the Chevelle and scratched the chalk of bird droppings off the trunk, traced the notch between the trunk and fender. Under the bend of the back windshield, on the shelf over the back seat lay the broken flies and June bugs that had been trapped in the car, the faded moths and bees and beetles, an old wasp wedged against the curved glass, its body as white and intricate as ivory.

As it grew dark and cold, Daniel let himself into the back of her car. He sat there and collected the dead bees from under the glass. They weighed absolutely nothing in the cup of his palm. And even though they were curled and blanched by the sun, it was hard not to be somewhat wary of the bigger ones. The old wasp with its sci-fi armor and jet-fighter wings, its stinger, its helmet eyes, the thing seeming to tremble in his hand as if highly keyed.

Daniel closed the wasp in his fist and held it and breathed into the collar of his shirt for warmth. When he heard the side door of the house open, his first reaction was to lay himself across the back seat and hide. He crouched down and held his breath and followed the crunch of shoes on the sidewalk and driveway. He heard the Bonneville's door being opened and closed, the engine starting, the car backing into the street and driving away.

Window by window the lights of the house came on.

He sat up and watched as the porch light flickered to life and Anna stepped out of the door. She came straight to the car, as if she knew where Daniel would be. She seemed out of sync in the light, her movements not quite linked to the sound of her steps. She opened the door and the dome light left her face vaguely blue, as if her bones were pewter under her skin. "Scoot over a little," she said.

The boy turned slightly from her so she couldn't see his face, and it was almost comic, the way she sat there beside him as if a chauffeur were driving.

"You saw your father just now?" she asked.

He nodded and said, "Yes."

She looked at him. "I don't know what we should do anymore, Daniel, do you?"

He didn't know what to say, and soon the chance to say anything was gone. All he knew was that it didn't matter what happened, as long as something happened to take them away from all of this. He put his hand on her knee.

"Other women can do it," she said. "Others let their husbands back and put up with so much worse—my mother did, my sister did, but I just don't know if I can."

She led him back to the house, Daniel a step behind her across the yard in the dark. As they walked over the grass, he rubbed the bees into ash and blew them from his hand as if he were blowing out candles. And as they reached the front steps to the house, he slipped the wasp into his mouth, as if trying to swallow fear itself, the soft bead of it rolling over his tongue and teeth. He stayed silent, swallowing and trading weak for strong.

And later, watching his window for his father, he wondered just how long before this so-called strength became a kind of fear. And then how long before the fear became a kind of hope or longing all its own? He only asked because there he was in his room with this first hope of his, that the wasp would stay down and swallowed away forever. And yet there was always this other hope, the one in which he spit it up again and held it in the cup of his palm, the wasp in his hand again, all glossy and wet and newborn as ever.

She became the scuff and creak over him again that night. Daniel lay awake in bed until his father appeared at the window, the boy lifting open the sash and beginning to give away all the secrets she'd trusted him to keep for her. He watched the orange glow of the man's cigarette and heard his father spit into the grass. Daniel didn't expect to cry right here, but he tasted salt in the back of his mouth and saw everything begin to swim and waver in his eyes. He tried not to exhale any long, shaky breaths, because he knew his father would lean up to the window and tell him not to start any crybaby stunts, Bob's voice half joking yet half not joking, Daniel unable to stop himself or his tears.

Bob tossed the cigarette to the grass and became by turns gruff and then angry with the boy, sullen and then gentle, saying he'd do anything if he just stopped with the tears. "Aw c'mon already," said Bob. "Where's that tough guy I used to know? He wouldn't carry on like this, now would he? He wouldn't make his father feel like an asshole."

Bob threw up his arms and walked out to the middle of

the lawn in exasperation to the moon and the trees. And then he just headed away to the street and his car around the corner. In the quiet of his room, Daniel wiped his face and tried to gather himself. He stood alone at the window and waited as his father came back across the yard to the house again.

"Are you done yet?" the man asked. "Because if you're done I want to show you something." He had a slip of paper in his hands and held it up to the window, then slipped it under the screen. "I want you to hold on to that for me," he said, "if it's okay with you."

It was too dark to read anything, but Daniel took the piece of paper and tried to look at it, his father explaining how it was a receipt for the ring. It was in a pawnshop, he said, and someday they would go get it for his mother.

Still later, in the middle of the night, Daniel would feel more than hear the sounds Anna made as she moved around the house. He watched the window for so long he began to dream of the bushes in the wind outside, his mother in his doorway, the muffled clank of pots and pans in the kitchen. And still later he woke, the windows pale with morning, and he went down the hall to the bathroom. All the lights were on in the house, and the rooms looked shell-shocked to be awake, as if they hadn't been put to bed that night, all the furniture and fixtures almost dazed and overtired.

He found his mother in the kitchen, where everything had been taken off the walls and shelves—the clock, the spice rack, the recipe books all taken down. The whole room had been dismantled into a jumble of dishes and pots and pans. She looked like she hadn't slept that night either, her face pale and drawn, her clothes the same as yesterday's.

He watched her from the hall, but she didn't see him right away. Instead she went down to the basement and came back upstairs with a piece of plywood. In the kitchen she wrote—MOVING SALE—in big black letters on the wood, front and back. And as she started to the living room, Daniel went to his room and watched from the window as she took the sign outside and propped it against the tree by the sidewalk, sunlight full on the lawn:

— MOVING SALE —
EVERYTHING MUST GO

She stood in the yard and looked at the house for a moment, as if she might not ever see it again, and Daniel waited for her to come to his doorway.

"What're you doing up?" she asked.

"I guess I couldn't sleep," he told her. "What're you doing, Mom?"

She was trying to be strong, but once again he felt the metal washer or coin come back up inside him as her chin started to shake. She left his room and went to finish what she'd started. With a marker and a roll of masking tape, she began with the sofa—$40—pressed the price on its arm. She tore a piece of tape—$5—for the coffee table. The mantel clock—$65 (OR BEST OFFER). In the kitchen she gathered the table and chairs and opened the cupboards and priced it all to sell. She carried a rocking chair onto the lawn, a magazine stand, a lamp, arranged them as if in a room with the walls taken away. She even laid an afghan over the arm of the chair.

It seemed like years since it'd been the home he'd once known, but now this was even worse. From his room he saw people cutting across the grass, saw them touch the chair in the yard, saw that mix of curiosity and sympathy in their faces as they came into the house. They browsed the kitchen and hall, and he heard the way they mumbled to each other that her husband had left. *Husband's the window washer*, they whispered, *drives the big Pontiac. Look at this place — no way to care for a boy, that's for sure.*

Daniel dressed slowly and then lifted open his window. He lowered himself over the sill, out into the yard and woods. He started to run and ran the mile into town, reached Livery Street, and found his father.

They drove back home in the Bonneville, and Bob found the insides of the house spread across the yard, the roof like the keel of a sinking ship. Cars lined the street and Bob pulled up and sat a moment, pinched the bridge of his nose. "Do you want to stay here or come with me?"

"I'll stay here," said Daniel.

"Can't blame you for that," he said to the boy. He winked and got out of the car. Bob crossed the yard to the front steps and cattle-called everyone out of the doorway and living room. "Show's over, folks," he said. "Time to go now."

He found Joelyn at the kitchen table with a bowl of cereal. She always appeared at the worst moment, that smile on her face. "I thought I heard you out there," she said. "So's this your shining moment or something?"

"Where's your aunt, Joelyn?"

The girl pointed at the floor, and Bob turned and started down to the basement. Anna stood under the boy's bedroom, between the lawn furniture and the furnace. "Hello, Bob," she said, her voice calm. "How about helping me with these boxes?"

He reached to her, but she pulled away from him and said no. She picked up a box of Christmas ornaments and carried it up the stairs, her heels rising out of her shoes as she took each step. In the daylight, Anna seemed so papery and frail that he put himself between her and Joelyn, the girl with that lie-in-wait smile of hers. She waved her hand around the room as if to show Anna and Bob what was left of their house. And Bob just nudged Anna toward the hall, and then he turned back to the girl. "I need your help," he said quietly. "I need you to go outside and make sure everyone's gone. Then just pull the place together, get all those things back in the house, and get Daniel to help—he's in my car."

And before Joelyn could say anything, Bob followed Anna down the hallway. She'd stopped in the boy's doorway and moved into the room, standing there looking at Daniel's bed and posters. She pushed the dresser drawers shut, and Bob watched as she stared at the wall.

"Why don't you come lie down for a little while?" he said.

"Because I don't need to lie down, Bob."

"Okay, Anna, so don't lie down—I don't care."

"You really are my nemesis," she said, turning to him. "I mean, everyone else is gone but you—*why?* Why is that, Bob? I mean, why are you always here? What do you want? Why do you keep coming back to torture me like this?"

"Must be all my charm and winning ways," he said and smiled.

They heard the front door open, heard footsteps approach in the hall. Joelyn appeared at the doorway, and her eyes darted from Anna to Bob. "Uncle Bob," she said, "I need to talk to you."

"Go ahead," he told her. "Talk."

"Well, I did what you said, but I couldn't find Daniel."

"You looked in my car?"

"I looked," she said. "I can't find him anywhere."

Part Two

CHAPTER EIGHT Daniel sat in the first seat of the bus and held his breath, half expecting the Bonneville to appear at any moment over the crest of the street. Outside on the sidewalk, the bus driver stood talking with the woman from the drugstore. Daniel waited and held the armrest and watched the driver and the street. He poked the lid of the ashtray—a peach pit inside, a secret little brain surrounded by ash and mold. He flipped the cover closed and tapped the window lightly, as if that might bring the driver back into the Greyhound and start them out of here.

It was ten-thirty on the bank clock when the driver finally climbed up behind the wheel and pulled the lever to close the door. The engine droned under the bus, and they began to swing around corners, past storefront windows. Leaving was the taste of diesel, the big turns out of town, and then the slash of guardrails. There were maybe a dozen people on the bus that morning, and Daniel heard the rustle of newspaper and shush of voices behind him, an empty soda can rattling across the aisle. At first his eyes itched, then they burned, and the boy squeezed them closed and felt that roller coaster of hills, his head against the tinted glass. He touched his shirt pocket for the receipt, took the slip of paper, unfolded it, and read the address, the claim number, the fine print on the back, in bold: *Avoid selling under unfavorable circumstances. Don't make hasty decisions regarding your jewelry, diamonds, and gold.*

He put the paper away and patted the house keys in his pants pocket, the coins, the fold of money—two hundred and forty dollars—a fortune in dirty windows and heavy buckets, all those nights with his father outside in the dark, not to mention his own scheming and stealing and lying to his father and mother. Yet it would be forgotten by returning the ring to her, everything forgiven after the ring.

A few more miles, and he pictured his mother on the seat next to him, the tap of foot or purse of lips, her signal ticks of anger. He rose above it this time. She could drink silence and stillness under the table, but her simmering routine meant nothing to him this time. The wipers whistled, the billboards passed, and he blew saliva bubbles and plucked details from the side of the road—a shredded tire, a crow on a fence, a lump of clothing or raccoon. These things helped when he wavered, when he sensed that sigh building up in her, that sound of yet another submission she had to swallow.

He imagined handing her the ring, pressing it into her soft palm. She'd look at him and then down at her hand and see her mother and sister there. She'd see Bayside and her father with all those dreams for them. She'd smile at Daniel as if a veil had lifted off her face, as if all this time she'd been only one gesture away from life.

. . .

The phone poles ticked past, their wires swooping up and down in a kind of flight at his window. The trees and houses rolled slowly by, and Daniel tightened himself against the slightest lift or drop of road. He wiped his palms on his legs and listened to the hiss and wheeze of the power steering, the groan of the engine, the rattle of loose metal somewhere near the driver. Daniel leaned forward against the slow reverse of his stomach, the warm floods of saliva in his cheeks. He fought every rotary and high turn into the next town, the next postcard view of a Main Street or milldam, a handful of people on a sidewalk, duffels and suitcases at the curb.

The driver opened the undertrunks of the bus and stowed luggage, took tickets, and the passengers filed up the steps into the bus. An older woman in a church dress, a man with a fedora and a newspaper; everyone headed down the aisle to the empty seats behind the boy. One last gulp of air, and the driver closed the doors and started forward again. "Hey, chief," the driver called up to him. "You all right over there?"

Daniel took his hands from his face and fell silent—he realized he'd been panting inside his head—and he looked up at the driver. The man angled the rearview mirror and kept glancing from the road to the boy. "Now c'mon, bud," said the driver. "You're not going to get sick on my bus or anything, are you?"

"No," he croaked to the driver. He managed a dismal grin, but the smell of diesel made him gag, and he quickly tucked his chin and mouth into the collar of his shirt.

"Hey there, pal," said the driver. "Here comes a little

fresh air for you. You'll feel much better in a minute." The man slid the vent windows open and fumbled at the small fan on the dash as he drove. "C'mon," he said to the boy, "no disasters."

Daniel slumped across the seat with his shirt still over his nose, his mouth working the saliva back.

"Look alive over there," said the driver. "You just need to talk to me, kid—c'mon now, get your head up and look down the road." He caught the boy's eye in the mirror and tried to distract him, tried to ask his name, and did he like school or baseball or anything? "So you're heading to New York City," he said. "What d'you got going on there? You have family meeting you?"

Daniel looked away and clenched his teeth, feeling his stomach lurch up to his throat again. "Hold it together," said the man. "Just a few more clicks and we're almost there."

The road widened and graded gently into a long, smoky view of the river valley below. The driver down-shifted to an off-ramp and another mile of streets—old clapboard houses and drab brick buildings, kids on the corners, and then a big sandcastle of a train station and bus depot. The driver announced Hartford and swung the bus around with a final release of air brakes at the gate. He opened the doors, gave Daniel a pat on the hand, and stepped down to open the luggage trunks, and all the passengers rustled out of their seats to the aisle, the steps, and the platform outside the bus.

Daniel stayed in his seat, his hands still clenched to the

armrest. He watched people carry their bags away into the station or the pay phones, some stopping to light cigarettes, the smoke trailing behind them. Strips of sunlight fell between the buses, blue swirls of exhaust in the light. The driver swung back up onto the stairs. "We have a layover, you know. Maybe you should get out and stretch your legs a little bit."

Daniel nodded to the man but didn't move, and the driver reached up over the visor and turned the scroll of destinations above the windshield.

"You might feel better — walk it off, get some fresh air, some blood moving."

"Is it okay if I just wait here?"

"Sure," said the driver, "of course you can. Just as long as you feel better, that's all."

The man took some paperwork from under the dash and said he'd see him back here in a little bit. He tapped the handrail in front of the boy and climbed down from the bus, folded the doors closed, and then crossed to the main hall of the station. The bus grew quiet and empty and almost dark. Everyone was gone and Daniel slid out of his seat and stood in the aisle, his legs wobbling as he began to walk to the back of the bus. He pushed open the narrow door of the restroom and retched long, yolky strands into the toilet. He pinched them off at his lips and wiped his fingers on the calves of his pants.

Back in his seat, he rested his eyes and waited for the driver to return. His mother tended to arrive at times like these, of course, when things were quiet and the minutes seemed to stand still. He sat there and told himself not to open his eyes to her or that look of hers, her face full of every doubt he'd ever had about himself and his feelings. It became a kind of contest, and he kept his eyes blind for so long that he became the statue, the creepy person made of marble.

Nothing touched him but the passing of buses, the watery talk of people on the sidewalks, a hint of cigar smoke like the smell of burning leaves. The bus doors opened, and still he kept his eyes squeezed shut. He heard people climb the stairs and brush past his seat to the rows behind him. He felt suitcases being loaded under the bus and more passengers shuffling past, and then a stillness in the doorway, a sense of someone looking over the handrail at the seat next to him.

And when he opened his eyes, he saw a lunch bag. The driver had put it there. "Didn't mean to wake you," said the man. "But in case you're hungry."

The driver stepped down off the bus again, and Daniel lifted the bag from the seat. It had the cool weight and shape of a soda can inside, and he took out the package of chips, the sandwich, the can of Sprite. He waited to catch the man's eye, but the driver didn't turn to him as he closed the trunks. Daniel felt the weight of something else inside the bag, and he found a little toy airplane with a pilot and bombs, propellers that spun.

The driver walked around the outside of the bus, checked the tires, adjusted the mirrors, and then finally slipped in behind the wheel without so much as a glance at

Daniel. He turned the engine over and closed the door, stoked the gears, and then drove quietly onto the streets and the wide highway. Daniel balanced the plane on his knee and waited until the driver flipped the sun visor and saw him in the mirror at last. "I wasn't sure," said the man, "but you're not too old for the toy, are you?"

The boy shook his head and said no.

"Good," said the driver. "Now if you're hungry," he said, "you might start out with the soda and chips and see how your stomach does, okay?"

"Thank you," said Daniel.

The driver shifted and changed lanes, and the sound of the engines ran through the floor and seats. Whenever Daniel felt the motion of the highway beneath him, he took the little plane and banked its wings with the graded turns and speed of the Greyhound. He glided high above the interstate, high above the towns, the passengers crowding up the narrow stairs at each stop. They stepped like penguins down the aisle to seats behind him.

Then it was back to the highway and that drone of engines again. And soon enough the city turned everything into brick and concrete, New York piling up like so many stacks of nickels and pennies in the light.

The bus arrived in a great hangar of a building, and Daniel said goodbye to the driver and followed everyone to the hall, to the escalators, and then to the sunlight of the avenue through the front doors. There was a line of taxicabs along the street, and some policemen, a hot dog cart, the smell of burnt salt. Past the shoeshine thrones at the corner, past all the people and cars and trucks and noise, the boy went along with the flickering crowds.

He tapped his pockets and realized he'd forgotten his plane and sandwich on the bus. He stopped as if to go back, but just looked at the Tinker Toy girders of the bus terminal. He told himself to keep moving and turned and walked away. Pigeons leafed up around him from the curbs and gutters, and he went over the subway grates, steam rising into his face. He weaved his way along the busy sidewalks and felt as if he was a balloon tied with a string to his own wrist somehow, the boy at once hollow and high and bobbing along after himself through the city.

CHAPTER NINE The doors—wide bronze double doors —hushed open to the touch, the long aquarium counters inside. His eyes adjusted to the dim light and high ceilings, the glow of necklaces and rings and wristwatches behind glass. The place looked like any jewelry store, except for the case of knives and guns at one counter, that thrift-shop clutter of old silverware, of camera and office equipment along the side wall. A subway rumbled under the floor, and a guard appeared from a darkened corner back by the door. He was broad and bald and smiled in a way that made Daniel check his fly.

"Something I can help you with, little man?" The guard's mouth seemed full of marbles, and his suit bunched up at the shoulders and arms and had a shine to it, a green-fly sheen at the cuffs and lapels. Daniel had the receipt in his hand and tried to explain about the ring, but his lips and cheeks went wrong, one of his eyebrows twitched.

The guard looked at him and started to laugh. It was a great gobble of a laugh, as if the man was choking to death. Just then a set of half doors at the back of the showroom pushed open, and a saleswoman appeared. Daniel glanced at her, at the guard, at the windows facing the street. He almost started to run for the door as she walked behind the counter to them, her fingernails long and red and tapping the glass, the guard still chuckling over the boy.

"What's going on, Lou?"

"Customer for you," said the man. He turned and leered so close that Daniel teetered back a step from him. "Now listen," said the guard, "I don't want any funny business out of you, twitchy—got it?"

The woman stood at the counter and smiled at them, as calm as a den mother. "Leave him already," she said. "You're scaring the poor kid."

The guard tsked at the boy and went back to his stool in the corner.

"Let's just ignore him," she said to Daniel. "We'll see if he goes away—now what can I do for you, honey?"

Daniel stepped up to the counter with the slip of paper in his hand. "I'd like to get a ring," he said and flattened the receipt on the glass.

The guard started laughing again, and she turned and said, "Be quiet already, Lou." She smiled at the boy. "Don't mind him," she said. "He's our resident troll, is all."

Her smile was strained, as if her shoes were too tight and small, and she said, "Let's just see what we've got here."

She opened a pair of bookkeeper's glasses and tipped the paper to the light, her lips moving slightly as she read the receipt to herself.

"Where'd you get this, sweet pea?"

"My father gave it to me," said Daniel.

"And did your father give you money for it too?"

"Yes," he said, taking the fold of bills from his pocket to show her.

"That's all right," she told him. "I believe you—let me go find your ring." She took the slip with her and headed through the slatted doors again, and Daniel waited at the counter and looked at all the jewelry under lights.

"*Pssst*," said the guard. "Over here."

The man motioned for the boy, but Daniel turned away to the case of pearls and pens and flasks in the fishtank lights. He chewed his lip and walked toward the back as the guard came closer. "So who's the ring for?" he whispered. "Don't worry, you can trust old Lou. I won't tell anybody."

Daniel shook his head, and the saleswoman elbowed her way through the doors, a large flat tray in her hands. She set it onto the counter in front of the boy, and he looked at all the rings in tight slotted rows of velvet. There must have been a hundred shining stones, each with a numbered tag attached to it by a string. The woman flattened the receipt on the glass and began to turn the little tags with her fingernails, Daniel just standing there, trying to look away from the full scoops of her breasts. She squinted over the tiny numbers and told him, almost absently, about sapphires and diamonds. And then there it was—the ring. She removed it from the tray and dangled it on her fingernail in front of him.

He'd never seen it before, and it was small and dim compared to what he'd imagined. His mother had told him how it was supposed to glow in the light, but the metal seemed almost dull, almost gray to him, and the whole thing seemed so simple and modest that he'd never have looked at it twice, let alone picked it from the tray with all these others.

The saleswoman slipped the ring onto her finger as far as her knuckle. She modeled it for Daniel. She asked him what he thought, and he just stood there, taking his hands from the counter, unsmudging the glass with the cuff of his shirt.

"What's the matter?" she said. "Don't you like it?"

"Are you sure it's the right one?"

She smiled and looped the tag off and held the ring out over the countertop to him. "Go on," she said. "You can take a look at it, if you want."

He felt his heart stumble in his chest as he slowly reached his hand to her. She placed it in the cup of his palm like a dime. The ring was much heavier than he thought it would be, almost sturdy in his hand, the diamond set in claws. The whole thing wasn't half as delicate as he'd pictured, not half as beautiful or large or important as he'd imagined, either.

He fingered the bead of the stone and raised it to the light, listening as the woman described what he was seeing: a lovely ring, a perfect diamond, fancy-cut and set in an old European style. Someone had it resized recently, she said. But before that, I'd say someone had worn this ring every single day of her life.

Daniel looked up at her, and she smiled and shrugged.

"But then again, what do I know?" she asked. "The truth is, every ring in this place is a tragedy of one kind or another. Happy rings don't end up here."

A subway rumbled under the floor again, and she offered Daniel a jeweler's glass from her pocket. And when he looked in the lens, the stone trembled like a star in a telescope. As he stared at it, the woman slid a calculator across the top of the counter. She started to tap some numbers with the nail of her thumb and explained the vault fee to him, the back interest, the sales tax, and then the reappraisal. He tried not to react, but he didn't have enough money, and he never would, and all he could seem to do was nod his head at her.

She took the tray of rings and said she'd be back in a jiffy. And when the doors flapped open again, she led an older man around the counters to Daniel, the man moving as if he were all hinges and wires under a rumpled suit. The man didn't say a word as he took the claim ticket from the counter. "Aren't you a little young to be shopping for rings?" he asked, his voice gruff.

"It's for my mother," said Daniel.

"That's none of my business," he said, and he turned to look at the saleswoman.

She tucked her hair behind her ears. "Let's let Harry take a look at the ring," she said and opened her hand out to Daniel. "It's a beauty," she told him. "Now let's all have a look, please?"

Daniel placed the jeweler's lens in her palm, and she smiled and tipped her head to the side. "Don't try to be cute," she said. "We need your ring for a minute here, okay?"

Daniel stared at her and waited, and then he took a single step back from the counter.

"What's his problem?" said the old man.

"I don't know," she said. They stood there and never took their eyes off him.

Daniel didn't move. He just stood on the carpet and felt frantic inside—they were going to take the ring from him.

"I thought you said he had money," said the old man.

"He does," she said. "Maybe he's just scared."

"I'll give him something to be scared about," the guard said. "Let me handle him—the little turd."

"Oh, don't hurt him, Lou."

"I'm not going to *hurt* him," he said and turned the keys in the door with drama. "I'm going to *kill* him."

"Come on," she said to the boy. "What's the matter, sweetie?"

Daniel stared at her and took another step back. He looked down at the ring in his hand and then closed his fists. Everyone started to move in on him, it seemed, the woman and old man coming around the counter, the guard spreading his arms, Daniel backing slowly into a corner. "Here, kitty-kitty-kitty," said the guard.

"What's with everybody?" the old man yelled. "Just grab the little fucker."

Daniel ducked under the guard's arms and circled away toward the old man. The woman half lunged at Daniel and the old man—nothing but cords and springs inside his suit

—caught the boy and wrapped his arms around him, lifted him off the ground.

"Don't just stand there, you idiots," the old man hollered, the boy struggling against him. "Get the ring from the kid."

Daniel twisted and kicked against the old man, the man's arms as hard and mean as wire. The guard rushed forward and grabbed Daniel by the legs and pulled. "Hold still," he said. "Little fricken monkey, isn't he?"

Daniel kept kicking at the guard, and the woman tried to pry one of the boy's fists apart with her nails. It was the wrong hand, and she went to his other fist, but Daniel arched his back and knifed himself sideways at her hand, his teeth jamming onto her thumb. She screamed and actually smacked him across the face.

His ear rang and burned, and she yelled, "He just bit me!"

The guard laughed, and Daniel jerked away from her and caught the old man with the back of his head. The boy rocked forward once more and cracked the old man hard in the chin, the two of them falling to the floor. The woman screamed again as the man and boy fell, and the ring bounced out of the boy's hand and onto the carpet. She saw it and started for it immediately, the ring lying there across the showroom, and Daniel scrambled on all fours after her.

They reached it at the same moment, but the woman stomped her shoe over the ring and squared herself to the boy. "Do not even *think* about it," she said, grinding her toe into the carpet.

He felt paralyzed by her voice and just looked at her,

his mind racing. The guard took the boy by the ankles and hauled him away from the woman, the ring still there under her foot. "What the hell is your problem?" he said to Daniel.

The old man had blood on the front of his shirt, and Daniel looked from him to the guard and started kicking his legs to try to get loose. He broke free and just charged her, threw himself at her knees, and she fell against the glass counters — and there, embedded in the carpet, was the ring. He scooped it into his hand and ran for the front door.

But it was locked, and he was cornered and feral again, all three of them approaching him now. The boy pressed himself behind the guard's stool, his back to the wall.

"And just where d'you think you're going?" said the guard.

"It's in his right hand," the old man said, blood running from his nostrils. "You two hold him down and I'll get it."

They closed in on him, and Daniel clapped his hand over his mouth and stood wild-eyed before them. He clicked the ring on his teeth and didn't make another move, his lips pinched tight.

The guard tipped the stool to the side. "His mouth," he said. "It's in his mouth."

"No shit," said the old man. "Just *get* it already!"

The guard grabbed the boy and held him, pinched him by the back of the neck. He started shaking Daniel back and forth, saying, "Spit it out, asshole."

"Get his mouth open."

"I'm trying."

"You're useless," said the old man. He took Daniel by the hair and tilted the boy's head back, forced his lips and teeth apart with his salty fingers. "Lift your tongue," he barked at him with disgust. "Let me see."

Daniel opened his mouth and moved his tongue out of the way. He held his jaw open for them, the guard still pinching his neck.

"Stop," the woman said. "I think he's swallowed it!"

"Bullshit," said the guard. "Just cough it up, kid."

"I'm telling you," she said. "It's *gone*."

"Nothing's ever *gone*," said the old man. "Stick your fingers down his throat, if you have to, *squeeze* him or something."

The guard turned the boy's face up to the light and looked inside Daniel's mouth again, and then he turned and smiled at the woman and the old man. "What d'you know," said the guard, *"Breakfast at Tiffany's."*

"I'm gonna call the cops," said the woman.

"Good," said the old man. "And somebody tell this kid he'd better wipe that smile off his face before I do it for him."

CHAPTER TEN He gave the police his money and keys, then held out his hands to be cuffed. The sergeant shook his head and told him to just move along. "Never mind that," said the man. "This isn't a TV show, you know."

They took him away in the police cruiser—two officers, everything orderly and quiet—and Daniel felt that uneasy smile on his own face, that sneaking smile and feeling of satisfaction. They called his father and brought Daniel to the hospital for x-rays. A nurse took the pictures and later shook the gray foil sheets up to the ceiling lights: they showed the boy's ribs, the gauze of his lungs and stomach, and the ring so bright it might have blinked or beeped like a satellite. It'd take anywhere from a few hours to a few days to pass, said the nurse, and she joked with them, suggested prunes, some canned corn, a good long walk around the block.

The two policemen drove him across the city to the precinct station. They filled out paperwork and brought him to a room upstairs, where they said he could wait for his father. Daniel sat at one of the tables and laid his head on his arms and felt incredibly tired all of a sudden. They left him alone in the room, and he tried to wish away the click of heels in the hall, which he knew would come, his father's zippered boots. Daniel both did and didn't want his father to arrive for him, just as he both did and didn't want to go home again. He stared at the lights on the ceiling, the green filing cabinets against the walls, the shades, the brick wall outside the window—and he slowly fell asleep.

His father's easy voice outside the door woke him, the man a blur behind the pebbled glass. When the door swung open, Bob and the sergeant laughed as if ducking into a bar together. "He's back here," said the sergeant, "back where we keep all the riffraff."

Under the hard light of the room, Bob looked smaller and older, and Daniel tried to gauge how tired or angry or unforgiving the man might be. His father flashed that crooked game-show smile across the room at him. "There he is," he said, "my little jailbird."

He stood a moment and then opened his arms to Daniel. "Hey?" he said. "You ready to go or not?"

Daniel smiled weakly, shied around the desk, and buried his face in his father's stomach, the weight of the man's hands pressing onto his shoulders. "That's enough of that now," said the man. "C'mon, let's buck up a little here, kiddo."

Daniel felt his father's hands turn him toward the door and the hall outside. They said goodbye to the officers and opened the door onto the hallway together. The floor ran long and glossy to the stairs, and the man's heels went so sharp and hard that the boy looked for little crescents in the tile. Downstairs, through the bustle of people, they walked out of the station and into the dark of night. The windows in the buildings, the people, the taillights along the bulge of the avenue—everything overwhelmed him.

Bob roughed up the boy's hair as they went. "So, did they show you the x-rays?"

"No," said Daniel, "but I saw."

"I'll bet," said the man. "But you feel okay, though, right?"

Daniel nodded and looked up at his father. And, standing at the corner, he realized that whenever he expected his father to be angry or severe, the man became almost amused and comforting. Instead of harsh, his father grew almost gentle, almost jovial and happy. The traffic lights dominoed green to yellow, yellow to red, and Bob bumped him forward and stepped off the curb.

Daniel followed his father toward the boxes of lights and buildings across the avenue. They walked under the fire escapes, past the tenements, the garbage cans, the doorways and black iron fences. Bob went along and said the car was out here somewhere.

"Don't worry," said Daniel. "I'm fine walking."

"Spoken like a free man," said Bob.

They went the length of a warehouse, its loading docks and doors, Daniel walking under his father's hand. And as they passed another cross street, Daniel wondered why his father didn't ask him about the money or the ring or any of this; the man just walking along the half-lit streets, the patches of cobblestone, the brick walls of buildings.

"Dad?" he said, finally.

"Yes, Daniel?"

"Are you mad?"

"I'm not sure," said the man. "Why? Should I be?"

"I don't know," said Daniel. "You could be, I guess — if you wanted."

"All right, lemme just think on it a little more," said the man.

They passed another block and the creamy glare of the Bonneville appeared under a streetlamp. Daniel stopped short beside his father — there was someone in the car. He saw the dark outline sitting and leaning against the passenger door, a head resting on the window. "Now don't get your hopes up," said Bob. "It's not who you think it is."

"Who is it?"

"Don't ask," said the man. He put his hand on the boy's shoulder and said, "Really, don't even ask."

They approached and Daniel felt a chill. His father grinned and went ahead to sneak up to the car, the keys in his fist as he rapped the window just behind her. And she jumped away at the sound, her face so pale, her hands up to the glass — and Bob yelled out to Joelyn, *"Gotcha!"*

Bob opened the back door, and Daniel stared at her as he slid over the newspapers and stiffened rags on the back seat. Bob closed the door behind him, and it was quiet in the car, just Daniel and Joelyn as Bob walked around the car.

"Did you know I'd be here?" she asked, turning to the boy.

"No," he said.

Bob circled the front of the car, and she said, "I made

him take me. That way I knew he'd bring you back to your mother."

Daniel looked at her as if he didn't believe anything she said; and as she started to say how worried his mother had been, Bob got to the driver's door and folded himself behind the wheel. "Everybody all right in here?"

Neither of them said a word, and Bob smiled and turned the ignition. He pulled the headlights on and nosed the car forward from the curb. Bob unrolled his window and slid the car onto the avenue and away. He looked over at Joelyn and then up at Daniel in the rearview. "So who's hungry around here?"

Daniel pulled himself up to them, his feet on the empty bottles as if standing on ladder rungs.

"What d'you say?" said Bob. "You hungry back there?"

"I could eat," said the boy.

"All right," said Bob. "That's the spirit. And how about you, Joelyn? You mind if we stop for a bite to eat?"

She sat pressed against her door and looked at Bob and that smile of his. "Sure," she said. "I mean, people have to eat, don't they?"

Bob said yes and gunned them through the traffic and lights, and Daniel leaned back again, spread his arms over the seat, and let the city whiffle past him in the open windows. They drove past Chinatown and soon the avenue widened and began to lift away from the ground, lift away and rise into a bridge, a great scaffold of beams and cables and black open water below, a slur of lights strung above. The road tipped them like a Ferris wheel toward the smear of Brooklyn, and they swayed along with the noodle turns to that clockwork beat of expressway—*ga-domp, ga-domp, ga-domp, ga-domp*—Manhattan like an amusement park in the distance, Brooklyn like a shipwreck below.

Bob cruised with his wrist over the steering wheel, Joelyn leaning against her door away from him. She reminded Daniel of his mother, the way she sat there with that same quiet anger when his father was like this, the man aimless and swashbuckling as he drove. It both thrilled and horrified Daniel to be on the loose with his father, to see him become large and reckless with the Pontiac, the kind of man who should have had streets named after him, statues in his likeness.

They slowed and veered sharply down the ramp, drove to the sea-bottom streets of Brooklyn and Greenpoint. At a stoplight, the engine idled high, with a burnt smell of rubber and oil. "All right," said Bob, "so who thought I'd have us lost by now?"

The girl turned to him. "You mean we aren't lost?"

He laughed and told the boy to lean himself forward and take a look at some things—take a look at this school, for instance, and this church, and the brick arch of this swimming pool over here. Bob steered around a corner and coasted past another church, a set of steps where he said he'd first met Anna.

Daniel watched the darkened entrance of the church glide past and tried to imagine his mother pushing open the doors and walking down those steps, leggy and slim as in the old photos. These were the same sooty old streets she always said she'd wanted to leave. Bob showed the boy how the names of the streets ran in alphabetical order — from Java to India to Huron to Green, Freeman, Eagle, Dupont, Clay, Box, and Ash — Ash being nothing but a darkened foundry dock.

Bob spun the car around in a dead-end lot, the piers in ruins around them, the warehouses dark and empty, the wharves buckled and crumbling. He pulled over to the end of the asphalt, where the city stood across the river, everything close and clear in the night air. "Piss call," said Bob.

And out of the car, Daniel followed his father to the dock, the broken slabs of concrete and weeds and car tires, the river like oil under them. Bob stood and pissed over the side in an arc that poured loud into the water below. "What's the matter," he said, "stage fright?"

"I don't have to go," said Daniel.

"Just keeping me company?"

Daniel took a few steps away and looked at the lights on the water and waited for his father to finish.

And when the man shivered and zipped his pants, the two of them stood with their faces raised to the air. The river curved away to the left and the bridges twinkled green in the distance. In their youth, said Bob, they used to spend a lot of time down here, he and his mother. "It was pretty ratty back then too," he said. "But we didn't seem to care."

In the car again, they drove and found a busy little diner in the shape of a train car. It had big wraparound windows, the walls aluminum and quilted and shiny, the lights bright inside. They took a corner booth and Bob slid in beside Joelyn. He leaned back and hooked his arms over the seat, damp patches of maroon under his shirt. He always tried to face out on a room, it seemed, always seemed to watch everyone else, the man always looking for a better party.

It was almost ten o'clock, but the lunch counter and nearly all the tables were full, the place loud and alive with voices and cutlery. A waitress took their orders and hurried away to the kitchen in her short skirt, her ponytail switching down her back as she went.

Joelyn curved away from Bob like a plant toward the window, and the man slowly turned to her and tilted his head slightly. "You just stay quiet over there, Joelyn."

"I didn't say a word," she said.

"I know," he said, "and *still* you talk too much."

Daniel braced himself for the moment that he knew was about to come, that cross look on his father's face as he turned to the boy. "Anyway," said the man, "tell me — what's a bus trip to New York like these days? Is it a nice ride? How long's it take? Three hours or so?"

Daniel nodded but knew his father didn't care how long or how much money the bus ticket cost. Bob was just getting his shots in, throwing his little jabs to keep Daniel off-balance. "Expensive little meal," said Bob, "wouldn't you say? That lunch of yours?"

"I had money, Dad."

"So I gather — just not quite enough, isn't that right?"

The boy shrugged.

"Don't shrug me off like that. Answer your father."

Daniel didn't say anything, and the waitress approached carrying their dinner plates. She recited each dish as she laid it before them — grilled cheese and tomato soup for Joelyn; hot dog and fries for the boy; the meatloaf special for the man of the house, an extra side of cole slaw. Bob tried to catch her apron bow as she turned to leave, and he smiled at the woman, at Daniel, at Joelyn.

They tried to ignore him and began to eat in silence. And when they were done, the waitress tucked the bill under Bob's plate. He took out his wallet and stood, finally, and Joelyn slid out of the booth to use the restroom. He told her to give his name to get a good seat, and she went away toward the kitchen, Bob leaving a tip on the table and paying the bill at the front door. He bought cigarettes from a machine in the breezeway, and out in the parking lot he hit the pack against the inside of his wrist, peeled the cellophane, and brushed it from his fingers like a soap bubble.

Daniel watched his father trick the lighter open and closed, a new cigarette between his lips. There was a phone booth across the lot, and Bob started walking toward it without a word, Daniel following. He watched the man tuck the receiver to his chin, slip dimes into the phone, and then dial and wait as the phone rang.

"We had a little car trouble," he said to Anna. "The guy at the garage says we'll be back on the road in the morning."

Bob winked at Daniel. "No," he told her, "he's still in the restaurant with his cousin — we just ate. Everyone's just ducky. Most of all, I didn't want you to worry, Anna — okay?"

He smiled and blew smoke up and away and into the

air and said they'd see her tomorrow. And then he just hung up the phone, as if this were nothing. "Well," he told the boy, "looks like I just bought us a night on the town."

They went back to the car and stood together and saw Joelyn in the bright windows of the diner. She walked down the aisle, past the tables, and out through the doors. "Here comes trouble," said Bob. "Let's just swing her by the tail a little—what d'you say? Let's see how long before she squeaks."

In the car again, and Bob spun them back around toward the murky streets and the factories and scrap yards of Brooklyn and Queens. He must have loved these kinds of leftover ends of places, because he always seemed to find them, always seemed to stay and revel in them. Daniel knew that the man might drive all night like this, the Bonneville like a ghost past all the beleaguered warehouses and bodegas and barrack gates of the world. They rumbled over stretches of cobblestone and took maze-end alleys and streets that led nowhere. Another car became a sign of life, while a traffic light seemed a sign of civilization itself.

Daniel rode in the back and pretended not to notice Joelyn, that growing silence and anger of hers. She leaned against her door and fidgeted with the handle as Bob turned down another dark street. The blocks whisked by, and they passed under the stonework of a bridge. "You know," she said, almost casual, "it's getting kind of late."

"Yeah?" said Bob. "So?"

"Don't you think we should start heading back soon?"

"Actually, Joelyn, I'm not sure I'm up for that much of

a drive tonight." The man smiled at her, and she glanced back to Daniel and then turned to Bob again. He put his arm over the top of the seat.

"I don't understand," she said.

"What's to understand?" he asked. "I just think I'm too tired to drive — I'm not sure it'd be safe. I mean, it's been a helluva day, don't you think? The long drive? The traffic? What d'you say back there? One helluva day, right?"

Daniel wedged his hands between the seats under himself. He wanted to stand up to his father and say — and say what? What could he ever really say to him? He couldn't say a single thing to the man, in the end. All he could do was look out the windows like a coward and wish he could step out of himself and leave that person with them, like an empty costume. The real Daniel — whoever that was — would huddle in some doorway and watch this other boy being dragged away by them. The real Daniel could start home, where he was supposed to be.

"Bob," said the girl, "I can drive."

"Not my car, you can't."

"But we could be halfway home by now," she said, her voice beginning to crack.

"Oh, now really? Is that right?"

"Why are you doing this to us, Bob?"

She turned in her seat to the boy and looked so angry and raw that he had to look away. "You know," she said, her voice quiet now, "you know you can always tell him too — just say that you want to go home, that you don't want her to worry."

Daniel didn't answer, but she held her gaze on him as if she could convince him. But what she seemed to convince him of, really, was that he suddenly wanted, more than anything, to stay with his father. And the harder she tried to push, the more he didn't care how or where or why—only that they were together for what he suddenly felt might be the last time like this.

"Bob," she said, "*talk* to me."

"What, Joelyn?"

"Why are you doing this?"

"I don't know," he said. "Maybe it's just too long of a drive."

Bob had a smirk on his face when he turned to glance back at the boy. They slipped along a short bend in the roadway, a long stone curtain wall angling like a wedge to the right of them. Joelyn looked terrified as they glimpsed the hills of a cemetery, all dark inside, all pillars and crosses and hunchback domes. She crossed herself and touched her fingers to her lips, and the hair on Daniel's arms crawled inch by inch to his neck. He didn't know for sure, but he thought they'd been here before, as if this could be the cemetery where they'd buried his aunt and his grandmother.

Bob turned around at the big iron gates and passed a service station, a garage, a fire station, and then a motel, the Cityview Motor Inn. He pulled up and parked near a row of shrubs in front, took his keys from the ignition and bounced them in his hand.

"Well?" he said. "What's your preference? A room of your own, Joelyn? Or a cot in ours?"

Daniel saw her pause before she looked at Bob. "Why are you doing this?"

"Room or cot?" he said, his voice flat, cold.

"I haven't got money for a room, Bob."

"Well, then, it looks like we're bunkmates," he said. "Shall we?"

They took a room on the top floor, rode the elevator in silence, and walked along the carpeted hall with half-shell sconces and numbered doors. The room itself was stale and airless, its ceiling peaked at the windows and gables of the roof. A pair of beds sat on one side, an armchair on the other, a painting of seagulls over the dresser. Bob tossed his keys onto the nightstand and went into the bathroom.

They could hear that long pour of the man into the toilet, Bob calling for someone to get those windows going. He couldn't even breathe, he said, it was so stuffy. Joelyn quietly followed Daniel across the room. The boy worried about her silence and asked her to hold the curtains aside for him so he could get the windows. She seemed like the saddest person in the world to him, an orphan, a lost dog, but he didn't have the patience for her either. He unlocked and lifted the window, the air cool, the cemetery in blackness below, the city in the distance.

"Daniel," she whispered. "Do you hate me?"

"No," he said.

The toilet flushed and his father stepped into the room. He was buckling his belt and taking the cigarettes and lighter from his pockets. They watched him shake the pack and pull a fresh cigarette with his lips, his lighter clicking open. He went over to the bed and set the cigarette backward on the nightstand and then stopped short and scowled at them. "What's the hell's everybody looking at?" he asked. "Buzz off already, the both of you."

Daniel turned away to the window, Joelyn still holding the drapes in her hands, the cloth yellow with nicotine and sun. She seemed frightened of the man as she stood there, as if she knew she brought out the worst in him somehow. She kept her eyes to the floor as she waited and then crossed the room and closed the bathroom door behind her.

"Now what's the matter?" said Bob.

Daniel shrugged and went to the chair by the window, his father sitting on the edge of the nearest bed. Bob bent forward and unzipped his boots. He slowly peeled off his socks and lay back over the bed with a long sigh, the cigarette still on the nightstand, as if he'd completely forgotten it.

"You going to sleep, Dad?"

"Eventually," said the man, "but first I'm gonna close my eyes and relax a minute."

Bob lay there with his hands folded across his chest, his toenails as thick and yellow as horse teeth. And the cigarette uncoiled a thread of smoke up into the lampshade. Daniel watched the ash bend and go limp as the cigarette burned down, the boy pinching the filter off the wood. There was a black scar on the edge of the nightstand, as well as ash on the floor.

"Where you think you're going with that?" said the man.

Daniel set the cigarette in the ashtray on the dresser and carried the ashtray back to his father. He set it down on the nightstand and rubbed the ash into the carpet with the toe of his shoe. And when the doorbell rang, Daniel turned, his mind flashing to his mother in the hall, maybe. His father sat up in bed and said to get it. It must be the guy with the cot, he said. He tossed his wallet to the boy. The bell rang again, and Bob said, "What're you waiting for, numb-nuts? Answer the door already. And have a dollar ready for the guy when he's done."

They watched the porter roll the little bed into the room, and Daniel stood at the door with his father's wallet in his hands. It was warm and shaped to the man's back pocket, the leather soft and smooth and worn to almost nothing along the fold. He handed the clerk a dollar and closed the door behind him, and then Daniel turned and slipped the wallet into his father's boot.

Bob lay quiet, and Daniel waited for the bathroom door to pull slowly open, for Joelyn to step into the room again. She opened the door, finally. She'd washed her face, her skin flushed and thin as she crossed the room, the blue of veins in her cheeks. She pressed her lips into a smile at Daniel and went to the cot, took off her shoes, turned the bedcovers down. The metal springs creaked as she climbed onto the mattress and pulled the sheets and covers around herself.

Bob opened his eyes and leaned up on his elbows to see her. "What're you doing?" he asked.

"I'm going to sleep, Bob."

"What d'you mean, no slumber party?"

She said no and turned toward the wall. Bob looked over at Daniel and smiled and mugged his face at her, her back to them. The boy watched and stayed by the window as the curtains filled and emptied into the room, the hum of traffic from below.

"Let the boy sleep in the cot, Joelyn — go on, take the other bed at least."

She moved slightly under the covers and said no. "That's okay," she said and lay still, the blankets pulled up to her chin.

Bob said good night and looked over at Daniel and shrugged. He rested back against the headboard of the bed, his feet crossed at the ankles. "So maybe you should go sit on the bowl," he said to the boy. "Just see if the spirit moves you or anything."

Daniel left gladly and closed the bathroom door and sat on the radiator by the sink. In the middle of the door was a hole the size of a fist, darkness coming out of it. Daniel just stared up at the empty circle and waited there with the bathtub, with the interlock of tiles, with the old newspaper folded behind the toilet. He heard his father and cousin, heard the hush of their voices start through the door, but he didn't move, didn't care. He just sat there and waited and felt nothing, just empty and dark, the radiator cold and hard under him, like bones, as if he were sitting on the backbone of some animal.

He ran the water in the sink and washed his hands and his face. And when he bent to take a drink, he caught a glimpse of himself in the chrome neck of the faucet — a small raccoon-eyed boy, his face stretched and strange like a funhouse. He didn't seem at all like the hero he'd hoped to be, but just this sad and scared and lost little kid. He pressed his eyes with a towel and went back to his father and cousin in the dim light of the room.

They were huddled so close together that they were practically touching, Bob sitting on the end of the bed, Joelyn below him in her cot, neither of them seeing or hearing him come out of the bathroom. Whatever it was they were saying, it was serious and private and urgent in some way. And when they saw Daniel by the dresser, they broke quickly from each other and looked guilty to the boy. His father stood up and shifted his weight on his legs, his feet and ankles cracking like knuckles.

"So," he said to the boy, "any luck?"

Daniel leaned against the dresser and shook his head. "No," he said, "no luck."

Joelyn turned away and pulled the covers over herself again, and then Bob turned as well. He lit a cigarette near the window and looked back at the boy. "At least the neighbors are quiet," he said and smiled, "right?"

Daniel shook his head, and Bob stared at him.

"You'd tell me," he said, "wouldn't you—if you had some luck?"

"Yes," said Daniel.

"I mean, I was a card player too, you know."

Daniel nodded and said he knew.

"Now what's in the drawers over there, anyway?" he asked the boy. "Take a look and see if there's a deck of cards or something."

Daniel slid open the dresser one drawer at a time and

said there wasn't anything—a Bible, a book of matches, a shirt button.

"Well," said Bob, "pass me that Bible."

Daniel brought the book to the man, put it on the nightstand, and looked at his father. What were they going to do, he asked.

"Well," said Bob, "you're gonna go to sleep. And I'm gonna sit and read for a while."

Daniel kept his eyes away from the man and started to get undressed. His father switched on the reading light, sat in the chair, and fished a half-pint of whiskey from his pants pocket. He could conjure these bottles at will, it seemed, pull them out of glove compartments and couch cushions and the thin air itself. Bob sat and edged the drawer of the stand open, tapped his cigarette ash inside, and opened the book on his lap as Daniel climbed into bed. "You don't think the light'll bother you, do you?"

Daniel said no and watched his father's shadow on the wall and ceiling, the man seemingly bent across the room like a stick in water. Daniel lay there and listened as Bob leafed through pages and smoked and tamped his cigarette into the drawer.

"Dad?" he whispered finally.

"Go to sleep, Daniel."

"Are you going to be here in the morning?" he asked.

"I hope so," said Bob. "Why, you know something I don't?"

Daniel closed his eyes and listened to his father turn the pages—the sound like embers in a fire—and eventually he slept. He'd wake twice that night, each time like a dream within a dream. The rustle of voices waking him, his father in low tones, his cousin all treble, her voice sharp in the room. "He's going to wake up and hear you," she said.

And the room fell quiet. It could have been anything, whatever they were saying, but she was telling him no. She kept saying it over and over — "No, Bob." And his father's words were indistinct to Daniel, like a voice from the room below. Daniel stretched in the covers so that they'd know he could hear them and stop. He heard the springs in the cot, his father standing up to close the window, the air cold now and fresh. Bob sat carefully in the chair, that gun-click of the lighter in the room again, that kindling sound of pages being turned.

In the middle of the night, he'd wake a second time. His father had fallen asleep in the chair, the reading light over the man's shoulder, Joelyn in the other bed now. She lay there in that pretty, perishable sleep of hers.

Daniel slowly climbed out of bed and moved toward his father. He stood breathless over the man, studied him under the light, the dirty pocks and pores, the dents and darkness around the eyes, that yeasty smell of his sleep. And without a thought, he began to wish that each breath would be — right then and there — his father's last. He stood over the man and kept wanting him dead and gone and far behind them. It was like a prayer, yet it was also the greatest fear that he had, the fear like a wish for his father to simply become a thing that was finished in their lives, like a picture or trophy, a trinket they could set, harmless, on the mantel.

It was all he seemed to want as he stood there, to let all of this ache and anger end, to let them all somehow be released.

Daniel reached down and placed his hand on the man's arm and just held it until Bob woke and smiled, happy, up at him. "What's the matter?" said the man. "Was I snoring?"

"Dad, why don't you sleep in bed?"

"Sure thing, pal."

The Bible fell to the floor, but Joelyn didn't move. Daniel led his father back to the other bed and watched the man lying there in his wrinkled clothes. He shut the reading light and sat on the warm edge of the chair in the dark, the boy listening as his father's breaths went slow and deep again.

He waited and watched and became attuned to every stir and possible scatter of sleep in the room. He was wary of either the girl or his father waking and finding him like this, standing up from the chair, beginning slowly, noiselessly, across the carpet. He felt he barely existed anymore, felt himself as insubstantial as a ghost. And inside the bathroom, behind the door and the lock and the hole the size of a fist, Daniel's feet went numb with cold from the tiles. He stood and shivered and listened in the dark for them. And then he spread the old newspaper on the floor and began his life as the goose who laid the golden egg.

CHAPTER ELEVEN

He slept what was left of the night with the ring on his thumb, his thumb in a fist, and his fist hidden under the pillow under his head. In the morning he woke to the keening sound of an airplane passing low over the motel. The sun was full in the curtains, and he could hear church bells. All the muddled sounds of morning, of traffic and chirping birds, it all slowly filtered in through the window.

The room, he realized, was empty. His father and cousin were gone, and he sat up in bed, called toward the bathroom, and looked at the doorway, at the rumpled cot, the chair, the lamp. He turned to each as if the furniture might answer him. He felt a sort of sadness, a kind of panic or desperation in the face of the dresser, in the sconces on the wall, the stains and cigarette scars on the carpet.

Daniel kicked the covers off the bed and went to the window. No matter what else happened, his father would never leave without the Bonneville. He'd desert his son before his car—and there it was, that creamy slope of the hood and trunk, its grill nosed into the bushes.

People passed below outside like extras in a movie, a

man with flowers, another with a dog on a leash. A few cars in the lot, some litter in the street. Daniel looked along the avenue and the sidewalks for any flash of his cousin's blond hair or his father's slant of shoulders. He pulled on his shirt and shoes and headed quickly down to the Pontiac before it could go anywhere without him.

He draped himself over the clammy skin of the fender and hood and looked for his father or his cousin on the sidewalk. He kept waiting for them to appear, kept watching as another airplane sailed in over the cemetery, its wings correcting as it passed low behind the motel. He knew enough to keep himself between the car and his father, Daniel feeling something like compassion for the old Bonneville. And as he watched the street he took the ring and held it in his hand, as if that might bring them back sooner. It didn't—in fact maybe it even kept them away. The sun rose slowly across the trees and buildings.

His father had a way of leaning forward as he walked, and the man was halfway up the hill before Daniel recognized that scissored waltz of his across the avenue. Bob had a grocery bag in his arms, a bride's veil of cigarette smoke behind him in the sunlight. A quick flip of the cigarette into the gutter, and Bob flashed a cocky smile when he saw the boy by the car.

Bob called out from across the street and crossed to the boy, that smile still on his face. The man cut through a gap in the hedges and came up to the car. He had breakfast and newspapers in the bag with him, he said. All kinds of treats, he told the boy as he set the bag on the hood.

Daniel leaned against the car and made his mouth into a line, his father saying that they lost the Duke last night, John Wayne.

"I got all the papers so we can read," said Bob. "Looks like cancer," he said, "seventy-something years old—that's probably long enough anyway, right?"

Daniel shrugged to his father and raised his face toward the cemetery and trees across the street.

"Aw, for Crissakes," said Bob. "Don't tell me you're pissed already. It's still early—I mean, what could I have done by this time of day?" He threw up his hands and huffed at the boy, waved open the handkerchief from his pocket in surrender. Bob laughed to himself and wiped his forehead and neck with the cloth, and then he leaned on the fender alongside the boy, the two of them shoulder to shoulder. He followed the line of Daniel's eyes across the avenue to the cemetery and just stared at the crosses and crypts with his arms folded.

"You know what?" he said. "I'm not gonna be drawn into it this time. I'm sorry for whatever it is I've done, but I'm not gonna fight with you—I'm just not."

Daniel looked down at his father's shoes, the leather like faces.

"And besides," said the man, "I went and got some of those little pies you used to like, back when you were young and nice to your old man—bet you don't even remember those days now, do you?"

Bob lit a cigarette and stared at the side of the boy's face for what seemed a long time. "You know," he said, "you've got some pretty good-size ears there, don't you?"

Bob went to flick at the boy's ears, and Daniel shifted against the car. He moved a step away and didn't say anything.

"Don't worry," said Bob. "I have them too — the better to hear you say nothing with, apparently."

Bob finished his cigarette and stretched back and then popped the boy on the back of the head — not hard, but hard enough. "Knock it off with the attitude," he said, "you hear me?"

Daniel rubbed his hair and looked up at the man.

"So how'd you sleep last night, anyway?"

"I slept fine."

"Good," said Bob. "Glad to hear it. Now what about the other end of things, any progress?"

Daniel shook his head and said no.

"I don't have to keep asking all the time, do I?"

"No," said Daniel.

"You're sure?"

The boy nodded and said yes.

"So how should we do this, then? D'you want to just give me the ring when you're ready?"

Daniel nodded again and felt his voice would break with the slightest word. He swallowed and glanced up at his father. The man gave him a pat on the top of his head. "So we'll leave it at that, okay? Now why you so mad, anyway — just worried I left?"

Daniel surprised himself and said yes.

"Well," said Bob, "I'm afraid you won't get rid of me

that easy." He pushed himself off the car and kicked the creases back into his pant cuffs. He stood there and adjusted his belt and spit into the hedges. "So anyway," he said to the boy, "what about your cousin, where's she?"

Daniel looked at the man. "I thought she was with you," he said.

"What's that supposed to mean?"

"Nothing," said Daniel, "but she wasn't there when I got up—that's all."

Bob turned and looked back to the motel again. He raised his hand against the sun and squinted up at the windows and roofline, standing there as if pricing a cleaning job. "You mean, she's not up there?"

"No," said Daniel, "she's not."

Bob pursed his lips and glanced away to the street and cemetery. He looked back up at the motel again, as if he didn't quite believe this yet.

"Do you think she's really gone?" asked the boy.

"I don't know," said Bob. "One can always hope, I guess." He smiled at him. "Right, kid?"

"But was it you, Dad? Did you make her go?"

Bob looked down the avenue at the cemetery again. "Not that I know of," he said. "I mean, I wasn't *that* bad, was I?"

"You must have done something else," said Daniel. "Why else would she leave?"

"Damned if I know," said the man. "I mean, why would she come in the first place, anyway?" He spit on the ground again and Daniel just looked at him in silence, his father seeming nervous.

"Don't look at me like that," he said. "I didn't do anything to her."

Just then another plane approached, and Bob turned as it sailed in toward the cemetery. The wheels opened from the belly of the fuselage, and Bob and Daniel watched the wings teeter and coast over and behind the motel, the two of them standing together and staring at the sky. Bob waited a long moment before he turned to the boy. "Well," he said, "I sure hope there's an airport close by."

Daniel smiled. He couldn't help but smile.

"So I guess I should go settle up now." He pointed at the grocery bag and told the boy to have a pie, and then he started across the motel and into the lobby.

Daniel half expected his cousin to step out of the doorway or alley or wherever else she might have been hiding. And the longer he looked for Joelyn, the more relieved he began to feel when she never showed. He began to will her away, actually, for her own sake, as well as for the sake of himself, for the sake of his father and mother. Just the thought of his mother at home, just the idea of her waiting and worried and angry in the house, the telephone staring at her, the curtains hanging there, the way she'd stand behind them and look out at the empty yard and street—it made him sick.

He heard the snap of his father's lighter and turned. The man stood in the shade of the motel awning, one more fresh cigarette between his fingers. Then Bob walked slowly across to the boy and the driver's side of the car and asked if there was any sign of her. Daniel said no and followed his father around to the front of the car. The man fit the cigarette into the grill and reached under the hood, raised it open. He tossed the car keys to Daniel and pulled the dipstick from the engine, wiped it between his finger and thumb. "How about grabbing one of those quarts from the trunk for me?"

Daniel got the oil, the funnel, the can opener, and he watched the man pour the oil like honey into the engine. Bob dropped the empty can into the bushes behind him and told the boy to wrap the funnel in newspaper before he put it away. Then he opened the air filter and lowered the idle with the nail of his thumb and then closed the hood and took his cigarette from out of the grill again. The boy gave the keys back to his father.

"All right," said Bob, "I guess you and I should have some sort of a talk now, shouldn't we?" He leaned against the back of the car and hooked one of his boot heels on the bumper and told the boy to pull up a chair.

Once again they leaned shoulder to shoulder against the car and looked out at the cemetery and the avenue. Daniel still watched for Joelyn on the sidewalk, and the old trees seemed to untwist as they rose out of the ground on the street side of the wall, their shadows like blankets over the sidewalk and gutter.

"So let's do a little thinking here," said Bob, "shall we? Because at the bottom of everything, at brass tacks, you're gonna have me to blame for all of this—you understand that, don't you? I mean, that's pretty clear by now, isn't it? I'm the one who's supposed to know better, right?"

Bob waited for an answer from the boy, but Daniel

didn't know what his father was really trying to say. And he didn't want to guess. He heard that spare tone in the man's voice, something like pain or sadness, but he was afraid to understand it any more clearly than that. They stood together and turned to look at the motel, at the street, at the cemetery gates in the distance, as if each might sneak away at any moment.

Bob ground the soles of his shoes into the sand and asphalt, a loud crackling sound, and Daniel looked up at him. "Does that mean we'd just leave her?" he asked.

Bob hesitated—they both knew that he'd meant Joelyn, but they'd both skipped ahead to his mother and just leaving her and not going home. That it was even a *choice* made it seem as if they'd already strayed across some boundary, already wandered into something completely wrong yet irresistible. The two stood in the parking lot, aware that they were just this side of some great catastrophe. And as this came to them, they felt almost gleeful for a moment together. She'd never forgive them for this, but still neither wanted to go home just yet. The boy looked at his father and tried not to smile.

CHAPTER TWELVE They called from a roadside truck stop, and the boy said, "It's me, Mom—Daniel."

"And where are you?" she asked, her voice quick and strong, not at all small or quiet as he'd imagined it would be. He stood in the booth and looked out through the streaky glass at the Porta-Johns, the dumpsters, the other cars. She waited, and he felt his mouth open and close, as if everything might come out of him—the bus ride, the police station, the surprise he had for her of the ring, all of it.

"I'm with Dad," he told her.

"I know," she said. "But where—why aren't you here yet? Is the car okay?"

He glanced up at his father, at the way the man leaned against the doorway, his weight locked on one leg. "I don't know," he said, and she stayed quiet and kind to him. She seemed to be waiting for him to come around to her, but all Daniel did was turn and finger the coin return slot. For his father's benefit, he started to roll his eyes at her.

And she said, "Stop. Just stop."

It seemed as if she could see him, see the way he was, and he froze. "Daniel," she said, "listen to me—I want you to come home now."

He held still, and his father's hand came to the back of his neck. The man signaled for them to speed it up. "I'm sorry," Daniel said to his mother. He cleared his throat. "But I have Dad right here," he said. "Will you maybe talk to him now?"

She didn't say anything, and the boy listened for the next hint of her voice on the other end of the line. He turned the steel cord in his hand and looked at the glass of the booth, the window smudged like cellophane. He waited and knew that whatever she said, she would be simmering and angry and unendurable to him. He could practically feel the cold as he waited.

"Mom," he said, finally, "you still there?"

"Where am I supposed to go, Daniel?"

"Will you just talk to him now?"

"Yes," she said, "I will—just give the phone to your father now, please."

He slid the receiver to his chest and looked up at his father, the man seeming so tired and ashen around his eyes. He held the phone to the man's hand. "She wants to talk to you," he whispered. "Come on, Dad, here."

Bob shifted slightly, but nothing came from the man—unless silence was something, which it was. At the bottom of everything, they were a family of silence—nothing but blind, black, coal-crumbling silence, his father never anchored or steady like his mother, his mother never sanguine or loose like his father, but still they were silence.

"Dad," he said, "talk to her for a minute, please."

Bob took the phone, and the boy swiveled under his father's arm and was free. He left the booth and kept going, kept brushing his way through the tall grass and flowering weeds beyond the car. Crickets and grasshoppers spurted from the ground around him. And when he looked back, he saw his father digging the loose coins from his pockets, the receiver tucked to his shoulder.

"It's not what you think," Bob told her. "It's not anything, Anna, really."

"I don't want to hear a word of it," she said. "I truly don't. All I want is to see the car pull into the driveway and have the boy get out of it, Bob, and come home."

A truck passed the booth, and he waited and listened for her, heard the gargle of other voices on the line. He switched the phone to his other ear and turned to check on the boy out in the grass. "So, Anna," he said, "I'm thinking we're gonna be away for a couple of days, me and the kid — just a little AWOL, that's all."

"Tell me something," she said, "did I ever do anything to deserve this from you? I mean, did I ever ask for anything? Did I ever say no to you? Was I that bad of a wife? I mean, do you think I ever wanted us to be unhappy like this?"

He said no to her. "Of course not," he told her.

"Well, then just come home, Bob."

"I don't think I can," he said. "Besides, I told the kid."

"So *un*tell him."

"No," he said. "I don't want to, Anna — I guess it just comes down to that in the end, doesn't it? Sort of a Cussler's Last Stand?"

She started to say something, but he said goodbye and

pressed his finger to the tongue of the cradle. All the coins fell inside the face of the phone, and Bob winced and looked at the trees beyond the booth. He started back to the car, the boy already there waiting for him. They leaned against the trunk together, as always, and a long moment passed. Daniel slipped his hand into his father's.

The man looked down at him and smiled. "How's it going, kid?"

"What did she say?"

Bob took a deep breath. "I don't know," he said, "same thing she said to you, no doubt."

Daniel kept his hand in his father's hand and waited. "What did you tell her?" he asked.

"I guess I told her the truth—I said it was all your idea." He glanced to the boy again and winked and stepped away from him slightly.

"Seriously," said Daniel.

"You really want to know?" said the man. "I told her we were gonna have a last hurrah out here together—just you and me."

"And what did she say?"

"Oh, you know your mother—she just loved the idea."

Daniel waited for his father to continue. He knew the man would rather leave it there, but Daniel wanted him to step up and say it, once and for all, just spell it out clearly, whatever it was, just put it into words—say that he was leaving, that this was goodbye. Daniel stared up at his father until the man turned to him. "What?"

"What else did you say?" he asked.

"Nothing," said the man. "What do you expect me to

say, Daniel? I mean, what could she say? And what exactly could I say?"

Bob reached over to the boy and pushed him gently away from the car. "C'mon," he said. "Let's get going."

Bob dug the keys from his pocket and circled to the driver's door. "Not to worry," he said to the boy. "Always easier to get forgiveness than permission anyway, right?"

Neither said anything for miles, the Bonneville all momentum and mood as they drove old post roads away from the city. A fill-up at some gas station, a couple of sodas and some snacks, some Slim Jims, some peanut butter crackers and Table Talk pies for the road, and the car seemed to glide through streets and towns, the boy and his father catching this glimpse of themselves reflected in storefront windows, this glow of chrome and cream-white paint in the sunlight. It was mid-afternoon, the speedometer like a pressure gauge, the odometer like a clock, and the heat off the tar on the asphalt ahead. Daniel leaned against his door and blinked the wind and light out of his eyes, watched his father's hands on the wheel, Bob driving in silence.

A fork in the road, and they banged a right under a railroad overpass, wandered alongside tracks for a mile or two before the tar gave out. Bob rattled them down another mile of dirt and gravel until the road itself washed into a field of demolition piles, old debris and brush and trash, mounds of dirt and broken concrete. Bob rolled to a stop at the edge of the weeds, the dust drifting through the sunlight. He shut the engine and sat for a moment before turning to the boy. "Now what?"

Daniel shrugged and smiled. "Piss call?"

"You got it," said Bob.

They left the doors open and wandered away from each other into the field. Daniel stood with his back to the man and painted the sand dark and then buckled his pants. Half hidden in the brush, he stood there and checked for the ring in his pocket as if he'd forgotten it for a while, the stone like a bead under the cloth. He heard his father at the car and started back to him, the man leaning against the trunk with his eyes closed and his face to the sun.

"So, why don't you drive?" said Bob. "I'll take shotgun for now."

Daniel looked at his father, the man circling around to the passenger side of the car. "Go on, get in there," said Bob. "Let's see what you've got."

It was like putting on his father's clothes, climbing in behind the wheel, the Pontiac too big and awkward for him. Bob reached under the seat and slid it up so the boy could reach the pedals and see over the dash. He told him to turn the key and put her in drive and go slow. "Just try not to crash," he said, "okay?"

The steering wheel sticky in his hands, Daniel touched the gas and jerked them forward, his father starting to laugh. "Keep going there, bubba."

Daniel sat straight and held himself tight as he steered the car back from where they had come, over the washboard of dirt and gravel. His father lit a cigarette and told him to slow up a little. With a bump, the road turned to asphalt, and the tires went quiet and smooth again. Another mile or two and they curved around to the railroad overpass, back to the main road. Bob had him pull over to a skirt of sand on the side. "Nicely done," he told the boy. "Now put her in park."

Daniel smiled and kept smiling as his father drove the service roads to the highway. And on the highway, speed became distance, and distance became a destination all its own, and Daniel, as if by reflex, tried to hold details from the road—a crow, a house, a long fairway of grass alongside them—all the things turning slowly into feelings for him, if he could only hold them long enough as they passed.

His father nudged him to look at some birds flying. "See the crows?" he said.

Daniel nodded—there were two or three perched on the guardrails, as well. "Very intelligent bird," said Bob. "Smarter than a parrot, you know. You can actually teach a crow to talk. I bet you didn't know that, did you?"

His father glanced over at him and smiled. "I mean, you never see them on the side of the road dead, do you? You know why? Because they work in teams. Like I said, a very smart bird, always one of them up in a tree or something, and he goes — '*Caaaa! Caaaa! Caaaa!*'"

A few more hours, and they ended up at a bar and grill for dinner, Bob with quarters for the boy after they were done eating. Daniel stood at the pinball machines, as ever, while his father switched from beer to whiskey. Daniel watched his father in the mirror on the wall behind the bar, and he came back and climbed onto the stool next to him. He sat next to the man until he noticed him, finally.

"Hey," he said to the boy. "Everything okay?"

Daniel nodded and said yes. "How about you?" he asked.

Bob laughed a little and said sure. He finished his drink and set the empty glass away from himself. It was almost dark by the time they got in the Bonneville again. Bob had a cigarette and touched the ash to his open window as he drove. They rode the dark two-lane out of town, all the dips and curves past fields and fences, the sky barely blue, and the moon almost full and transparent over the hills. Bob put the heater on and leaned back with one arm over the seat, Daniel riding with his window open and his eyes closed.

It was dark as he felt his father nudge him awake. "Did I sleep long?" he asked the man.

"No," said Bob, "not too long, at least—not long enough to miss anything, anyway."

They floated behind the taillights of another car, and Daniel caught the scent of pine trees along the side of the road. He didn't want to ask about anything, just wanted to move forward without knowing where or why or how. In front of them, the driver threw a cigarette from the window, a splash of orange on the black road.

A few more miles, and Daniel cleared his throat. "Where are we?" he asked.

"I'm not sure," said Bob. "I think Pennsylvania some-where? Ohio? Does it really matter?"

Daniel looked at the man in the glow of the dash and

the headlights, and he sank into his seat as he realized that it didn't matter where they were at all.

"I guess it matters more where we aren't," said Bob, "doesn't it?"

Daniel watched a strip of houses pass, the lights in the windows and on the porches and streets. "I guess," he said, "but still, can we stop somewhere?"

"We can do anything we want, Daniel."

A billboard appeared in the headlights, the beginnings of the next town, and they kept to the shadowy edges of office buildings and strip malls, the parking lots all empty, the stores all closed, the streetlights all a sickly yellow. Bob slowed and eased into a gas station by the side of a highway overpass. They filled the tank and bought some sodas and crackers, some cheese in a jar. And they asked if there was a place they might stay around here. The attendant looked puzzled but said to try just down the way. There was a motel, he said, a little past the highway. They drove to it, the place in a whitewash of lights on the side of the road, a big sign on the lawn in the shape of a shooting star.

Indoor Pool   *Air Conditioned*

S T A R L I T E
M O T O R   C O U R T

Color TV   *No Pets*

They pulled up to the main building, which seemed to hover on a small hill, its roof upswept and shining and edged with brushed steel. The office had a similar space-age feel to it, a small colony of outbuildings curving along the driveway behind, a few other cars parked out in the dark.

At the front desk, they rang a little bell for the night clerk to appear. Bob paid and signed the ledger and asked about the pool and where they might get some swim trunks for the boy. The clerk shrugged and said to try the lost and found by the door. They took the key and thanked the man and proceeded to fish a deck of playing cards from the box, some fresh socks, and then a pair of Hawaiian shorts — "*Voilà*," said Bob. They were five sizes too big for the boy, but Bob waved them open and held them up and said, "Perfect."

They got in the car and pulled around to the room and took their things inside. It was surprisingly nice, everything kept tight and neat and blue. In fact, the whole place came in shades of blue, the walls more diluted than the carpet, the carpet and beds as bright as Popsicles, even the ceiling as pale as the sky.

"Wow," said Bob, "I'm speechless over here."

They stood and looked at the room, and Bob said, "C'mon now, let's get changed before they close the pool down on us."

"What are you going to wear?"

"I'll swim next time," he said to the boy. "Just hurry up —chop-chop."

The man waited outside on the front steps with a cigarette and then led the way, Daniel feeling skinny and small behind him, his trunks held up by the belt from his pants. The night was cool and dark, and they could hear the murmur of televisions as they passed the other rooms, trucks on the thruway, crickets and frogs. And that strange glow of light beyond the last cottage was the round dome of the pool house. The windows were fogged over, and a humid smell of chlorine thickened as they got closer.

They could hear voices and laughter from inside—a whole crowd, it seemed, the sounds multiplied by tiles and glass and splashes of water. Through the doors and the room was bright and warm, and another family stood at the shallow end of the pool, a mother and two daughters in the water, a father at the lip of the steps, a home movie camera in his hands. All of them had stopped to turn to the door, and Bob waved his little hello. He and Daniel circled to the diving board and the deep end of the pool and watched without quite looking at them.

The girls started splashing with their mother again, and the big tungsten light came on over the camera, that ticker-taping sound of the super eight starting up to speed. And in the background of that other family's movie, Daniel thought, there might be this scrawny kid in loud-flowered shorts. He'd be in and out of focus in the distance, on the diving board, his hands up, this boy begging his father not to shoot him from the side of the pool. And his father would be slowly taking aim with his finger. There'd be this moment, this gunpoint smile, and then the boy would clutch his stomach and fall over dead into the pool, the porthole lights shining under the water.

It would all be there—the boy and his father on film, the two of them coiled safe and tight on a plastic reel somewhere, proof of them together like this.

.   .   .

136

And later, back in the room, they ate pizza and drank sodas and played crazy eights and Indian poker. This, they knew, was their time together — brief and perfect and doomed — almost too perfect to seem real. And still later at night, lying in the dark, they tried to sleep through the distant pass of trucks on the thruway. Daniel's eyes burned from the pool.

He rolled toward the man and could see his father lying motionless, like a cutout in the darkness. He suddenly missed him, suddenly felt that he had been the one who had made it this way, made his father unable to go home again, made him unforgivable to her now. He lay in bed, forever anxious for a face in the window, a hand cupped to the screen, an orange point of cigarette light outside, yet anxious to be safe at home, as well, his father outside the house in the night again, where he was meant to be.

"What's the matter with you?" said Bob, out of the dark.

Daniel lay there and stared at the outline of his father in the other bed.

"What is it, Daniel?"

"Why, what do you mean?"

"I mean, just lie still already," said the man. "Close your eyes and stop fussing."

"Dad?" he asked.

"What, Daniel?"

"Can I ask you something?"

"No," said Bob. "Go to sleep."

CHAPTER THIRTEEN

One day they'd be peeling off some turnpike for gas or breakfast, and the next would bring another speeding ticket to add to their collection, all the carbons tucked under Saint Christopher like souvenirs from Pennsylvania, Ohio, New Jersey. Three days passed like this, the Bonneville running sleek and suave, a Texaco map folded open between them, and the back seat littered with soda cans and sandwich wrappers. They hit a turtle by accident and skipped school and work and slept in their clothes, stayed one night at a rest area, Bob on the road before dawn. A few more sweeps of land, another blur of corn, of highways, of lunch stands and trucks and clouds, the road always flirting with rivers and ponds.

They found mountains and pines and the prettiest little lake, Bob keeping the water to their left for the whole loop of shoreline and folded hills. And soon they started to pass the same stone bridge, the same cottages, the same views across the water.

"Maybe it's just me," said Bob, "but d'you ever get the feeling we've been here before?"

There were spits of rain on the windshield, and he

pulled into the parking lot of an old general store. It looked like part of a set — the weather-beaten store, the big farmhouse, the barn, the silo — all the pieces arranged on the lawn, a pair of marriage trees near the front porch of the house. The grass ran from the edge of the road in one long swoop to the edge of the lake. Bob wandered from the car to the yard. It was drizzling now, a fine mist, and Bob just stood there with Daniel and gazed across the lake for a few moments, the clouds over the water, the wind in the trees.

The boy looked at his father. "It's going to rain," he said to the man.

"No shit, Sherlock. What gave you the first clue?"

Daniel smiled weakly and took a deep breath of patience for his father, as if he alone understood the man — that his father did the best he could, that he didn't mean to be harsh or cruel, that he just didn't think things through all the time.

Bob spit into the grass and led Daniel across the lot to the store. Sleigh bells rang as they opened the door, and one step inside had Bob staggering and swooning over the place, his hand clutched to his chest. It was love at first sight — the aisles a warren of food and toys and racks of clothes, piles of tent kits and fishing tackle, lawn chairs.

Daniel felt a smile hanging on his face, and his father clapped his hands. "What's the matter with you?" said Bob. "Grab us a cart and c'mon already."

Bob filled his arms with soup cans and candles and bug spray and dumped everything into the basket. He sized himself and the boy with a pair of cowboy shirts with pearl snaps on the chest and fancy stitching. Daniel tried not to encourage his father, but there was shampoo and shaving cream and underpants and toothbrushes for them, foot powder, Pop-Tarts, swim trunks. He wheeled the cart along after the man and tried to slip things back to bins and shelves as they went.

And just by the way the girl at the register set aside her magazine and smiled, Daniel knew his father would want a performance out of him. She was Joelyn's age and had long brown hair and straight-across bangs, a round face, a soft voice when she said hello. Bob started in about the lake and the rain and the store itself as she rang up their things and put it all into bags. When she was finished, he paid and asked if he could ask a question.

"Of course," she said.

"Well, we were wondering—you wouldn't happen to know of a place to stay around the lake, would you?"

She looked at them both, from one to the other, and seemed confused. "Do you mean *besides* the camp?"

Bob tilted his head to one side. "Camp," he said and placed his hand on the back of his son's neck. "Now let's think," he said to the boy. "Did we know about any camp?"

Daniel shrugged and made a cartoon of his face and said, "*Camp*—what camp?"

The girl smiled at them and said that there was a camp attached to the store. They could rent cottages and sailboats and things, she said. She reached for the display of postcards by the magazines—photos of loons and sunsets on the water, little Davy Crockett cabins lining the lakeshore. "It's kind of rustic," she said. "But people seem to like it."

Bob nodded, turning serious and looking to the boy. "Sounds good," he said. "I mean, we're sort of like people, aren't we?"

"I think so," said Daniel. "At least sometimes we are."

"Well, then, should we sign up?"

"Sure," he said and smiled at to his father.

The girl stepped around the counter and walked them to the entryway with their bags. They'd have to go to the manager's office, she said. She pointed to the big farmhouse across the driveway. The rain had opened up and was coming down hard. The three of them all stood under the eaves of the store, the air cool and effervescent. "You can wait here if you want," she told them. "Until the rain lets up a little, at least."

"That's all right," said Bob. "We won't melt or anything—right, kid?" The man put an invisible rope around Daniel's neck and gave him a tug, the boy pulled along on a leash.

They ran the bags to the car and were drenched by the time they hit the porch. Daniel dried his face with the front of his shirt, his father already knocking at the door. Bob shook open his handkerchief and dried his hair and face. They watched the house, but all the windows stayed dark.

"Doesn't look like anybody's home," said the man. "Does it?"

"You want to wait?" said Daniel.

Bob shrugged and put his handkerchief away. He opened the storm door and knocked on the glass this time. They waited again, and Bob glanced back at the boy and then tried the handle. The door swung quietly open, and

Bob clucked his tongue and stepped inside the house. He called hello into the front hall and stairway and cocked his head to listen.

"Dad," whispered Daniel from behind him. "What are you doing?"

"Gee," said Bob, his voice quiet, "where d'you suppose everyone is?"

"I don't know," said the boy, "but come out of there."

Bob smiled. "Why are we whispering?"

Daniel watched in horror as his father started to drift down the hall, past the mirror, the coat rack, the darkened staircase inside. Once more, how awful to be pulled along in his father's wake, but he couldn't leave him alone in there. The old floor creaked as he edged into the foyer, his father as calm as a sleepwalker through the doorway into the dining room.

Daniel tried to call him back, but Bob just picked an apple from a bowl on the table. He offered it out to the boy.

"Put it back," said Daniel.

And Bob started to bring it to his mouth, but Daniel stepped up and stopped him. He pried the apple from his father's hand and placed it carefully in the bowl with the rest, with the scatter of mail, the empty plate and drinking glass on the table. The boy had to physically pull him away from the house. He pushed him through the rooms and hallway and back out to the porch.

The man laughed and let himself be pushed and prodded the length of the porch by the boy. There were wicker chairs, and Daniel turned his father by the shoulders and sat him down. "Stay," said the boy. "Just stay there."

"Can I have a cigarette?"

"Yes," said Daniel. "But don't go anywhere."

Bob scratched the lighter up from his pocket and hunched his shoulders as he lit a cigarette.

"You shouldn't smoke so much."

"Thanks," said Bob. "Anything else I should know, while you're at it?"

"Just try to be nice," said Daniel. "That's all."

Bob leaned back and hooked his boots on the porch rail. The wicker crackled as he locked his legs. He looked across at the lake, and Daniel stood there against the house like a guard, the boy watching that his father didn't move.

The rain began to ease off, gradually, and Bob finished his cigarette and flipped it into the grass. "We sort of had a spread like this where I grew up," he said. "No lake or store or anything, but we had the same hay barn and silo."

Bob stared out at the lake, and Daniel watched him, waiting for the man to offer more. But he didn't. "So, Dad, what happened to it?"

"I don't think anything happened to it," said Bob. "I mean, my brother's still around. He still runs the farm and everything, I imagine. You've been there—you were little, but we took you a couple of times."

And like all his father's mysteries—the farm, his side of the family, what he did in the service—he hadn't hidden this so much as never volunteered it to anyone. Bob looked at Daniel and stood up and went over to the porch column, tapped it with the toe of his shoe. "You know what?" he said to the boy. "I have to go back to the store for a minute."

"Why?" said Daniel.

"I think I forgot something."

Daniel started to move forward with his father.

"No, you just stay here," said the man. "It's like a guy can't even take a shit in peace anymore. Don't worry, I won't go anywhere."

He left the boy on the porch and in the store bought a post-card of the lake. He asked to borrow a pen from the girl at the register. He asked about the mail. He guessed it would take two days for a card to reach home, then it'd take a few hours for her to drive to the lake, and then he just went ahead and lit the fuse:

Anna,

> *Why don't you come join us here when you get this? We'll be waiting for you.*

Love always, Bob

He addressed the card and set the pen on the counter and asked the girl about postage. She had stamps and a pile of letters to go out that afternoon. She added it to the rest, and Bob said, "I'd like it to be a surprise for the boy. So don't say anything, okay?"

They ended up with their choice of cottages and got a one-room cabin at the farthest end of the camp. The manager gave them preseason rates and coupons for lunch and dinner and boat rentals. He showed them maps and brochures, gave them mimeographs about water safety and event schedules. When Bob and Daniel left the office, they took a two-cent tour of the camp, coasted the Bonneville past the sheds, past the playground, the fire pit, the stacks of cord-wood, everything still wet with rain. Bob circled them along a cul-de-sac of campsites and trailers under the trees.

A small rise, a break in the trees, and they curved onto a panorama of the lake and the tree-softened hills beyond. Bob stopped the car a moment and watched the clouds and the spots of sunlight moving over the water. "Pretty nice," he said to the boy, "isn't it?"

Daniel said yes, and Bob rolled them forward, both of them wincing at each rock and rut that caught the under-pipes of the car. Another curve, another last string of camp-sites, and then a gazebo came into view. There were people standing under the roof, a half dozen or so, and they all watched and waved as the Bonneville paraded past. Bob gave them a little toot and rode the brakes down the hill to the lakeside.

At the water's edge, the cabins all backed away into the woods, the water smooth and brown in the cove, a few docks, a swim float. They were completely alone down here, and they opened up the cabin, the curtains, the win-dows, took in the lake and hills from the porch.

The cabin itself was the size of a garage and opened on three sides like a sleeping porch, the metal screens making the view seem as faded and silvered as an old photograph. Bookshelves lined one of the walls, a table in one corner, a couple of narrow beds side by side in the other.

"A perfect gangster hideout," said Bob. "Don't you think? Just lay low a couple days? Let the heat cool down a little bit—right, partner?"

Daniel nodded and looked out over the lake. The

cabin grew quiet, and everything seemed to slow. The water gently slapped against the dock below the little porch, and even the sunlight seemed thick and ambery in the room. Bob tested one of the beds and lay back across the mattress, his feet still flat on the floor. He didn't move or open his eyes, and Daniel watched, as if his father had fallen asleep already, just like that, hands folded over his chest, his eyelids fluttering against the light.

"Hey," said Bob, his eyes closed, "you still there?"

Daniel waited and said yes and saw his father smile slightly.

"So, listen," said the man. "I'll give you a dollar to take my shoes off for me."

Daniel stared at him and didn't say anything.

"All right," said Bob, still lying there, not moving, barely even breathing. "How about ten? How's that sound? C'mon, be a pal already—that's five bucks a shoe, you know."

"No," said Daniel.

Bob groaned and said, "You're gonna break me, kid, but let's say twenty. That's my final offer, though—I mean, I'd do it myself for that kind of money."

Daniel went to the foot of the bed and unzipped the man's boots for him. He eased them off by the heel, set them neatly on the little rug, and stood up again.

"So what's the chance you can do my socks now too?" Bob wiggled his toes, and Daniel moved away from the man and watched him from across the room.

"That's what I was afraid of," said Bob. He looked over

at the boy and smiled and then made himself more comfortable on the bed.

"I owe you," said Bob. "Now I'm gonna rest my eyes a few minutes. Just don't let me go too long if I sleep, all right?"

Daniel stood in the room. He didn't move, and within minutes his father's body flinched across to sleep. He watched the rise and fall of the man's stomach, and outside a pair of sailboats stood motionless on the water, the crayon-colored sails in the sunlight. He remembered the ring in his pocket and thought how his mother would like this place. It'd be just the thing for her, he thought. She could rest and read and go for walks with them, as if all she'd ever wanted was to have the kind of life that included quiet, aimless walks in the woods.

The fart-purr of a motorboat approached and passed, and Daniel started to move toward his father again. He had the ring in his hand and reached it out slowly and held it up to him as if somehow controlling the man with it, as if daring him to break whatever spell this was. And Bob snored softly, Daniel taking pains not to wake him. He moved about the room carefully, ate crackers and cheese, and knew that the man would be angry for having slept so long. The trees smudged in the dusk outside, and a mineral taste of lake weed and pine seeped into the cabin. As it got dark, Daniel switched on a reading light in the corner and browsed through the paperbacks and puzzles on the shelves, the guidebooks to birds and plants, a dictionary with flowers and leaves pressed in it, an old *Farmer's Al-*

manac, and then a *Guinness Book of Records,* which he took down from the shelf. It was worn and the pages had yellowed, but he sat by the light and dog-eared all the things he thought his father might like to hear later:

> *The longest recorded attack of hiccoughs was that afflicting Charles Osborne of Anthon, Iowa, from 1922 to present. He contracted the hiccoughs while slaughtering a hog 55 years ago. His first wife left him and he is unable to keep in his false teeth.*

> *The worst reported case of compulsive swallowing, Mrs. H, aged 42, found to have 2,533 objects in her stomach, including 847 bent pins.*

> *Swami Maujgiri Maharijj stood continuously for 17 years while performing penance. He leaned against a plank to sleep.*

He could sit and read stories like this all night, each like a little fable or fairy tale. The heaviest man being buried in a piano case. A Chinese priest growing his fingernails for twenty-seven years. So many different ways to live in the world. And the moths pattered softly against the screens until he turned off the lamp and went to sleep.

In the morning they hiked up into the woods together. Daniel led them along a dry streambed of stones and sand, the air cool and damp under the trees. From a clearing, the lake lay shining and flat below, the clouds and the shadows of clouds flooding over the water and the hills. It was beautiful, and Daniel waited and listened for his father to come trudging up the path below him. He began to hear that telltale jog of keys in the man's pocket, and Bob appeared in the distance with a walking stick, his breathing heavy and labored as he picked his way between the stones and trees.

"Fuck," he said when he saw the boy. "I mean, pardon my French, but I'm too old for this crap."

Daniel smiled and pointed for him to see the lake below.

Bob turned and looked back. "That's good enough for me," he said. "Let's stop and sit for a while, before you kill me—literally."

They moved into the shade, and Bob took Pop Tarts and little red boxes of raisins from his pockets. He produced a Slim Jim and a roll of Life Savers, and he and Daniel sat and ate breakfast under the trees. They stared at the clouds and the light, the air cool from the woods like a cellar. "I keep thinking how much your mother would like it here," he said to the boy. "I mean, what's not to like, right?"

"Do you think she's okay?" said the boy.

"No," said Bob, "I don't, actually. I really can't fathom her being too happy with us right now, can you?"

Bob stood and kicked the blood into his legs, as he always did, and he and Daniel started back down to the camp again. They followed the streambed and came out of the woods to the fields, the sunlight warm and the grass and air as sweet as bread. On the dirt road to the lake they passed other campers and said hello, like normal people, but then in the dining hall Bob wrapped sandwiches in paper napkins to take back to the cabin. They ate alone on their little porch, like hermits.

When they were finished with lunch, Bob lay in bed and closed his eyes again. Daniel cleaned the plates and pulled a chair toward the window. Taking his book, he sat and started to read aloud to his father:

Mrs. Marva Drew of Waterloo, Iowa, between 1968 and 1974, typed the numbers one to one million on a manual typewriter. She used 2,473 pages. When asked why, she replied, "But I love to type."

The record squat for pole sitting is 399 days by Frank Perkins from June 1, 1975, to July 4, 1976, in an eight-by-eight box atop a fifty-foot telegraph pole. He was observed by motorists passing by.

"What a nut," said Bob as he lay there, his voice dry and half asleep. "At least in jail you'd get TV, right?"

Daniel looked at the man, and Bob breathed out deep and waited for the boy to start again. "Keep going," he said, and Daniel flipped through the pages and pictures and began again for his father:

Princess Pauline stood only 23 inches tall and weighed 9 pounds at her heaviest.

Dave Mann of Eastbourne, England, ate 130 prunes — without pits — on June 16, 1971, in 105 seconds.

"I'm sorry," said Bob, "but how many prunes was that?"

Daniel looked again. "A hundred and thirty," he told the man.

"And what was his name?"

"Dave Mann," said Daniel. "Why?"

"Do me a favor," said Bob. "Just look up 'Longest on a Toilet Bowl' for me now—I'll bet good old Dave's got that one locked up too."

Bob stood up out of bed, and Daniel watched him walk across to the bathroom. He heard the toilet flush, and when Bob came out he had changed into swim trunks, a towel around his shoulders. Standing pigeon-chested in the room, the man looked at the boy and said, "Well? How about a little swim before dinner?"

And in some ways, this was what Daniel wanted most to remember, the two of them walking down to the dock and standing in the sun, just working up the nerve to jump into the water. It would be so cold, he knew, and he watched his father swing his arms in circles as the man counted down from ten and dove out, at last, into the lake. Bob swam under water with long frog kicks, his body pale and glowing as he went, the water like a thick skin over him.

Halfway to the swim float, he broke the surface and turned to Daniel. "Simply lovely," he called like a queen. "Do come and join me," he said in a falsetto. "It's quite lovely, actually—quite warm, quite delightful."

Daniel swung his arms and counted down, and when he hit the water, the lake felt so cold it seemed electrified. He gasped and howled and chopped his way across to his father. Spokes of light turned around his head when he opened his eyes in the water, and Bob already stood on the float. He reached over the side and lifted Daniel out of the lake with one strong pull. They stood on the plastic turf as the raft swung away on its anchoring, a submarine sound of oil drums under them as they caught their breath.

Daniel unclenched his jaw and let his teeth chatter, and the man laughed. It was a good laugh, kind and happy, and Bob said, "So I guess I lied, huh?"

Daniel looked at him, and Bob said, "Cold, huh?"

Daniel nodded, his father laughing again.

"Other than that," said the man, "it's been kind of a perfect day for us, hasn't it?"

A shiver passed through Daniel, and Bob said they should swim back before they got all warm and comfortable.

Back on shore, Bob wrapped a towel around the boy, that mentholated feel in their skin from the cold. They stood on the dock and watched the light drain from the sky, the cottages and trees growing indistinct and dark around the lake, the water still and polished.

In the cabin, Daniel put on his new cowboy shirt and combed his hair and watched his father shave at the bathroom sink. The boy stood in the doorway and found himself holding his breath. In fact, he felt he'd been holding his breath all along, almost afraid to really breathe. Bob splashed himself with aftershave, his neck and cheeks, and then he dried his face, put on his new shirt, the one with pearl snaps like Daniel's.

"If they could only see us now," he said, taking a teacup from the table and crossing the room. He reached under his bed pillow and a pint curve appeared in hand. He twisted the seal off the cap and said cheers to the boy.

Daniel pressed his mouth into a line. "I'm going to wait outside," he said.

"Hold on a second," said Bob. "You ever taste this stuff before?"

Daniel slowly shook his head and said no.

Bob poured some whiskey into the cup and held it out to the boy. "Come here," he said. "Who knows, someday you might wanna say you had a drink with your father."

"I don't want to, Dad."

"Sure you do," said Bob.

"No," said Daniel, "I don't think I do."

"Here," the man said. "Just don't tell your mother— the woman would shit a pickle." He pressed the cup to Daniel's hand and said, "Take it already."

Daniel took the cup and raised it to his lips and just drank the whiskey for his father, his whole body convulsing with the taste and feel of it. But then it was done, and Bob could laugh and clap the boy on the back, always hitting him a little too hard, always trying to toughen him up.

And now Daniel could go outside. It was almost dark, the other cabins empty and quiet. Everything about the lake and woods seemed remote and gloomy to him. He wandered down into the side yard and stood at the far end of the Bonneville, the ring in his hand again. The woods, the lake, the sky, everything got dark, and he waited behind the car until his father came out to the porch.

They drove halfway around the lake for dinner and ate

in a family-style place called Rosie's. And afterward, outside in the parking lot, Bob suggested they check in with his mother. She answered in one ring, and Daniel didn't say a word to her, the receiver to his ear. He glanced up at his father and shrugged to the man, as if the phone was just ringing on her end of the line, no one picking up.

"Daniel," she was saying to him, "say something." Her voice became almost desperate and raw as she went on and on to no one. "I can hear you breathing," she said.

He pressed his lips tight and felt cruel and hard and didn't care—but then he did care too and wanted so badly to hear her voice, even if it was shaking and brittle and choked with tears. If nothing else, at least now he could feel some of what she felt.

Bob lit a cigarette and poked the boy's shoulder. "Maybe she's not there," he said. "We'll try later?"

Her end of the line went instantly still—she'd heard.

Daniel tried to swallow, his throat thick as clay, and Bob coughed into his fist. And then a car passed on the road, and she said, "How could you?"

When he still didn't say anything, she lashed out and called him a liar and a thief, just like his father—and he couldn't bear to hear this. It took all his strength to slip the receiver from his chin and hang it up into the cradle, all of the coins falling inside the phone.

He felt his father lean over to check the empty slot. Bob put his hand on the boy's shoulder. "What did you expect?" he asked. "All sunshine and flowers from her?"

"Don't touch me," said Daniel. He hated everything

about the man, and he threw his way out of the booth and walked across the parking lot toward the car. They shouldn't have called, he knew, and he slipped the ring out of his pocket and held it as if to secretly apologize to her.

Bob followed him, and Daniel touched the car and turned to look at his father. "I want to go home," he said.

Bob smiled at the boy and said, "No, not yet."

"Why not?"

"Because I said so, Daniel."

"Well, why can't you just leave us alone already?"

"I know," said Bob. "I should have done that. I should have just gone — but I didn't."

Daniel looked away at the parking lot and the lights and wished he'd told her where she could find them. They rode back to the camp, to the cabin, the lake, all of it so quiet now. Never had Daniel heard or felt such quiet, the moon bright over the far hills on the other side of the lake. Bob suggested they go to the fire, as if this was the day's last formality.

"You can go," said Daniel. "But I'm tired."

They'd lie in their beds that night and wait a long time for sleep to come, each of them just visible to the other in the light from the moon.

Bob took a deep breath and let it out slowly, like steam escaping. "You gonna hate me forever?" he said.

Daniel rolled in bed toward his father and that voice of his from the dark.

"You know," said the man, "it'll be fine. You'll see, you'll borrow fathers. And that'll be better for you, much better — not having me around all the time, not needing to check over your shoulder to see if I'm watching you or not, not having me busting your ass every two minutes. I'd be terrible for you. I mean, let's face it: I already am terrible for you, aren't I?"

"I don't understand," said Daniel.

"I don't exactly understand, either," said Bob. "But I know lots of guys who never get out from under their fathers' thumbs, that's all. And it'll be good for you and your mother when I'm gone. You'll be able to be your own man, and you'll be better than I'd have ever let you be."

In the morning, Daniel couldn't understand why they were hiking into the woods again. They went higher this time, all the way to the crest of the hills above the camp. They had breakfast under the trees and watched the slow tumble of clouds, the lake appearing different from yesterday—still beautiful, but hazy and seemingly far away. There was an air of waiting, as well, as if they were putting off an ending that they both wanted yet didn't really want. Bob smoked a cigarette and started back down again, into the fields and camp. They took sandwiches back to the cabin and lay in the room after lunch, the light languid and drowsy.

They swam out to the float and stood in the last light of the afternoon. And back in the cabin again, Bob shaved and pulled a bottle from his sleeve, fixed himself a drink, and smiled and sat with the boy. They watched the lake turn grainy and dark.

Daniel sat another few minutes and let himself out to the porch and side yard. He couldn't name what he felt, beyond cold and damp from the air and grass, the wind rising off the water. The windows of the cabin stayed dark, just as all the empty cottages along the shore stayed dark, the lake still and smooth.

He had wanted so badly to have his father come home, just as he'd wanted to give the ring to his mother. But now, with the ring in his hand, he'd just as soon throw it into the woods or the lake, just let his arm hang out of the car window and let it fall away. It seemed just another kind of lie to him now.

Almost completely dark, and then there she was, a faint crunch of footsteps on the gravel. Daniel watched the dirt path and heard and then saw her walking past the other cottages. She moved deliberately, straight toward the Bonneville. She didn't see him in the side yard, and he, for his part, didn't run or call or move to her. He held his breath as she climbed the steps to the cabin and crossed the porch, her shoes on the boards. There was that pleasant glide of his father's voice from the dark of the cabin, and the lights came on in the windows.

He stood on the outskirts of the yard and heard the pneumatic pull of the screen door opening and closing. He pictured them inside, imagined all the things they could say to each other, all the different ways they could be in that little room with each other, all his life seeming to balance on this one moment. And as long as it didn't end, they could always step onto the porch together and call for him. And waiting outside like this, he found himself watching the windows of that cabin, as if anything was still possible.

EPILOGUE Years from here, each time they think him dead and gone and far away behind them, each time they believe they are safe at last, that they have forgiven him his many slights and sins, all his greedy lies and neglects forgotten—then there he is again, narrow as an arrow, the man with the sweepstakes smile and sly charm. It might be a birthday that brings him around. A certain song on the radio. A spoon falls to the floor and they think of him. The roof leaks, the car breaks down, and he's there at the door, his hand raised to the window to break the glare.

He is welcome to visit as long and as often as he likes now; they could never turn him away again. That was his to accomplish, and he's done it so completely that it almost qualifies as a work of art. And it's true, Daniel and his mother are just glad to see him. He seems so frail and thin and, in an odd way, precious to them as he sits there on the couch. The truth is that they have so little time with him. They swallow all the hard resentments and offer salted nuts and fresh cans of beer for him to balance on his knee as he sits and listens to all he's missed. They catch him up on work and school and Joelyn and everything else that is small and light enough for him to carry away. He's always on his way somewhere else and has to get going soon, so they try to make the most of what little time they have together.

They never ask him where he goes now, because they know he's lost to them. Let him send his postcards from Lake Tahoe. Or Montreal. Or Fort Lauderdale. His notes say nothing, except that he's still alive, and that he thinks of them. In the end, the postmark, his choice of paper or picture, the words he misspells or scratches out, these things tell them more about him than he ever does. They know more about his life when he trades his Pontiac down for a Dodge or pulls up to the house in a Cadillac.

At a retirement party for one of her friends at the store, there's a birthday cake for Anna. She's forty-six years old, and everyone's hiding behind racks of clothes to surprise her. Even Daniel is home from college and goes with his mother and her friends for dinner in the next town over. It's late by the time they get home. And just as they let themselves into the front door, they hear a great crash in the kitchen. It's unsettling—a sickening, unsprung sound. Someone's in the house, they think, but then they find that it's the cuckoo clock that has fallen to the floor. Daniel picks up the little house, and she helps untangle the chains and pinecone weights. They hang it back on the wall and try to start the pendulum, but the maple leaf won't catch again.

And first thing in the morning, the phone starts ringing. The fact that he's died on her birthday is nearly too much to believe, nearly too perfect. "He always had to get the last word," she says, her voice almost bright and happy.

She can't remember the last time she visited the farm where Bob grew up, and she gets lost on the way and calls Danny from a service station. There are cars lined up in front of the house, and someone comes out as she pulls in. He comes across the yard to Anna with that familiar, crooked smile on his face, a sturdier version of Bob, a bit more weathered than his brother had been. "You made it," he says and hugs her.

He holds her away and says she looks great. Anna smiles, and Daniel thinks she looks soft today and pretty, her face young and flush, as if she's carried something for a long time and has placed it down and become light and lovely and alive again.

"Danny," she says to the man, though she is suddenly undone by tears. She steps back and wipes her face and laughs at herself, smoothes her jacket. The man turns to Daniel. "And you must be Daniel."

He crosses the front of their car and shakes Daniel's hand. "I don't think I've seen you since you were five or six years old," he says. "But let's go in and meet everybody."

It's a great rambling farmhouse with a wraparound porch, a barn in back, a silo. He leads them into the front rooms, and everyone stands in the kitchen as he makes the introductions—his wife, Eileen, daughter, Maggie, sons, Jeffery and Alex, sisters, Margaret and Anne. Then there's Herby and Trish, and Francis and Matthew, and Monsignor Michaels in his priest's collar, and Anna seems to know them all. It's warm in the room, everyone talking out of turn, all these people who belonged to Bob. Danny brings chairs for Anna and Daniel, and there's coffee and drinks and pierogies and ham on the table.

It's almost time for calling hours, and the priest gets everyone to start out the door. The funeral home is in town, a big white handsome place with scalloped siding and a turret. It's impressive and austere and immediately inside is a coatroom, a vestibule, and then a parlor opening off to the left. And it's a surprise to see his father lying there, at the far end of the room, a clutter of flowers, some church candles, some folding chairs. The coffin shines black like a piano, and everyone's hushed, almost ignoring him, as if he's in the bath and they don't want to disturb him or look at him impolitely.

After a few minutes in the doorway, Daniel takes his mother's hand and they go to him. He remembers how this was exactly what he wished, the thing he seemed to always be waiting for, but moving down the aisle to the man, he just feels lonely for his father. And up close, the man doesn't look at all like himself, his face smoothed with makeup, his skin orangey at the temples. One of his eyes is slightly open and catches the light like glass.

He's surprised that his mother doesn't say goodbye from the funeral home; instead she follows everyone back to the farm. They all raise a toast, and someone brings a snapshot and sets it on the table: it's Christmas in the photo, and Bob's in a bright white shirt and rabbit-fur hat with flaps. He looks heavy and happy and drunk, with that lopsided smile of his.

Daniel sits and listens to it all, how his father was as a boy on the farm, how he left for the service, how stupid and selfish and wonderful he could be, all these pieces of the man that won't lie still.

As someone says, he was no saint. But then again, what fun's a saint to have around anyway? And they laugh, and Danny's saying that no one could stay mad at him, everyone around the table nodding and smiling in agreement, including Anna.

It's dark outside when his mother starts her goodbyes. She's in the living room, and Daniel can hear that silver in her voice, happy and easy now that he's gone, as if it's safe for her to have feelings again, as if she's allowed herself to be in love with him again.

Daniel feels a hand on his shoulder, his uncle. "I've got to run out to the garage a minute," he says. "Can you give me a hand?"

He follows his uncle out to the workbench in the garage, Danny saying how good it was to see him and his mother. "Now I can't say when I'll see you next," he says.

There's a small paper bag on top of one of the boxes stacked there, and he picks it up and hands it to Daniel. "I thought you should have these," he says. "It's what your father had with him when he died."

Daniel takes the bag and will take it again and again over the years. A moody glide of a car, a sleepless night, and he'll idly glance at the shelf and take down his father's effects. Each time is slightly different. Maybe it's just him, but something always seems to catch him by surprise, as if these things all had a life of their own. He keeps them in a coffee can with some old photos of his father and mother, a work slip for windows, and then, of course, the ring, part of himself and his own mystery now, or so it comes to feel.

A deep breath, and there's his father's wristwatch, a Bulova with an expandable band. The time is 11:19—though it ticks once or twice each time he handles it. His father's keychain has only two keys on it—a house key and a pink-tinted GM key—one side of the green plastic dangler reads, COMPLIMENTS OF SAVOY BEAUTY SALON, and the other side is a zodiac, KEEP US IN MIND FOR THE FUTURE.

The man's wallet is soft and tan and tri-folded. It's stamped by Amity Cowhide and has fourteen dollars inside, nine ones and a five. There's a carbon to a money order for 175 dollars and 00 cents. There's a VA card, a driver's license, and a Social Security card made of sheet metal. And then there are all his memberships—the American Legion, the Elks, VFW, National Ukrainian Home, Knights of Columbus. There are phone numbers on pieces of scratch paper, addresses to his dentist and his tax accountant, a dry cleaning slip, an appointment reminder from Dr. A. P. Sharon, Orthopedist, 6 Clinic Drive. A coupon worth fifty cents toward filter, lube, and oil change. A business card for a Tropicana Hotel and Apartments—*Your Home Tonight, centrally located, 5 min to ocean*. And then there's a red plastic coin, GOOD FOR ONE BEER, B.P.O.E. NO. 574.

Along with everything else, there are two photographs.

One is a school picture of Daniel, his mother's handwriting on the back: *12 Years Old*. And the other is a passport photo of a woman—it's faded and blurry and, most of all, it's not Anna. He goes through the wallet so many times, not that he knows what he wants to find anymore, only that it never seems to be there.

THE

POETRY

OF

FRENCH CANADA

IN

TRANSLATION

THE POETRY OF

FRENCH CANADA

IN TRANSLATION

Edited with an introduction by

JOHN GLASSCO

TORONTO/OXFORD UNIVERSITY PRESS/1970

PUBLICATION OF THIS BOOK WAS ASSISTED BY
THE CANADA COUNCIL
AND THE DEPARTMENT OF CULTURAL AFFAIRS OF QUEBEC

© Oxford University Press (Canadian Branch) 1970

SBN-19-540167-0

Printed in England by
HAZELL WATSON AND VINEY LTD
AYLESBURY BUCKS

Contents

*Where the translator's
name is not given,
the translation
is by John Glassco.*

* Émile Coderre.

FRANÇOIS HERTEL

SAINT-DENYS-GARNEAU

RINA LASNIER

ANNE HÉBERT

GILLES HÉNAULT

YVES PRÉFONTAINE

GÉRALD GODIN

PAUL CHAMBERLAND

ANDRÉ BROCHU

ANDRÉ MAJOR

Introduction

Anthologies of translations lie under handicaps from which other collections are free. Above all they are subject to inevitable gaps and a corresponding want of proportion and balance in their survey of the field. There is no remedy for this: the anthologist has only the choice of what is available—and the choice is made still harder in the case of translations of poetry, where minor poems have often been excellently rendered and major ones either skipped or spoiled. This is especially true of the poetry of French Canada where translation, while often inspired, has always been capricious and sporadic.

Any formal review of French-Canadian poetry itself would be thus out of place here; moreover, this has already been so well done, in French by Guy Sylvestre in his *Anthologie de la Poésie Canadienne-française* and by Gilles Marcotte in *Une littérature qui se fait,* and in English by A. J. M. Smith in his introduction to *The Oxford Book of Canadian Verse*—to say nothing of the valuable studies of Gérard Bessette and Gérard Tougas—that the reader need only be referred to them. The present anthology can do no more than give the English reader his first extended view of the beauties, development and direction of the poetry itself.

This view will reveal both its limitations and its excellencies. It will be seen that the poetry of French Canada is a poetry of exile—from France and North America alike—and that the note of desertion, of nostalgia, of the *dépaysé*, recurs constantly, forming a kind of ground-bass to themes of avoidance, retreat and

escape. This feeling of abandonment, first by France and then by a native élite, is only too well founded in historical fact; and the poets of French Canada—who rather than her religious and political leaders have always been the true spokesmen of her reality—have expressed with varying degrees of intensity the spirit of a people whose pride and conservatism, religiosity and restlessness, sentimentality and neurosis, have united and interwoven to form the defensive armour generally assumed by peoples whose normal evolution has been checked and stifled for any length of time. For the Conquest was the first and supreme experience of French Canada, and its perpetuation in various forms of control and isolation, no matter how or by whom imposed, has given a certain uniformity to her literary attitudes. The three constant sources of poetic inspiration have thus continued to be Nature, the Self and Death; the passions of love and liberty play almost no part in it, for women, as Jean Le Moyne has pointed out, are considered exclusively as mothers, and liberty is conceived not as individual freedom but always as a transference of power from an English to a French ruling class.

It will be noted, however, that within these limits French-Canadian poets have accomplished marvels of form, insight, music and grace. The work of Nelligan, Morin, Choquette, Grandbois, Saint-Denys-Garneau, Rina Lasnier and Anne Hébert is of the first, or almost the first, order of poetry; but the measure of its worth is in its transcendence of the historical situation, of that French fact which, however fundamental to the life of the people itself, was nonetheless something that these poets

assimilated and surmounted: the single-minded passion by which they did so is the measure, indeed, of their poetic stature. It is still too early to assess the corresponding stature of their successors of the present day, though it is safe to say that *'le créateur, le poète, qui donnera au peuple canadien-français son image'*, the genius so hopefully announced and awaited by Saint-Denys-Garneau in his *Journal*, has not yet appeared. Brilliant, eloquent, impassioned and exploiting all the resources of new and exciting techniques, they seem too often preoccupied by political and national ideas, by the one incandescent ideal of a beleaguered Quebec—and it is a truism that politics and nationalism have somehow never managed to make really good poetry. Also, the dead hand of surrealism—an influence no less pernicious than any other worn-out poetic method—is still hovering over them, with its obsession with the magic of dissociated images, its facile surprises, its meaningless sonorities. Nevertheless, the greater part of this anthology has been allotted to the younger poets; for the renaissance begun by the *parti pris* and Hexagone groups is in fact, as Alain Bosquet has pointed out, the only significant development of French-Canadian poetry since it emerged from the prison of the self-regarding self under the leadership of seminal poets like Grandbois, Hertel and Hénault. The voices of this renaissance, which are the collective voice of the future of French Canada, are what is important and what must be heard, even in the unequal and opaque medium of translation.

The translation of poetry is often decried. It has become

fashionable to repeat Robert Frost's remark that what gets lost in the process is 'the poetry itself'—or, as Sir John Denham put it rather less succinctly 300 years earlier, 'the subtle Spirit of poesie evaporates entirely in the transfusion from one language to another,' though he adds the saving qualification, 'unless a new, or an original spirit is infused by the Translator himself.' This infusion remains the mark of good translation; and difficult as it is, the operation must always be ruled by the architecture of the poem itself, which is necessarily laid bare. Faithful translation especially, which can seldom hope—and in the opinion of some should never try—to reproduce the music or magic of the original, is in fact the strictest examination a poem's intimate structure can undergo, an ultimate screening that may leave it nothing but its intellectual content or 'meaning', its images and inner pulsation; for Mallarmé's clever riposte to Degas is only half true: poetry *is* made out of words, but poems themselves—as Mallarmé must have known—do not *begin* with words but with ideas, concepts, formulations of emotion. The scales of translation are thus weighted in favour of a poetry marked by clarity of thought and expression, spare and striking imagery, and a simple internal movement: the work of Virgil, Dante, Villon and Baudelaire, for example, lends itself admirably to versions in other tongues, while that of Catullus, Tasso, Hugo and Verlaine does not. Rimbaud's richly allusive prose-poems are almost unreadable in translation, though his sonnets and 'ballads', owing to their comparative simplicity, come through quite well.

But it is not only the ideas and progression of a poem

that are exposed by translation : the temper and complexion of the poet himself are so mercilessly revealed
as to justify the wry old equation of *traduttore, traditore*.
This betrayal, which is part of the translator's enforced
role of analytical critic, is everywhere apparent in the
present anthology. The fustian of Crémazie, the smugness
of the poets of the *Terroir*, the rhetoric of much of the
jeune poésie—all these are indeed *traditi*, as they were
bound to be. For the good translator is obliged, whether
he likes it or not, either to take the line laid down by
Lord Roscommon in that ingenuous couplet,

> *Your author always will the best advise;*
> *Fall when he falls, and when he rises rise,*

or to yield to the temptation to beautify and 'improve',
and thus perhaps carry the process of betrayal still
further.

Why then, it may be asked, make translations of poetry
at all? If the result is a loss, a depreciation, a betrayal,
surely the expense of effort, the dizzying labour of trying to transmute the essence of that most incommensur-
able thing, a poem, might be better applied elsewhere—
even in following Ezra Pound's advice to 'make it new',
that is, to misread the text in a fit of inspired illiteracy
and make another poem altogether. But is not this question only another way of asking why poetry itself should
be written? The poet, as Saint-Denys-Garneau found, is
aware sooner or later that in pursuing his vocation he is
exposing, depreciating and betraying himself, and finally
failing to express the reality of his experience; but this
does not stop him from writing poetry. In the same way

the devoted translator of poetry will not be balked: he is possessed by the necessity of making a *translation*—in the older, religious sense of a conveyance or assumption, as of Enoch or Elijah—of the vision of reality he has received from a poem, and of communicating his experience to those of another tongue; and when he wholly succeeds, as he sometimes does, the sense of achievement is that of poetic creation itself. At the worst, he has made a bridge of sorts.

The history of serious translation of French-Canadian poetry is short, covering little more than a dozen years and comprising only the collections of Jean Beaupré and Gael Turnbull (1955), P. F. Widdows (1960), F. R. Scott (1964) and Peter Miller (1964), although isolated groups of poems have appeared from time to time in books, newspapers and the little magazines; and almost all the poets represented in these collections date from within the last twenty-five years. Of translations done before 1950 there is little worth preserving except for antiquarian reasons, and going back further, one has only to read the translations done around the turn of the century, with their faded prettiness, poetic diction and Victorian tinkle, to appreciate the treatment that the poetry of French Canada has received within the last ten years.

The leading figure in this field so recently opened up is undoubtedly F. R. Scott, whose early renderings of Garneau, Hébert, Hénault, Trottier, Pilon and Giguère are still outstanding. His taste, fidelity and grasp of the movement of each poem are always admirable, and his

versions could serve as models; he is Canada's first artistic translator of poetry. The joint work of Beaupré and Turnbull—whose little mimeographed pamphlets, produced in Iroquois Falls in 1955-6, are now collectors' items—has a place of honour as the first example of collective poetry translation in this country, while Widdows and Miller, in their selections from the work of Émile Nelligan and Alain Grandbois respectively, gave English readers at least a glimpse of two of the most important poets of French Canada. Since then the translation of French-Canadian poetry has been immeasurably enriched by the work of such English-Canadian poets as Fred Cogswell, John Robert Colombo, G. V. Downes, Louis Dudek, R. A. D. Ford, Eldon Grier, Ralph Gustafson, George Johnston, Jay Macpherson, James Reaney, A. J. M. Smith and Francis Sparshott.

The present anthology was not, however, made from book or periodical printings alone, though these sources have all been consulted and drawn upon. More than three-quarters of the translations in this book have never been published before, and such a high proportion of new work may be taken as a hopeful sign for the future.

The leading principle of selection has been the viability of the translation itself. Thus, the space occupied by any poet has little relation to his importance vis-à-vis any other; for instance, Paul Morin has almost twice the space given to his contemporary René Chopin—but only because the latter, while quite as good a poet and only slightly more difficult to render, has somehow had less attraction to translators; the same circumstance accounts for the insufficient representation of the work

of Suzanne Paradis and Jacques Brault, and for the no
less regrettable omission of Cécile Chabot, Clément
Marchand, Alphonse Piché, Gérard Bessette and J.-P.
Filion: *non omnia possumus etiam omnes*. Versions of
important poems that by reason of their intractability
have failed to make good poetry in English have generally
been excluded; on the other hand fine re-creations of
less representative poems have been regarded as their
own warrant; so that, in a sense, this is an anthology of
poetic translations rather than of translations of poetry.
The possibly undue space given to Crémazie, Fréchette
and a few earlier poets should be regarded mainly as an
acknowledgement of their historical importance.

The original poems have not been printed. It was felt
that the traditional juxtaposition of original and translation not only hinders the enjoyment of the translation
as a poem in itself, but tends to turn the original into a
study-text, the translation into a crib, and the essential
poetry of both into a lesson in language or an occasion
to compare techniques. The translations in this collection
are presented as things that must stand on their own,
dependent on their own poetic merits, owing to their
originals nothing but the inspiration that has here found
a partial rebirth.

JOHN GLASSCO

Foster, Quebec
17 October 1968

Acknowledgements

Most of the translations reproduced in this anthology are printed by permission of the author of the original French poem and of the translator; a few exceptions are listed below.

JACQUES BRAULT : all rights, Mr F. R. Scott

RENÉ CHOPIN : Mrs Simone Moore and the translators

ALFRED DESROCHERS : Les Éditions Fides and the translators

PIERRE FALCON : translator's rights, Miss Sybil Hutchinson

SYLVAIN GARNEAU : Librairie Déom and the translators

ROLAND GIGUÈRE Translations by Francis Sparshott : reprinted from *A Cardboard Garage* by Francis Sparshott, published by Clarke, Irwin & Company Limited. Used by permission of Clarke, Irwin & Company and M. Giguère. 'Polar Seasons' : all rights, Mr F. R. Scott

ANNE HÉBERT Translations by F. R. Scott : all rights, Mr F. R. Scott. All other poems : Éditions du Seuil and the translators

GILLES HÉNAULT Translations by F. R. Scott : all rights, Mr F. R. Scott

GATIEN LAPOINTE 'Le Chevalier de Neige (I)', 'Down to Earth', 'The First Word' : Les Éditions du Jour Inc. and the translators

ALBERT LOZEAU : Mr Fred S. Lozeau and Mr John Glassco

PAUL MORIN 'Music of Names', 'Perdrix', 'Synderesis' : Le Cercle du Livre de France, publishers of *Géronte et son miroir* by Paul Morin, and the translators. 'The Peacock

Royal': Les Éditions Fides and Mr John Glassco

'JEAN NARRACHE' Translation of 'Les philanthropes' from *Quand j'parl' tout seul* by Jean Narrache printed by permission of Les Éditions de l'Homme, M. Émile Coderre, and Mr F. R. Scott

ÉMILE NELLIGAN Translations by P. F. Widdows: reprinted from *Selected Poems of Émile Nelligan*, edited by P. F. Widdows, by permission of the Ryerson Press, Toronto, and Les Éditions Fides. All other poems: Les Éditions Fides and the translators

FERNAND OUELETTE '50 Megatons': translator's rights, Canadian Speakers' & Writers' Service. Translations by F. R. Scott: all rights, Mr F. R. Scott

JEAN-GUY PILON Translations by F. R. Scott: all rights, Mr F. R. Scott. All other poems: M. Pilon, Éditions de l'Hexagone, and the translators

SAINT-DENYS-GARNEAU Translations by F. R. Scott: all rights, Mr F. R. Scott. All others poems: Les Éditions Fides and the translators

PIERRE TROTTIER Translations by F. R. Scott: all rights, Mr F. R. Scott

It has not been possible to trace the present copyright owners of several of the original French poems. The publishers would be grateful for information enabling them to make suitable acknowledgement in future editions.

August 1606

Farewell to the Frenchmen returning from New France to Gallic France

This address to the members of Poutrincourt's second expedition to Port Royal—on what is now the Annapolis Basin—who returned to France under Dupont in 1606, is probably the earliest work in verse written in America north of the Spanish Empire. It was first published in France in 1607.

Go then, set sail, O goodly company
Whose noble hearts withstood courageously
The dreadful fury of both wind and wave
The cruel blows the many seasons gave
To plant among us France's glorious name
And 'mid such hazards to preserve her fame.
Go then, set sail, and soon may each attain
The home fires of his Ithaca again :
And may we also, yet another year
See this whole company returning here.

Worn with fatigue you leave us, and we share
With you an equal weight of mutual care;
You, that no dread diseases bring their doles
To make to Pluto offering of our souls :
We, that no fitful wave or hidden rock
Strike your frail craft with unexpected shock.
But here resemblance fails, the likeness ends,
'Tis you who go to see congenial friends
In language, habits, customs and religion
And all the lovely scenes of your own nation,
While we among the savages are lost

I

And dwell bewildered on this clammy coast MARC
Deprived of due content and pleasures bright LESCARBO
Which you at once enjoy when France you sight.

What nonsense! I am wrong! in this lone land
All his soul needs the just man may command
And will God's power and graciousness revere
If he will contemplate the beauty here.
For should one travel all the earth around
And test the worth of every plot of ground
No place so fair, so perfect will he find
That our Port Royal will not leave far behind.
Perhaps you would on open country gaze?
These sloping banks are washed by numerous bays.
One hundred hills as well would please your
    eye?
Below one hundred all these waters lie.
Do you then seek the pleasure of the chase?
On every side great forests it embrace.
Are gamey birds desired for your meat?
Each season does its ordered flocks repeat.
Have you a longing for a varied dish?
The bounteous sea will gratify each wish.
Love you the gentle prattling of the rills?
They flow profusely from th'enlacing hills.
Would you enjoy the sight of islands green?
Two city-size within this port are seen.
Do you admire loquacious Echo's rhymes?
Here Echo can reply full thirty times,
For when the cannon's thunder outward sounds
Full thirty times the reverberant boom rebounds
As loud as if Megaera furious sought
To bring this mighty universe to nought.
Would you survey deep rivers in their course?
Three here pay tribute with their wavy force,
Of which the Eel,[1] that sweeps the most terrain,

---

[1] The Eel River : now the Annapolis River.

2

Bears down the proudest billow to the main,
And almost deafens with her boisterous pace
Not the Catadupes,[2] but this wild race.
Would you, in brief, your enemies withstand?
No fear is here save from heaven's wrathful hand,
For with two bulwarks nature fortified
Our entrance road so well, the countryside
From every threat kept safe, can rest in peace
And season after season live at ease.

Corn still is lacking, and no grapes are found
To make thy name through all the world
     renowned,
But should Almighty God our labours bless
Thou soon shalt feel celestial plenteousness
Pour down upon thee like the early dew
That, softly falling, doth parch'd earth renew
In midsummer. And though we do not wrest
The richness of the gold mine from thy breast,
Bronze, silver, iron, that thy thickset woods
Guard as in trust, these too are richest goods
For a beginning; someday may be found
The gold that waits its turn beneath the ground.
But now we are content thou may'st supply
Both corn and wine, then afterward may'st try
A more ambitious flight (the grass that girds
Thy waters could supply a thousand herds)
And build the cities, strongholds, settlements,
To give retreat to pioneers from France
And bring conversion to this savage nation
That has no God, no laws and no religion.

O thrice Almighty God whom I adore,
Whose sun upon this countryside doth pour
His dawn, I pray thee, do not longer wait,

---

[2] Catapudes : people living beside one of the Nile's
cataracts.

Have pity on this people's poor estate,
Who languish, hoping Thy more perfect light
Too long, alas! withholden from their sight.

DUPONT, whose name is graven on the sky
For having stood with matchless bravery
Against a thousand ills, a thousand pains,
Enough to crush the spirit in your veins,
When you were left here with the governance
Of those who, in this country of New France,
Sustained with ardour equal to your own
The long and bitter absence from their home—
As soon as you shall come to greet your King
Remind him of those days of crusading
When his forefathers fought to Palestine
For love of Christian law, and held the line
'Gainst furious Saracen and all his host
Offering their lives along the Memphis coast
To whim of wind and wave in that dread land,
To dripping scimitar in sudden hand:
Tell him that here with little cost or blood
With which strong arms can taint the murderous
    sword
He may surround himself with equal glory
And add a greater grandeur to his story.

Go then, set forth, O Frenchmen of stout heart,
While now our sails are calling us to start
Toward the Armouchiquois, past Malebarre,
To find another port to serve as bar
To threatening foe, or as a post to extend
A sheltered welcome to the incoming friend
And there discover if New France's soil
Will justify our faith-inspired toil.

Neptune, if e'er thou hast thy favour cast
On those whose lives upon thy waves are passed,
Good Neptune, grant us what we most desire,

4

Safe berth in friendly port, so thine Empire
May thereupon be known in countless regions
And soon be visited by all the nations.

MARC
LESCARBOT

F. R. SCOTT

FOLK SONGS

These *chansons*, all brought from France in the seventeenth century, may now be regarded as an integral part of the early culture of French Canada.

The Miracle of the New-Born Babe

There are three mowers in the field;
Three maidens there the hay-fork wield.

Oh, I'm young and hear the wild melody,
I am young and free.

Three maidens wield the hay-fork there,
And one a little child did bear.

Oh, I'm young, etc.

And one did bear a little child,
And wrapped it in a kerchief white.

In a white kerchief it was sewn
And then into the river thrown.

5

When it was flung into the deep,
The little one began to weep.

Weeping still the infant cried,
'My mother, now a sin you hide.

You hide a sin, my mother dear.'
'My little child, how did you hear?

Who made you speak so wonder-wise?'
'Three angels out of Paradise,

Three angels who in Heaven pray,
One was white and one was grey.

One was grey and one was white,
One appeared like Jesus Christ.

One like the Christ was meek and mild.'
'Come back to me, my little child!

My little child, I cannot wait.'
'Oh, mother dear, it is too late!

It is too late, my mother dear,
My little arms now disappear.

Now my little arms have dropped,
Now my little heart has stopped,

My little voice no longer cries,
For my soul is in Paradise.'

Oh, I'm young and hear the wild melody,
I am young and free.

REGINA SHOOLMAN

Isabel

Fair Isabel is walking
Along her garden wall,
Along her garden wall
    By the island shoreline,
Along her garden wall
    By the water side,
       Where the ship lies along.

She met as she was walking
With thirty sailor-men.

The youngest of the thirty
Straightway began to sing.

'That song I hear you singing,
That song I'd gladly know.'

'Come with me then on shipboard,
I'll sing to you my song.'

When she was come on shipboard,
Then she began to weep.

'What is the matter, maiden,
What is it makes you weep?'

'My golden ring I weep for,
That's lying in the sea.'

'Fair maiden, weep no longer,
I'll dive and seek your ring.'

But the first time he sought it,
He brought her nothing back.

The second time he sought it,
The ring slipped from his hand.

And the third time he sought it,
The gallant youth was drowned.
The gallant youth was drowned
    By the island shoreline,
The gallant youth was drowned
    By the water side,
      Where the ship lies along.

JAY MACPHERSON

Nanette

One evening as I walked, by moonlight clear as day,
I chanced to meet Nanette, who went to bathe that way.

I said to her, 'Nanette, don't you get drowned, take care.'
Nanette went lightly by, she never stopped to hear.

Her foot she wetted first, then heart and head sank she :
Her body came ashore beside an apple tree.

O tree, O apple tree, you are bowed down with flowers,
But any passing breeze could bring them down in showers,
And any passer-by, fair maid, can have you now.

JAY MACPHERSON

The Transformations

I love a gentle lady, this long time past.
I'll go to see her Sunday, my love tell clear,
I'll ask the hand in marriage of my lady dear.

Well, if you come on Sunday, I won't be there,
I'll be a doe a-leaping, swift as I can :
You'll get no satisfaction from me, young man.

If you're a doe a-leaping, swift as you can,
Then I'll become a hunter, a-hunting deer,
I'll hunt the pretty fallow-doe, that's you, my dear.

If you become a hunter, a-hunting deer,
I'll be a carp a-swimming, neat as I can :
You'll get no satisfaction from me, young man.

If you're a carp a-swimming, neat as you can,
Then I'll become a fisher, to draw you near :
I'll catch the tricky carpfish that is you, my dear.

If you become a fisher to draw me near,
I'll be a bedrid patient, sick as I can :
You'll get no satisfaction from me, young man.

If you're a bedrid patient, sick as you can,
Then I'll become a doctor, your couch to cheer :
I'll nurse my patient tenderly, that's you, my dear.

If you become a doctor, my couch to cheer,
I'll be a holy sister, pure as I can :
You'll get no satisfaction from me, young man.

If you're a holy sister, pure as you can,
Then I'll become a father, your sins to hear :
I'll preach to touch that pious heart of yours, my
    dear.

9

If you become a father, my sins to hear,
I'll be the sun a-shining, clear as I can :
You'll get no satisfaction from me, young man.

If you're the sun a-shining, clear as you can,
Then I'll become a soft cloud, to clasp you near :
I'll clasp the shining sun that is you, my dear.

If you become a soft cloud to clasp me near,
I'll be Saint Peter guarding the gates above :
Those gates shall only open to the ones I love.

JAY MACPHERSON

White as the Snow

The maiden lies asleep upon a bed of roses,
Whiter than is the snowflake, fair as is the day :
Three captains come a-riding, to her their court
they pay.

The youngest of the three takes her by her white
fingers :
'Mount up, mount up, my princess, upon my horse
of grey :
To Paris I will bring you, in comfort we shall stay.'

And when they were arrived, the hostess asked the
lady :
'Ah, tell me, lovely maiden, speak freely without
fear :
Is it by force or willing that you are lodging here?'

The lady made reply : 'I am an honest maiden,
And from my father's castle carried by force away :
A captain brought me hither, at your fine inn to
  stay.'

When she had said these words, the captain stood
  before her :
'Eat up, drink up, fair maiden, enjoy good appetite,
For with a gallant captain you here shall pass the
  night.'

But halfway through the meal, the lady fell a-dying:
'Let every bell ring dirges, let solemn drums be
  rolled :
My lady's dead and parted, at but fifteen years old.'

'Where shall we bury her, this innocent fair lady?
Within her father's garden, under an apple-tree.
Pray God receive this lady, in heaven's joy to be.'

But when three days were past, her father went out
  walking.
'Raise up, oh raise the coffin, father, if you love me.
Three days I've lain as dead, for to save my chastity.'

JAY MACPHERSON

The White Drake

Behind our house there is a pond,
    Go down into the shade, my love,
Where three fine ducks swim round and round.
    Go down into the shade, my love,
    Into the forest shade.

Three pretty ducks are swimming close,
Where the king's son a-hunting goes.

A-hunting came the king's own son,
Armed with his great silver gun.

With the silver gun he took his sight,
Aimed at the black and killed the white!

Aimed at the black, killed the white one!
O cruel prince, what have you done?

O wicked prince, what have you done
So to have killed my handsome one?

So my lovely drake to slay?
Under his wing he bleeds away,

He bleeds away under his wing,
Out of his eyes diamonds spring:

Out of his eyes the diamonds roll,
And out of his bill silver and gold,

Gold and silver out of his bill:
His feathers fly at the wind's will,

All his feathers fly in the wind,
Three ladies gather them up behind;

Three ladies catch them as they fall,
To make a feather-bed withal,

To make a feather-bed whereon
    Go down into the shade, my love,
The traveller can lay him down.
    Go down into the shade, my love,
    Into the forest shade.

Right You Are, My Brigadier

One Sunday morning soft and fine
Two old campaigners let their nags meander;
One was a Sergeant of the Line,
The other a Brigade Commander.
The General spoke with martial roar,
'Nice weather for this time of year!'
    And 'Right you are,' replied Pandore,
    'Right you are, my Brigadier.'

'A Guardsman's is a thankless calling,
Protecting private property,
In summer or when snows are falling,
From malice, rape, or robbery;
While the wife whom I adore
Sleeps alone and knows no cheer.'
    And 'Right you are,' replied Pandore,
    'Right you are, my Brigadier.'

'I have gathered Glory's laurel
With the rose of Venus twined—
I am Married, and a General;
Yet, by Jesus, I've a mind
To start like Jason for the golden shore
And follow my Star—away from here!'
    'Ah, right you are," replied Pandore,
    'Right you are, my Brigadier.'

'I remember the good days of my youth
And the old songs that rang
So cheerily. In that time, forsooth,
I had a doting mistress, full of tang . . .
But, ah! the heart—I know not wherefore—
Loves to change its bill of fare.'
    And 'Right you are,' replied Pandore,
    'Right you are, my Brigadier.'

Now Phoebus neared his journey's end;
Our heroes' shadows fell behind :
Yet still the Sergeant did attend,
And still the General spoke his mind.
'Observe,' he said, 'how more and more
Yon orb ensanguines all the sphere.'
    And 'Right you are,' replied Pandore,
    'Right you are, my Brigadier.'

They rode in silence for a while :
You only heard the measured tread
Of muffled hoof beats, mile on mile—
But when Aurora, rosy red,
Unbarred her Eastern door,
The faint refrain still charmed the ear,
    As 'Right you are,' replied Pandore,
    'Right you are, my Brigadier.'

A. J. M. SMITH

14

The Battle of Seven Oaks

The famous 'troubadour of the North-West' and
voice of the Métis nation published nothing during
his lifetime; his songs, all occasional and generally
composed on the spot and to his own tunes, were
sung throughout the North-West long before being
written down. 'The Battle of Seven Oaks' celebrates
the victory on 19 June 1816 at 'Frog Plain' (*La
Grenouillère*, later the settlement of Kildonan and
now forming part of Winnipeg's Main Street) of
the Métis, or 'Bois-Brûlés', under Cuthbert Grant
over a party of the Hudson's Bay Company's new
settlers led by Governor Semple. Falcon himself
was present at the 'battle'.

Would you like to hear me sing
Of a true and recent thing?
It was June nineteen, the band of Bois-Brûlés
     Arrived that day,
     Oh the brave warriors they!

We took three foreigners prisoners when
We came to the place called Frog, Frog Plain.
They were men who'd come from Orkney,
     Who'd come, you see,
     To rob our country.

Well we were just about to unhorse
When we heard two of us give, give voice.
Two of our men cried, 'Hey! Look back, look
     back!
     The Anglo-Sack
     Coming for to attack.'

15

Right away smartly we veered about
Galloping at them with a shout!
You know we did trap all, all those Grenadiers!
    They could not move
    Those horseless cavaliers.

Now we like honourable men did act,
Sent an ambassador—yes, in fact!
'Monsieur Governor! Would you like to stay?
    A moment spare—
    There's something we'd like to say.'

Governor, Governor, full of ire.
'Soldiers!' he cries, 'Fire! Fire!'
So they fire the first and their muskets roar!
    They almost kill
    Our ambassador!

Governor thought himself a king.
He wished an iron rod to swing.
Like a lofty lord he tries to act.
    Bad luck, old chap!
    A bit too hard you whacked!

When we went galloping, galloping by
Governor thought that he would try
For to chase and frighten us Bois-Brûlés.
    Catastrophe!
    Dead on the ground he lay.

Dead on the ground lots of grenadiers too.
Plenty of grenadiers, a whole slew.
We've almost stamped out his whole army.
    Of so many
    Five or four left there be.

PIERRE
FALCON

You should have seen those Englishmen—
Bois-Brûlés chasing them, chasing them.
From bluff to bluff they stumbled that day
    While the Bois-Brûlés
    Shouted 'Hurray!'

PIERRE
FALCON

Tell, oh tell me who made up this song?
Why it's our own poet, Pierre Falcon.
Yes, it was written this song of praise
    For the victory
    We won this day.
Yes, it was written, this song of praise—
    Come sing the glory
    Of the Bois-Brûlés.

JAMES REANEY

From *The Old Canadian Soldier*

This poem was composed on the occasion of the
arrival at Quebec of the French corvette *Capri-
cieuse*, sent in 1855 by Napoleon III to establish
commercial relations between France and Canada.
The original of the Old Soldier was a certain M.
Evanturel, a veteran of Napoleon's peninsular cam-
paigns, captured by the English in Spain and by
them sent to Demerara and at last to Quebec, where
he died in 1852, three years earlier.

'As a poor soldier in my youthful prime
Long time I fought for you, O men of France;
I come now in my melancholy age
Here to await your conquering warriors.
Ah, how much longer must I wait for you
And take my walk upon this rampart's height?
When shall I see the dawn of that great day?
—Tell me, my son, are they not yet in sight?

'Who shall restore to us that glorious age
Which with Montcalm and all our victories rang,
Reviving in a young America
The deeds of old which our forefathers sang?
Those simple countrymen who left their farms
To come and strike and die in manly fight,
Who will repeat their doughty feats of arms?
—Tell me, my son, are they not yet in sight?

'Ah, could Napoleon, surfeited with glory,
Could *he* forget our miseries and our prayers?
He whose renown, that sun of victory,
Rises in radiance on the universe

And pours in torrents on the farthest climes—
Should we alone be bated of that light?
O heaven, what do I hear? The cannon's roar?
—Tell me, my son, are they not yet in sight?

'What! 'Tis the English banner, do you say,
Which, carried by yon vessel, comes again?
That banner I myself, one far-off day,
At Carillon did tear to rags! Alas,
Why did I not then, in the heat of war,
Rather go down into a glorious night
Than see it wave above our city walls?
—Tell me, my son, are they not yet in sight?

'The lilied flag, the glory of our fathers,
Since reddened by the life-blood of my King,
Carries no longer to the farthest shore
Alike the terror and the rule of France.
Th' invincible power of the tricolor
Unto new combats will *thy* soul incite,
For it is still the battle-flag of France.
—Tell me, my son, are they not yet in sight?

'I, an old man whose strength is almost spent,
Still dreaming of the happy days of old,
I still must celebrate, even as I die,
The blessed hope which animates my voice.
Oh, shall my sightless eyes see in the clouds
The proud flag at their masthead fluttering here?
Yes, for that vision God will give me sight!
— Tell me, my son, do they not yet appear?'

            But, one storm-beaten day
Upon these ramparts he was seen no more.
Death had, alas, struck down that hoary head
Which had so many times braved shot and shell.
But dying, as he held his weeping child

Close to his breast, he spoke again his prayer :
'Thine eyes shall see the dawn of that great day :
They will return—and I shall not be there!'

Even as thou said'st, old man! France has
   returned.
Upon our ramparts' height, see, in the clouds,
Her noble oriflamme in splendour float!
This glorious day when France's sons, our brothers,
Have come to greet us from our fatherland,
Is made our best-belovéd, happiest day.

And see! upon our walls that wavering form,
Feverish and shaken by the gusty wind—
The old Canadian at his post again!
The artillery of France has roused this ghost
Who rushes forth from out his dark abode
To hail the flag he waited for so long.

The ancient soldier thinks—pathetic dream!—
That France, so long abandoning our shores,
This day sends back her conquering warriors,
And is once more the sovereign of our stream :
His dusty corpse is quivering with joy,
And raises to the sky its grateful arms.

And all the old Canadians reaped in war
Rise also from their funeral couch, to view
The dear fruition of their brightest dream;
And that same night, from either bank was heard,
Mixed with the soft sound of the passing wave,
A long-drawn jubilation from the grave.

The Dead

OCTAVE
CRÉMAZIE

O dead, you sleep alone within your tombs,
Bearing no more the load of miseries
    Of the world wherein we live;
For you the heavens hold neither star nor storm,
The spring no perfumes and the sky no clouds,
    The sun no rays.

Inert and cold within the silent grave,
You do not ask if the echoes of the world
    Are grave or gay;
You hear no more the vain discourse of men
Which wastes our hearts and makes us what we are,
    Evil and wretched things.

The winds of suffering, the breath of envy,
No longer come to parch, as when you lived,
    The marrow of your bones;
For you have found in a cemetery's arms
All that our whole existence seeks in vain,
    You have found repose.

While we go on, full of the gloomy thoughts
Which keep our souls in daylong servitude,
    Alone and silently
You hear the song of sanctuary voices
Sent from above and passing o'er the earth
    To re-ascend the sky.

You demand nothing from the passing crowd
That gives not to the tombs which it forgets
    Even a tear, a sigh;
You demand nothing from the breeze which throws
Its scented breath over the silent grave,
    Nothing but memory.

All the fine pleasures which the soul can taste
Are nothing to you beside one faithful thought—
    That alms sent from the heart,
That charity which warms your frigid dust
And wafts your name, so kept in trust by prayer,
    To the Almighty's throne.

Alas, this memory friendship keeps alive
Dies in the heart before the body doffs
    Its mourning black,
And our forgetfulness before your tombs
Weighs on your fleshless bones more heavily
    Than the coffin's lid!

Our selfish hearts, given up to present things,
See in you but the pages of a book
    We have already read;
For in our joy and sorrow, we love only
Those who can serve our hatred and our pride :
    The dead serve us no more.

To our ambitions and our futile joys,
O dusty bodies, you can nothing bring!
    We put you out of mind.
To us, what does the world of suffering mean
Which groans beyond this vast and dreary wall
    That death has reared?

The Discovery of the Mississippi

I

The mighty river slept in the savannahs;
In the dim distance passed the caravan
Of the wild herds of elk and buffalo.
Clothed in the radiance of the morning sun,
The wilderness its virgin splendour spread
     Far as the endless skies.

June glittered! O'er the waters and the grass,
O'er the high places and the secret depths,
Fertile Summer intoned her savage love;
From North to South, from sunset's place to dawn's,
All the immense expanse seemed still to hold
     Grandeur of primal days.

Mysterious workings! Rocks with hairless brows,
Pampas and bayous, woods and caverns wild,
All seemed to quiver under a passionate breath;
A stirring in this sad wilderness was felt,
As on the day when hymns of the new-born world
     Throbbed in unending space.

The Nameless, throned in primal might, was there :
Splendid, and freaked with shadow and with light,
Like a huge reptile torpid in the sun,
Old Meschacébé, still untouched by man,
Dispread his shining rings, from bank to bank,
     Down to the southern gulfs.

Like a Titan's bandolier slung on the globe,   LOUIS-I
The mighty river took his limpid way   FRÉCH
From where the Bear to where Orion shines,
Bathing both arid plains and orange groves,
And joining in one marvellous nuptial bond
    The Equator and the North.

Exulting in the freedom of his waves
And in the mysterious woods which gave him shade,
The King of Waters had not yet laid down
(Wherever he had ta'en his wandering way)
The tribute of his mighty current save
    Before the sun and God!

II

Jolliet! Jolliet! What magic must have struck
Upon thine eyes when thy historic bark
Danced on the gold waves of the unknown stream!
What lordly smile have flowered upon thy lips,
What light of triumph, in that fiery moment,
    Glowed on thy naked brow!

Ah, see him there, prophetic and erect,
His face bright with Ambition realized,
His hand outstretched towards the embrownéd west,
Claiming this vast dominion in the name
Of the living God, and of the King of France,
    And of the civilized world!

Then, rocked by the swell and cradled by his dreams,
His ear attuned to the harmonious strand,
Breathing the sharp scent of the fragrant woods,
Skimming green isles and banks of opal sand,
He followed the winding thread of the pale wave,
    The wandering current's course!

Seeing him, from a core of floating boughs
Rose, like a concert, songs and murmurings;
Flights of water-birds started from the reeds
And, pointing the way to his fragile canoe,
Fled all before him, etching slender shadows
    In the water's luminous folds;

LOUIS-H.
FRÉCHETTE

And while he drove along with full-blown sails,
It was as if the distant river-trees
In perfumed arches leaning o'er his path,
Bowed to the hero whose bold energy
Had just inscribed once more our race's name
    In the annals of the soul!

III

O mighty Meschacébé, silent pilgrim,
Many a time, by starlight, have I come
To sit beside thy sleeping banks, and there,
Alone and dreaming under the mighty elms,
Have mused upon the curious forms that rise
    In the mists of evening.

Sometimes I saw, beneath the green arcades,
The cavalcade of fierce De Soto pass,
Offering its solemn challenge to the wastes;
Or 'twas Marquette, far-wandering o'er the plains,
Burning to offer a world to his own native land
    And souls to Almighty God;

Or, in the brushwood, my deceiving eye
Imaged the sparkle of La Salle's own sword;
Or a formless group of savage warriors,
Going I know not where, sombre and tragic-eyed,
Before a humble cross—O magic power!—
    Passed, bending the knee!

And then, steeping my soul in poets' dreams,   LOUIS-H.
I caught a glimpse, too, of white silhouettes,   FRÉCHET
Sweet phantoms floating on the waves of night :
Atala, Gabriel, Chactas, Evangeline,
And the shade of René, upright on a hill,
    Weeping immortal woes.

And so I put to sleep such memories . . .
But, amid those bright gleams of poesy,
The one that oftenest came to charm my eye
Was he who passed in a far-off gleam of glory,
That hardy pioneer whom our young history
    Denominates with pride.

IV

Jolliet! Jolliet! Two centuries of conquest,
Two matchless centuries have now gone by
Since the exalted hour when thy strong hand
Inscribed in one stroke on the mappemonde
These regions vast, this huge and fertile zone,
    This future granary of mankind!

Two centuries have passed since thy great spirit
Showed us the highway to the blessed land
Which God created with such lavishness :
May it still keep, in the foldings of its gown,
For the outcasts of all nations of the earth
    Both bread and liberty!

Two centuries gone! The virgin solitude
Is now no more! The rising tide of progress
Drowns the last signs of an extinguished past.
The city rises where the desert slept;
And the shackled river curves his mighty shoulder
    Beneath granitic spans!

No more the boundless forests : steam is there! LOUIS-H.
The sun of modern times shines everywhere; FRÉCHETTE
The child of nature has been evangelized;
The peasant's ploughshare cultivates the plain
And the gold surplus of his teeming harvest
    Feeds the effete Old World!

V

From the purest sacrifice, the marvellous seed!
Who of us could have dreamed this mighty work,
O Jolliet, and you ingenuous apostles,
God's valiant soldiers without pride or fear,
Who bore the flaming torch of holy truth
    To latitudes unknown?

O humble instruments of Heaven's will,
You were the guide-posts that make easier
The rugged paths humanity must tread . . .
Glory unto you all! Leaping the gulfs of Time,
Your names, ringed by exalted aureoles,
    Shall win immortal fame!

And thou, o'erflowing country of these heroes,
Dear Canada, thou whom I idolize,
I see the share which Heaven has granted thee
In the fulfilment of these mighty works :
O fated land, I view the future and I trust
    In thy new destiny!

January

LOUIS-H.
FRÉCHET

The storm has ceased. The keen and limpid air
Has spread a silver carpet on the stream
Where, on intrepid leg, the skater glides
With shimmering flame upon his iron shoe.

Far from her warm boudoir, a lady braves
Beneath her bearskin robes the biting air;
With a sound of golden bells her rapid sleigh
Flashes like lightning past our dazzled eyes.

And later, through the nights' ideal cold
While thousands of auroras in the sky
Flutter their plumage like fantastic birds,

In ambered salons—deity's new shrines—
T'orchestral strains, 'neath sparkling chandeliers,
The gay quadrille unreels its sinuous web!

LOUIS
RIEL
(1844–1885)

From *A Sir John A. MacDonald*

Sir John A. MácDonald doth govern proudly
The provinces from which his power flows;
While his bad faith perpetuates my woes—
And all his countrymen applaud him loudly.

Despite the peace he owes me, and despite
His pledge to honour in the deed and fact

What was our Pact[1]
And is my right,
For seven years now Sir John has warred with me.
A faithless man's a vulgar man, be he
Either a wise man or a witling born :
And so I hold him up to scorn.

He meant to cast into obscure disgrace
The Bishop of Saint Boniface;[2]
Then finding his mistake, he made a show of
candour
And sought to save his face
Before His Grace
By bidding this good Pontiff Alexander
Appease the Métis and their proper wrath,
And to be sure to let them understand
They'd followed the right path
In taking up their own defence,
Since the vile Schultzes[3] and
MacDougalls[4]
Had all received a rightful reprimand
For causing us, with their damned drums and
bugles,
Such dire alarms
When they took arms
Against us, *sans* authority
Of Her Most Gracious Majesty.

---

[1] The amnesty promised in 1869 to all Métis involved in the Red River insurrection.

[2] Msgr Alexandre Taché, Riel's early patron.

[3] Dr John (later Sir John) Schultz, a leading figure in the 'Canadian' party in Manitoba, and Riel's arch-enemy.

[4] Hon. William McDougall, Minister of Public Works in Macdonald's first cabinet. Appointed Lieutenant-Governor of Rupert's Land in 1869, he was ignominiously turned back at the border by an armed band of Métis.

He played the Bishop false, and then belied LOUIS
Him with fair words and with such *politesse* RIEL
    As cloaked his wickedness,
And pleased his party and his gang beside.

Despite his plots in their deceitful dress,
Despite his pride in his own cleverness,
He'll answer one day to a wrathful God
For all the injustice he hath sown abroad.
He's a fine speaker is the Parliamentary chief,
And sits among the great ones of the land;
But once Sir John's become so many grains of sand,
    God will arraign him at His Judgement Seat,
        Where he must stand.

    In eighteen hundred and seventy-three,
        With poor Lépine [5] in gaol
And Manitoba in her agony,
And I a hunted man with all men on my trail,
    Sir John offered me thirty-five thousand
        dollars [6]
    If for three years I would desert my nation
        In all her dolours,
    And leave my friend Lépine in tribulation,
        With bleeding feet and hands
        Captíved in iron bands! [7]

     *   *   *   *

---

[5] Ambrose Lépine, Riel's lieutenant throughout the insurrection of 1869-70, and president of the court martial which imposed the death sentence on Thomas Scott.

[6] This has never been confirmed.

[7] Lépine was arrested in 1873 on a charge of murder.

How happy was I one fine day to view LOUIS
Sir John laid low, with all his wretched RIEL
crew![8]

But still his projects were much narrower in scope
Than those of Edward Blake[9] and of
MacKenzie.[10]
When Blake closed off the future—and our
hope—
'Twas then, in a fine frenzy,
That he announced the Price of Blood,[11]
And, bidding justice cease,
Destroyed an innocent people's livelihood
By thus condemning, in its leaders, the Métis.

Almighty God! Protect Thy poor Métis
Almost abolished by the English race . . .

And as for you, Sir John,
I do not wish your death should be
Too full of suffering, of course;
But what I'd like to see
Is that you should feel some remorse,
Because, you Vampire, you have eaten me.

*   *   *   *

Canadians! The English whom you trust
Are neither generous nor just,
But quite the opposite.
Open your eyes, and be convinced of it!

---

[8] Macdonald's government was defeated in 1873.
[9] Liberal premier of Ontario in 1871.
[10] Alexander Mackenzie, who headed a Liberal
government in 1873.
[11] Blake's government offered $5000 for the apprehen-
sion of Riel and Lépine as the murderers of Scott.

Carthage ne'er boasted of her Punic faith,
Because her sons had still some self-respect.
But see the modern Englishman, erect
            In all his shameless brag
Of British justice and the British flag!
            Too well we see in all his actions
            How he aspires, if none gainsaith,
By every means to make us Anglo-Saxons.

But Lower Canada was never born to perish.
    Her bishops are all ready, I believe,
            To endure the loss of all they cherish,
            If need be, rather than to leave
            You, John, to do just as you please
    Whene'er you mean to make them hold their
        peace.

And the good God has given *me* strength and
    heart,
And I'll not die without declaring war,
            The war of sense and art
            And of the rights of man
            Against all that you are.
My strength is in my gift for suffering;
I am the man to leap into the ring,
            And give all that he can
            And more than John Bull reckons:
He has gored me all too often with his horn;
I'll beat him yet; and I shall have for seconds
Princess Louise and the Marquess of Lorne.

                *   *   *   *

            I laugh at those who place
            Vile flattery above
            The sacred love
A man feels for his native land and race;
And at Lord Dufferin I can laugh indeed,

That still-born child launched from old Erin's
    womb,
              Who did not come
Into the world headfirst, but by his bum.[12]

He and his wife have now re-crossed the ocean.
We saw them leave with no profound emotion . . .

           They've had illustrious successors
Sprung from the marquisate and royal line.
A poor and almost peasant stock is mine,
          But through it I pretend
        Unto the principality
Of moral principles, and will defend
          The Good against all bad oppressors;
             And this is why
I hate a policy that's based on Vice,
          And its employ
        Even in a Viceroy.

The unjust man lives peacefully in his house of
    clay;
    But its foundation will collapse one day.
Be sure that Washington is closer, in our view,
Than London, and your neighbours worthier far
    than you!

    If God saw fit to cut us off from France
    In spite of all the bonds of our affection,
    Remember also that the power she can
        advance
    May in a twinkling break old Albion's
        sceptre.
          Take care:
    I, I am watching you.   Beware!

---

[12] This reference is obscure.

Your whole empire, and all those who have LOUIS
    kept her   RIEL
Glorious, fall apart.   Too long and much too
    often
She's thrown false dice upon her mouldy
    coffin.

And all too long the children of New France
        Have borne the English yoke;
        And will not miss the chance
Of crushing a decrepit race, and so revoke
The rule of those who, in a pride not to be borne,
        Have governed them with such inveterate scorn!

THE *TERROIR*

The three following poems are sufficient to show the complexion of the 'poetry of the land', so famous in its own day and now so properly forgotten.

.LIAM

PMAN

-1917

The Ploughman

Behind two oxen or plodding Percherons
The man walks bent in the lonely field; his hand
Is riveted to the handle of the plough.
He is opening up the belly of the land.

Sunlight floods the base of the green hill;
The darling soil receives his fixéd stare :
Drunk with the heavy scent the fallow breathes,
He lines his furrows with deliberate care.

And, musing, sometimes he will sketch a smile.
His ear already seems to hear suspire
A sea of gold under a sun of fire;

He sees the harvest in his barn bestowed;
He dreams that an angel counts his steps the
    while,
And knows the ploughman shares the work of
    God.

The Haunted House

It heaves its gable under the grizzled moss,
And the great dormer, edged with wooden lace,
Is a kind of frame for the shattered window
    whence
I used to watch the splendid evenings pass.

Crying in the wind, the door has fallen open.
Caught in the trap of memory, I see
A faint light flickering from the blackened
    chimney
On icy ceilings and an empty hall.

On the sloping roof there is a shadow, leaning
In the window-frame . . . . The unseen evenings
    die;
The soul of a house so often cloaked in mourning,
Wrapped in its sadness, gazes at the sky.

Midday in the Fields

Noon. From the steeple of the parish church has
  pealed
The Angelus. The reapers drive the team
Under the birch-trees bordering the green field,
And fall to sharpening their scythes whose edges
  gleam
Under the day's hot kiss. Where the hay is piled
In stacks, the mother (modestly withdrawn)
Offers a milk-swollen breast to her newborn child,
And smiles—while under the Heaven's wide pro-
  found
Whose sleepy peace only the bells break in upon,
Her man has crossed himself, without a sound.

JOSEPH·ARTHUR
LAPOINTE

1878–1930

The Poor

They make no protest, these poor beaten curs.
We say : Poverty is virtue's best manure.
And they believe us, being simple and good.

They take the vilest burdens and the heaviest
loads.
We say : Work's the perpetual privilege of the
poor.
And they believe us, being simple and good.

They are hungry and cold; their hearts are stifled.
We say : Blessed are the poor in spirit.
And they believe us, being simple and good.

At last one evening, they see the portals of the
tomb.
We say : With what dignity the poor know how
to die!
And they believe us, being simple and good.

A. J. M. SMITH

Impressions of Snow and Frost

I

The trees are like white statues growing
Out of white sidewalks and by white rooftops
    swirled
With a foam of heavenly whiteness : Look, it is
    snowing!
Snowing as if the clouds had broken against the
    wind and curled
Backward and were all falling in thousands of
    snowflakes and all going
To cover the black earth of this old and sinful
    world.
The fields, where the snow has all day long been
    falling,
Look from here like a lake of curdled milk; a trine
Of silvery bells on the roads where the snow is
    balling
Tinkles an instant in the wind's cold whine;
And the little children are calling out gaily,
    calling
For joy of the sky's white powder upon this land
    of mine.

II

A snowflake melts in a tear upon my window.
I close my book in the middle of a page
To watch the snow out of the white sky falling,
And follow its slow and spiralling pilgrimage.
It is soft and alive, fantastical and doting,
Gliding and floating, eddying and flying,
Now gay, now grave, like a poet versifying
Who follows the wild vagaries of his whim,
As either a little listless wind comes blowing
Or a new breath all of a sudden keeps it going!
Yet all this ends, for the snowflake and for him,
In a long fit of weeping and in water flowing . . .

III

Today, my window is nothing but white leaves
Frozen in blanchéd tremors on the glass,
Frost-flowers, fruits of rime and silver sheaves;
Trees made of silver-gilt, entwined together,
Seem to be waiting for a wind to pass,
Quiet and soft and white. Calm little frame!
Where in the drowned repose of sleeping water
This garden lies insensible as in death,
Your scene will melt in the warmth of the first
    flame
Like the pure dreams our youthful spirit lost,
And all the hopes and illusions mourned below
    our breath:
On the heart's window, fragile flowers of frost . . .

ALBERT
LOZEAU

In these long winter evenings when the eyes,
Wearied of books, fix on the window-pane
Where the frost draws, with slow mysterious pen,
Under the influence of the raging wind,
In gardens and woods forever white and calm
The marvellous flower and the fantastic palm—
These evenings, in his solitary room,
Comparing the darkness lurking in his mind
With the white splendour of the things of night,
The poet, isolated from mankind,
Thinks of the grand peace of December's tombs,
And of their ermine shrouds, so noiselessly
Heaped up and shining under the moonlit sky.

ÉMILE
NELLIGAN

1879–1941

The Ship of Gold

There was a gallant vessel wrought of gold,
Whose tops'ls raked the skies in seas unknown;
Carved on the prow a naked Venus shone,
With wind-tossed locks, in the immoderate Sun.

But ah! one night she struck the famous reef
In treacherous Ocean where the Siren sings.
Ghastly, a slanting hulk, she twists and swings
Down the profound Abyss, her changeless
    shroud.

She was a golden ship whose glassy hull
Betrayed the treasure-trove for which the three
Foul Captains, *Hate, Disgust,* and *Frenzy* strove.

What rests at last after the hasty plunge?
What of my heart's lost fate, poor derelict?
—Foundered, alas! in the black gulf of Dream!

A. J. M. SMITH

Autumn Evenings

ÉMILE
NELLIGAN

See here the tulip, and see there the roses,
Where in the park Love sports beneath the trees,
Sing in the long rose-red, unruffled eves
Under the bronze and marble's massive poses.

Gaily at night have sung the flower-beds
On which the slanting moonbeams pirouette,
And gusts of wind blow heavy, desolate,
Troubling the white dream of the lonely birds.

See here the tulip, and see there the roses
And lilies dusk-empurpled, crystalline,
Gleam sadly in the sun that now declines;
And now the pain of things and creatures closes.

My shattered love is bruised and raw; but see,
The quivering nerves grow still, the hurt reposes.
And the lily now, the tulip and the roses
Watch my soul bathe in memories, and weep.

P. F. WIDDOWS

By the Fireside

ÉMILE
NELLIGAN

In the old winters when we still were small,
In dresses, boisterous, pink, with chubby looks,
Our big and long-since vanished picture-books
Showed us the world; we seemed to own it all.

In groups around the fire at evening,
Picture by picture, ah! how happily
We turned the pages, starry-eyed to see
Squadrons of fine dragoons go galloping!

I once was happy, one of these; but now,
Feet on the fender, with dull, listless brow,
I with my always bitter heart descry

Flame-fashioned pictures where my youth goes by,
And, like a passing soldier, rides abroad
On life's black field, gripping a bloody sword.

P. F. WIDDOWS

The Muses' Cradle

From childhood's cradle I have shaped this other,
Where sleeps my Muse while birdsong trills above
    her,
My white-robed Muse, my one and only dear!

Those golden kisses at day's kindly close ...
But hush! already at our door I hear
The harridan Distress creak her black shoes.

P. F. WIDDOWS

Evening Bells

Some evenings I roamed the moors, beyond the bounds
Of my home village, lost in the great rosy hills'
Calm pride, and down the wind the Angels shook the
    bells
Of churches in long waves of melancholy sound.

And in a shepherd-poet's dreamy, romantic mood
In the perfume of roses I used to breathe their prayer,
While in the dying gold my flocks of mania
Aimlessly wandered through forests of sandalwood.

Thus in this life where I follow my lonely path
I have kept in my mind a corner of old earth,
That evening countryside whose glow I see again;

While you, my heart, within your private reach of
    moor,
Recall the long-ago angelus, voiceless, faint:
That winging of bronze birds flown from the chapel
    towers.

P. F. WIDDOWS

Castles in Spain

ÉMILE
NELLIG

Fierce in my pride, for bravery renowned,
In dreams I march like a conquistador,
Flying my conquering labarum before,
To storm the gold and bronze-embattled towns.

Like a royal bird, a vulture, eagle, condor,
I soar in dreams to the gods' territory
And scorch beneath the sun my two-winged glory,
Seeking the Treasure of the skies for plunder.

I am no hospodar, no great bird of prey,
Hard put to it in my warring heart to stay
The vicious Angels raging to destroy;

And my high dreams like waxen candles melt
Before this hundred-walled eternal Troy,
Love's city impregnable, by Virgins held.

P. F. WIDDOWS

The Idiot Girl

The bells of Holy Week, she tried
To find them all along the roads;
On the sharp stones her poor feet bled
As on her evening quests she roamed,
  Ah! fol derol day,
On the cruel stones her poor feet bled;
'Try in your pockets,' people cried.

'No, no, nearer the skies of Rome :
I want to find the bells, the bells,
        I want to find the bells,
And I will hold them in my hands' :
Ah! fol derol lol derol day.

ÉMILE
NELLIGAN

Then she would go among the shaws,
Alone she went at evening.
She dreamed of the cathedral towers
And of the bells that in them ring;
        Ah! fol derol day,
She dreamed of the cathedral towers,
Then suddenly, confused and hoarse
Her voice far off came clamouring :
'I want to find the bells, the bells,
        I want to find the bells,
And I will hold them in my hands' :
Ah! fol derol lol derol day.

By winding byways one sad dawn
They found her : in a ditch she lay.
On that night when the bells return
The idiot girl had passed away;
        Ah! fol derol day,
On that night when the bells return
Her golden dream came true, as on
And on the brazen clangour came :
An angel put the bells, the bells,
        On high put all the bells
Put all of them between her hands :
Ah! fol derol lol derol day.

P. F. WIDDOWS

The Parrot

ÉMILE
NELLIG.

In her last days the poor Negress
Had kept, through old age and distress,
This bird with its gay jauntiness.

They lived down on a hideous back
Street in a rickety old shack,
Together, out beyond the tracks.

On her black shoulder it would shrill
Away in its old fair-time style
Of the great days remembered still.

The old dame trembled at the words,
Thinking that through the pretty bird
It was her lover's soul she heard.

He was a poet, with a veiled
Ironic wit, and had beguiled
Africa's over-credulous child :

Into her parrot's soul, when dead,
He would be safely spirited
And lodge there secretly, he said.

And so the old bald-headed thing
In the last light of evening
Would start her wild-eyed questioning.

The bird laughed, screeching all the time,
From morn till eve, all the long time,
'Ha! Ha! Gula, those loves of mine!'

She died of it, in a hoarse scream,
Thinking that underneath the stream
Of the glib, mindless chatterer's theme

48

The dead man used this mocking art
To taunt the love of her old heart :
She died of it, the bitter hurt.

ÉMILE
NELLIGAN

The bird wept at her funeral,
Then built itself a ramshackle
Stone nest within a ruined wall,

And became haunted, seemingly;
For when night sang her melody
Illumined by the spangled sky

One would have said, seeing its distress,
The spirit of the poor Negress
Wept in the bird, all tenderness.

P. F. WIDDOWS

Roundel to my Pipe

Feet on the fender by firelight,
With glass in hand, good pipe, content,
Let's keep our friendly precedent
And dream alone, this winter night.

Since heaven has grown so virulent,
(As though my troubles were too slight!)
Feet on the fender by firelight,
With glass in hand, let's dream, content.

49

Soon death, by my presentiment,   ÉMILE
Will drag me from this hellish site   NELLIGA
To good old Lucifer's; all right!
We'll smoke in that establishment,

Feet on the fender, by firelight.

P. F. WIDDOWS

The Poet's Wine

Green gaiety, everything blended in a quick
Burst. O beautiful May evening, bird-choirs bringing
Their modulations to my wide window, singing
As my relinquished heart-hopes sing, changing music.

O beautiful May evening, joyful May evening!
A far-off organ chants its melancholy chant,
And the twilight rays, like purple rapiers, slant
Into the day's heart, perfumed in its dying.

How gay I am, how gay! Into the singing glass
With the wine! Keep pouring, never stop pouring!
Let me forget that the days are triste and boring,
The crowd contemptible and the world an ass.

Gay, I am gay! Exalted in wine and art! . . .
How I dream of the lofty rhymes I shall make,
Rhymes trembling with the sighs of funeral music,
Winds of autumn passing through the haze, distant,
   apart.

Kingship of the bitter laughter, and the rage ÉMILE
NELLIGAN
Of knowing that one is a poet, pierced by scorn;
Of being a heart and not understood, forlorn
To all but the moon's night and thunder's equipage.

Ladies, I drink to you, smilers along the way
Where the Ideal beckons me to her pink embraces,
And to you, gentlemen, with your sombre faces,
You who disdain my hand, I drink especially.

When the blue pricks out its coming splendour of
    stars
And as it were a hymn praises the golden spring,
What tears have I to shed over the day's dying?
I, on a dark path, in the dark of my young years?

Gay, I am gay! Inexpressible May evening!
Ridiculously gay, can it be that I've—
Not drunk either—that I'm happy to be alive?
Has it at last been healed, my old wound of loving?

The bells cease, and the evening scents follow
    after
As the breeze takes them, and the wine rustles and
    throbs.
I am more than gay, hear my resonant laughter!
So gay, so gay, I am breaking into sobs.

GEORGE JOHNSTON

Old Fantasist

At her window among her potted plants, from cold
and bluster sheltered, she pulls her Japanese
shawl around her, Miss Adèle, and reads one of these
Dumas novels, as she did as a twenty-year-old.

And all her boudoir is a distraction of bizarre
odds and ends, cloister of ancientnesses, herself
the type of her own cult, encrusted, like her shelf-
borne vases, onyx, portraits, books from everywhere.

On the random cushions a scar-faced Persian tom
purrs his contented thunder while his fading dame
coaxes her sad heart among the ochreing pages

unaware, in the pangs of her closeted sweet
dream, of a passing mocking face, an outrageous
organ-grinder's face, magnificent, out in the the street.

GEORGE JOHNSTON

Before Two Portraits of my Mother

ÉMILE
NELLIGAN

I love the beautiful young girl of this
portrait, my mother, painted years ago
when her forehead was white, and there was no
shadow in the dazzling Venetian glass

of her gaze.   But this other likeness shows
the deep trenches across her forehead's white
marble.   The rose poem of her youth that
her marriage sang is far behind.   Here is

my sadness : I compare these portraits, one
of a joy-radiant brow, the other care-
heavy : sunrise—and the thick coming on

of night.   And yet how strange my ways seem,
for when I look at these faded lips my heart
smiles, but at the smiling girl my tears start.

GEORGE JOHNSTON

RENÉ
CHOPIN
1885–1953

Grotesque

See, 'tis Pierrot, affecting still
    The domino, the wry grimace,
The lantern jaw whose painted mouth
    Incarnadines a powdered face.

Shivering beneath her balcony,
    Lost in a dream of Columbine
(Who has refused him) he ignores
    The snow descending, floury-fine.

A grinning clown lashed by the wind,
    With fingers pinched and blue he goes
To wipe a tear away—then rubs
    The end of his frostbitten nose.

Polar Landscapes

The arctic heaven stars its crackling dome.
The frosted night-wind's gusty exhalation
Touches each constellation
And sets its light asparkle: the Swan, the Goat,
    the Ram.

A gauzy veil across that glass-clear sky,
One distant scarf of mist floats and is gone;
The silvered crystal moon
Plunges beneath the sea her doused enormous eye.

Strange architecture, whose familiar look　　　RENÉ
Of drift and ice-block soaring stage on stage,　　CHOPIN
Sketched on a printed page,
Stared from the safe pulp of some picture-book,

Appears enormous now : minster or hall,
The cave-worn polar pack! as we have seen
Thrown on a shadowy screen
The high faint image of a castellated wall.

Its vast façade holds on the seaward side
A portal, broadly stepped with ledge on ledge
Carved by the water's edge,
Untrodden reef emerging resplendent from the tide.

Colossal courses form that toppling height
Beyond whose pillared azure cloister blaze
Deep halls and passageways,
Where countless lustres hang their blue crystalline light,

Jewels and pins, whose metals never fade,
False stones amassed in treasuries unexplored
Among whose glittering hoard
Long since by Undine hands the Thule cup was laid.

　　　　*　　　*　　　*　　　*

In that far region of the polar stars
Rears the cold hell of tall convulsive capes;
And I see the twilight shapes
Of fleets that sailed the world in immemorial years,

Sheer cliffs stumbling over a stagnant sea,
Lakes spreading from a silver cataract;
Rough dolmens table-capped,
Vast cromlech-scattered plains, menhirs and tumuli.

White sacrificial bears with foaming mouth   RENÉ
Shall yawn with lust and tedium to behold   CHOPIN
The sun at midnight, gold
Among the promontories of the distant south.

*   *   *   *

The proud Explorers, captives of the floe,
Exiled forever in their icy tomb,
Had dreamed of deathless fame.
The Pole, a sphinx, still waits inviolate in the snow.

On a snowy isle, hope gone, provisions gone,
Owning defeat, they cut their names at last
In murderous conquest;
Disconsolate, resigned, they died as night came on.

Aurora's rich magnetic folds descend
On Chaos' awful pit; their bright fringe streams,
Shot with prismatic gleams,
And sumptuously beguiles the heroes' tragic end.

Their fires went out, their blood ran slow and cold.
And did their pale dreams show them there, remote
Beyond the bergs that float
On hushed seas, village steeples where their knell was tolle

Or, hell-borne harvest of a useless yearning,
The sun-drenched vine against the ancestral wall?
Or summer's miracle,
The fruitful field? the ash, the grates of home burning?

FRANCIS SPARSHOTT

Propitiation

The season of clean cold dissolves. In a flurry of wings
Its startled swans are gone from my empty shores.
My heart gives way, the dyke is down,
Its rivers spread to the sea.

In my soul the spring sap rises, blends with my tears
Its hidden water, love's exciting drink
Of dreams and torment spills in my cup
A bliss too deep to be borne.

White dove, snow-dove, clean winged, lest I should die
Of this thirst that parches me, thirst for the love of spring,
I will hold you in reverent hands, with trembling grasp

Twist that weak neck. Poor Iphigeneia
Whose wintry flesh, whose maculate quill
Must stain this altar where I appease my gods.

FRANCIS SPARSHOTT

Perdrix

Thy sylvan gods, O partridge, are not fled :
Where humid mint refreshes and delights
Still their bold shouts and sudden headlong flights
Startle the groves fouled by the huntsman's tread.

Nymphs, goatish Satyrs, Centaurs limbed like
   roots
—Whether on Othrys or Laurentian hills—
Still haunt thy woods, and the flute's liquid trills
Measure the tread of the intruder's boots.

But when the dusk's translucencies withdraw,
On grotto, copse, and fount a hush descends—
Syrinx is silent . . . Arethusa sleeps. . . .

And thou, dun Sorceress with three-pronged claw,
Art once again, in thy palace of gold leaves,
The amber Dryad the cleft cedar keeps.

A. J. M. SMITH

PAUL
MORIN

The Peacock Royal

Some ancient gardener with an Eastern soul
Gave the proud sonorous name of Peacock Royal
To the odorous pink, whose every heavy petal
Is iridescent velvet, flame and metal.

I know the ardent purple heliotrope
Whose fiery perfume makes the senses reel
From Asia's warm seraglios to the gardens of
    Europe,
Know Persian jasmine, roses of Mosul,

The marigolds Orcavelle wore on her brow
The night she died of hearing a nightingale,
The scarlet aloes on the caravel
Pizarro bore towards the Spanish sky,

Green tiger-lilies growing in Samarkand,
Russet chrysanthemums, sunflowers on fire,
Hyacinths that star the blonde meadows of
    Holland,
Tulips of jasper and blue hortensias,

But I like best the sparkling in the shade
Of the cup transparent, of frailest crystal made,
Where blooms, voluptuous, violent and dark,
On its enamelled stem, the Peacock Royal.

Music of Names

PAUL
MORIN

TO RENÉ CHOPIN

You, René, and you, Paul Fort, who sang Racine
And the glorious name of La Ferté-Milon,
Let an old bard (whose memory still is green)
Add to your marble rhymes a quarry-stone.

You'll say, 'Only another stale pastiche
From our splendiferosententious Fraud . . .'
Fie! In this land where all the world plays false
I'd only publish a few truths abroad;

For, though of lively apprehension yet,
I like no longer (list, O Mantuan swan)
The astounding names of Ancienne-Lorette,
Gaduamgoshout and Ashuapmouchouan.

The Bulls (Saskatchewan?) sets my teeth on edge:
Farewell Lacolle and Hull and Chaudière-Station!
I'll drown me in the waters of Bourboule
(If I should not die first at Castor-Junction).

Never does one French name affront my ear,
Evoke my laughter or my nerves attack:
Even the most cacophonous are dear—
Castelnaudary, Izernore, Segonzac!

For, from the rudest sounds, this blessed tongue
Knew how to weave—even in the far-off day
Of Carcassonne!—the curious changes rung
In Romorantin and Locmariaquer.

O syllables, 'tis not your noble style
Nor place in history (Paris, it is not quite
You, nor Vendôme, Èpernon or Versailles)
Which cause my hand to tremble as I write . . .

No, it's the frail, the fairy vocable,   PAUL
MORIN
The elegance sharp and limpid whence arose
The word made magic, pure, ineffable,
Smelling of poppy and the briar-rose.

Oh, I would give Venice and Ispahan
For Brive-la-Gaillarde, their murmurous flow
For the azure of the oriole-note within
Maintes-la-Jolie and Azay-le-Rideau.

Islam, my former love (pink minarets!)
I put below Ailly-le-Haut-Clocher,
Or the velvet wasps of Fontenay-aux-Roses,
Or Alise-Sainte-Reine where the peachtree blows,

Yet of those liquid sorceries still would choose
The place where Dammarie-emmy-ses-lys,
In a clear rush of suave arpeggios,
Divides her perfume with Les Andelys.

Synderesis

PAUL
MORIN

A friend writes : 'Cease to rebel.
We're old, and all the books are read.
The women titter when we touch their hands,
and those whom memory recalls, in the gardens—
    well,
today they are either old or dead.
Think, is it not time to break the lease
of that cracked-enamel palace which is yours,
and where your bitterness has gone to earth
like some secluded Turk,
painted, obese,
who quietly tests the sharpness of his dirk
ere selling to the Jews his moulting peacocks, rings
    and ewers?

'Adipose Brummell, settle down,
and, if you can,
bend over without having to cough,
change the wing on your heel for a slipper.
Deaf, limping, colicky, myopic as you are,
your Pegasus has bartered sky for drinking-trough,
and at this stage (remember *Mérope*)
la vie est un opprobre et la mort un devoir.'

Not so.

My body is lusty and my very own :
my heart leaps up—a daily miracle—
when the dawn walks in shoes of mother-o'-pearl;
I can still weep, listening to Mozart,
and the spring of Bellerie
has never dried for me
whenever I open my Ronsard;
my eyes

still dazzle at a flight of doves,
at a pure brow, at fiery Erigo
in the constellated skies.

PAUL
MORIN

I am not he of whom you speak.

And yet—
if he were right?
Perhaps, upon the whole,
I am only a dodderer hiding his white poll
under the golden wig of a sick Petronius?
heroic tumults crowd my balding skull,
but the lyre I played on in my twentieth year
(silver and ivory then)
proffers my nerveless key
only three namby-pamby strings.

Gnôthi seauton
(the words wrought on
Delphi's temple-front):
thou'rt fat as a pig; cease then to play the elf,
do not insist on gathering roses:
it leads to arteriosclerosis;
and if thou'rt wise enough to save thyself
a heart attack,
thy dreams in moth-balls pack.

I greatly fear, thou venerable tramp,
'tis time thou shouldst discreetly put a damp-
er upon thy frolic fires.
Exchange thy walking-stick for a decent shopping-basket,
thy opera-hat (by Lock) for a notarial bowler
(pardon me, René, and my dear Rosaire!),
the plastron for the dressing-gown besides,
and patent-leather pumps for slippers with clastic
    sides . . .

From foaming rapids lecherous,   PAUL
rainbow-hued, but treacherous,   MORIN
do thou emerge
towards the safe, the sensible river-verge
where saunter carelessly
the owner of the grocery-store
and eke thy janitor;
cease to officiate at the pagan altar,
and beneath thy roof
hide thee and slumber
like the complacent, placid cucumber.
All thy little household gods shall greet thee there,
thy rosary, pipe, and candy-pink pyjamas,
thy Saint-Simon and thy poor Anna
(*je viens, portant sur moi la fraîche odeur de l'ombre . . .*)
the sympathetic partnership that's made
by the double Haig-&-Haig and the fizzing soda-
    water,
sleepbringers with an over-obliging vertigo,
and thy bed
(Woe to the solitary dead!)
groaning, elastic,
the witness of thy windbroken Swedish gymnastic
so often,
and which looks so remarkably
like a coffin.

The Philanthropists

It's one of the sports of millionaires
And swell fun for the well-heeled guys
T'think up new ways of fixin' affairs
So's to steal all the limelight money buys.

They'll give handouts to hospitals anyday,
Welfare Societies and homes for the sick . . .
But it's all clipped off of our pay
At fleecing us they're too damn quick.

Newspapers build 'em up as philanthropists;
They're the big shots! They're sitting pretty!
But not a red cent really comes from their fists,
'Cause we're the poor dopes that sweeten their kitty.

Others who open nurseries and put statues up
Give Stations of the Cross and bells for churches
For their needy parents haven't a loaf or a cup,
Yet they're treated by all as though they were saints
    on perches.

And some who're nothing but pious deceivers
Screw their workers till they're ready to drop,
And then to attract all the true believers
Get a fat priest to come and bless their shop.

All the time he was preachin' around
Our Lord used to say : 'Don't profess
So's to have all your good deeds crowned;
What your right hand's doin' your left shouldn't
    guess.'

There's a helluva big change since th'Apostle's days;
Now they give with the right hand while the other
Keeps diggin' into our pockets in a hundred ways;
And this is how man now 'comforts' his brother.

F. R. SCOTT

GUSTAVE
LAMARCHE

b. 1895

Renunciation

And now let me move into my dark absence
distant from you as fish
drifting through unseen caves
or shy flamingo in the river reeds.
I would be to your groping hands
as a Prince in exile, a name
spreading in silence over a waste of seas.

G. V. DOWNES

ANTOINE
SAVARD

b. 1896

Saints of the Land

Saints of the rapids, floods and boiling torrents,
Saints of the tumpline, packsack and portage,
You holy martyrs of the paddle and oar,
Saints of the sunless icy dawn,
Fighters of storms, O white and holy snowshoers,
Blessed route-marchers on insatiate roads,
Saints of the snowstorm and the freezing wind
And all the brotherhood of dolour and death
And all the fellowship of cross and comfort,
O all ye nameless saints of man's communion,
Dead, so our race should give this land to God—
See! here in the forest are the treetrunks felled,
And here the clearing's happy, glowing coals,
And the first making of the land.
Lo, the first oxen ploughing the first meadow!
Lo, the blue underside of virgin loam,
The sowing planned, the harvest sure to come,
The pale and vaporous burgeoning of the grass;
And see the child asleep among the stalks
While the mother goes a-binding other sheaves;
And here, by axe and cutting adze well hewn,
The house arises from the timber's heart,
The house whose corners are so well dovetailed,
So joined they seem like fingers clasped in prayer;
And see, in the fields, the lofty Sheepfold raised,
The serene fold of the good, the perfect Shepherd,
The pastoral house whereto his sheep repair
When the bell sounds upon the steeple's neck.
So now, you saints whose holy relics lie
Within our altar-stones, come now ye Saints

Of all the brotherhood of dolour and death
And all the fellowship of cross and comfort,
O all ye nameless saints of man's communion,
Dead, so our race should give this land to God,
Come to this place, as it was so appointed,
Come to the field of your labours and your
    harvest-home.

FÉLIX-A]
SAVARD

ALAIN
GRANDBOIS

b. 1900

Heart

coloured signals flare
from prows of islands I hear
your hands, young lovers,
stirring from fire's centre
iron core of earth,
o innocence of flesh, May snows
melting in the long tides of the world
Suddenly among the myriad lights
I see huge waves, destruction
surging, unpredictable ground
roads swept, wrecked,
lowering red skies and already
the rough gold beast, waves whipping his feet,
flashes down shadowy curves
of golden dunes

crazy shipwreck
green gold miraculous blue
swamping the heart

G. V. DOWNES

68

The Ambiguous Dawn

ALAIN
GRANDBOIS

The slowly ebbing night
drains light from stars,
restores clear shape
to shoreline, meadows, lakes and wooded hills;
it is the end for sleepwalkers
staggering round roofs of invisible skyscrapers.

The end comes too
for poets and for the dying,
last lines, last rites, last agonies
of good and evil men
fade with the coming dawn
the shivering dance of the sun.

Dawn's paths are difficult;
exacting man
caught at the anxious crossroads
of the night
winds ropes of terror round
his own emerging throat,
seeking and shunning light.

G. V. DOWNES

Is it already the hour . . .   ALAIN
                                                                  GRANDBO

Is it already the hour
My tender fear
Is it the hour   the hour
Of tomorrow

Earth and sea
Glide into time
The rods of the sky
Roll gently
Bathed in oblivion

Where is that brow's whiteness
Where, the lost house
Where, on a soil
Not stealing away
Are the footsteps of today

The conspiracy of morning
Weaves in the silence
The endless journeying

Undefinable fingers
O vertical breath
O hollow of space

But where is the hour   my tender fear
Where, your soft snow
Fresh sister, compeer

The tunes of childhood
—Have they ever ceased
On the other side of the world
Out there, where your shadow hides its head

PETER MILLER

With your dress ...

ALAIN
GRANDBOIS

With your dress like a white wing on the rocks
With drops in the crease of your hand like an open
   wound
You laughing so freely head thrown back like a
   solitary child

With your feet passive and nude on the rough
   regime of rock
Your arms which stripe you with their nonchalant
   lights
Your faultless knee like the island of my childhood

With your youthful breasts erect in the verve of a
   voiceless song
The curves of your body plunging to the delicate sign
And this purest thing which your blood withholds
   for future nights

O my lover a dream already lost
O my lover already spoken for by death
O my lover a mortal moment of the eternal river

At least let me close my eyes
At least let me press the palms of my hands on my
   eyelids
Blind me from this at least

Spare me from seeing under the pall of shadows
The massive doors of forgetfulness
Slowly open and revolve

ELDON GRIER

Cries

ALAIN
GRANDE

All at once I saw these continents overthrown
The thousand trumpets of the ruined gods
The collapse of the walls of the cities
The horror of purple sombre smoke
I saw men frightful ghosts
And their gestures of the drowning
Covered the implacable wastes
Like the clasped hands of women
Like the great unpardonable transgressions
Salt iron and flame
Under a hellish sky ringed with steel
From the depths of volcanic craters
Spat the scarlet anguishes
Spat the long-departed days
Despair leaped into our hearts
The gleaming beaches of smooth gold the inexpres-
    sible blue
Of the seas and at the very end of time
The planets motionless   O rigid   fixed forever
The long silence of death

And I saw you each and all of you
In the little flower-decked cemeteries
At the elbows of the parish churches
Under the gentle swell of badly tended mounds
All of you   you and you and you
All of those I'd loved
With a violent and voiceless passion
I hurled my cries into the deep night
Ah they speak of hope but where can it be found
They say that we are denying God
When God is all we are seeking
Him only Him alone

Then in an avalanche of emerald ice
The caravans of the poles
Poured their frosty chaos
In the laps of the beautiful Americas
While we on that very day
With eyes tight-closed
—O lowly dream of gentleness of bondage—
We were seeking the pinewood undergrowth
To sing the joy of our flesh
O God in the treetop's swaying hands
How we have sought for Thee
At the hour of rest our bodies closed
Before desire came like a humming bee

Then the towering tropic palms
Sweeping away treacherous malarias
Bowed their unconquered heads
There was a wine-coloured boat
With a small white sail
And all the seas belonged to us
With their monstrous turtles
And the Roman lampreys
And the Labrador whales
And the islands looming out of coral
Like a photographer's proof
And those ice-sheathed rocks
At the tip of Tierra del Fuego
And all the splendid stretches of the sea
And the breathing of its waves
Sea   O Sea   O Beauty elect
What victories for our defeats

And the woods dense as the earth below
Where we walked together spreading out our arms
 Smothered us with their secret
Strayed memories and childhood lost
That morning sun as tender as a moon

ALAIN
GRANDBOIS

Ah in those legendary days ALAIN
GRANDB
Deep with the presence of the grass
Amidst the bars of our prison
She wept but with tragic reserve
And I declared a silent war

We were crushed beneath our giant ancestral trees
There were the solemn moments
When we were upheld by the darkness
When we were murdered on our knees
And our suffering fell short
Of entreaties fed with involuntary tears
And the shadows veiled our faces
Our naked feet bled on the edge of the rock
And daybreak laid its trap for us
Under the arches of the lofty cedars

The straining forests swallowed our sky
On the walls of trees like blazing cuts
The gentle streaks of freshwater springs
Stately labyrinths of octaves resting their brows
Mosses and stalactites formed from petrified waters
Bloody carnage of the grief to come
We were humble not speaking of poetry
We were bathed in poetry and did not know it

Our savage bodies fused in extravagant shame
Beating against each other
Like an assassination
When the frenzy of joy arrived
We were struck with wonder under the sun
Our sleep transformed us
Into corpses stiff and dry
In winding-sheets of a too-immaculate white
Ah springtime winds ah perfumes' delights
Open windows at the crux of city streets
You crave to see a single leaf

A bird the blue reflection of a lake
Ringed with spruce-trees and lungs free at last

ALAIN
GRANDBOIS

We took each other's hand
We went forward into life
With our forty years upon us
Each of us
Widowed twice or more
By as many mortal wounds
We had survived by a miracle
The demons of destruction

ELDON GRIER

Held and Secured

Held and secured and sentenced by the sea
I float in the trough of the long swell
The pillars of the sky weigh on my shoulders
My eyes are closed against the blue archangel
The weight of the depths is shuddering beneath
  me
I am alone and naked
I am alone and salt
I float adrift on the sea
Hearing the sunken gods' gigantic breathing
Listening to the final silence
From beyond dead horizons

The Fire's Share

ALAIN
GRANDI

Here the long swells of the sea
Here the heavens pitted with fires
Here the heart and the blood
Here tenderness and anguish
And I in my human nakedness
With my heart which beats like a harried beast
Hunted too long

The stars and their doings escaped me
No wizard I like the shepherds of Provence
I travelled I haunted the shadowy corridors
Of the pitiless cities of granite
I who was born for the tree and the mould
For the piercing odours of dawn
And to rest beneath towering lakeside grass
And to mark with passion
The final flutterings of my heart

Ah how long since grass and star
And the ivory flank of that blessed girl
Quartered me like a criminal
The choice was never mine
The days the nights slid over my body
Like the tepid tears of abandoned brides
I would dream of vertiginous towers
Of abysmal depths which struck
To the purple forge
At the core of the earth
I dreamed of vanished loves
Of arms that were white as the lightning
Of soft and sensual pleasure
Of the terrible escape
Beautiful red-mouthed girls
The eternal truths
Music   the twilight

All that seduces all that drowns ALAIN
The reach of space and the straining hopes GRANDBOIS
Hands shackled and ankles bound

Spirits dancing in the glade
Ah that night of cries and violins
When sin no longer existed
Desire was dead
And my youth
And my murdered cities
Florence with the periwinkle eyes
Shanghai and its hellish bordellos
Peking my passion
Quebec where I loved
Montreal where I suffered
My fabulous cities destroyed
And the speck of my native village
Far from the vital stream

It is useless to utter cries
Which will never reach the woman who deceived
     you
Every smile is alike
The Christ smile the Judas smile
And he who has never betrayed betrays his birth

The sea laps all my horizon
The sea which is infinite

ELDON GRIER

Close the cabinet of charms
Such games of mine are in the past
My hands no longer free
No longer drive towards the heart
The world I dreamed of creating
Possessed a light of its own
But now by this inordinate sun
My eyes have been blinded
I and my universe will perish together
I'll bury myself in the deepest caves
Night will claim me with its tragic snares
I will be out of reach of that other voice
I will bear with the deafness of metal
All will be frozen
Even my doubt

I know that time is past
Already the hillside swallows the day
Already my ghost is hailing itself
Ah those golden evenings   as I bend over the sweet-
     ness of lilacs I see them still
Still see the enchanting sails of darkness pitted with
     stars
Still see those riverbanks of an inviolate shore
I've loved too much the straight and unrepentant
     stare of love
I've over-adorned my women with matchless haloes
Tended my magic gardens like a fanatic

Once on the white of the house
Three immaculate cypresses
I saw them and am silent
My anguish extreme

But all this is past   ALAIN
GRANDBOIS
Let's close the cabinet of poisons
Blow out those lamps which burn in the void like
    dead fairies
Nothing will stir the shadows again
Night will no longer trail its morning of bells
Guiltless hands no longer be raised at the threshold
    of my house

But you   you whom I always saw walking the sea
    with your hairdress of brilliants
How straight you looked your pale face raised
You would walk encircled by the horizon
You would walk and slowly broach the barrier of
    the waves
Hands before you doves of the ark
You who were bringing us face to face with the
    archangel
You who were pure and sad and beautiful
You who smiled like a cripple

And the prophets would lay their gravid silence on
    the fluting of water
And there would be nothing but the great fraternal
    calm of seven seas
Like a mortal tomb

ELDON GRIER

The Butchering

Sensing above him a different moment come,
Snout up, snubbed like a Picard clog,
With convulsive leap from under, the Yorkshire hog
In panic scrambles the enclosure's straw and scum.

On his hide the tightening cable fire scrawls.
Tickled, he grunts and sneezes from the chaff.
The ears like cooking ladles slope above
The bistre eyes where realization sprawls.

Into the dazzling sun of morning dragged,
He understands as the knife-edge reaches doubt
That under him the ground deprives his feet; he
    staggers

Then gets up; the raucous call, as he dies,
So to the country pours such sadness out
A dog's howls join the uncommitted cries.

RALPH GUSTAFSON

Appeal to Remembrance

Close your fingers sleepless on your breast.
Your eyes. So may your body counterfeit
The dead, their future claim and their regret.
The air O barely let your breath attest!

Your strength was vain. Your loveliness is waste.
For others' grinding is the golden wheat.
Enfold your fingers. Close your eyes. Your sweetness
Clay and salty wet rehearse. Graced

With the empty stars, the arching night accept.
Be death. Those vast avowals nothing kept
For all your stock of valiance, passion, pride.

Only within your heart's own final truth,
Burn on the altars of the gods of youth
The immortal witness of the dreams you hide.

RALPH GUSTAFSON

Stoning Land

ALFRED
DES ROC

Against the livid light of early dawn
Darkened by scouring mist and coming rain,
The winter woods of rusted firs retain
The broken brown of fields they edge upon.

Worse for the breakfast left, the men have gone
In the damp that clothes the air, thinking to gain
Something of profit out of the large disdain,
The gift of wheat-fields filled with stone.

Dug out of the furrows, onto the flat dray
Dragged by steady Percherons, they pile
The stones and go on, gripped in their backs, clay

On their feet. Sometimes, dropping his mudded
    freight,
One of them, like a spring burst from its mortise,
    his whole
Muscled torso arches back from the weight.

RALPH GUSTAFSON

I Am the Dwindled Son

ALFRED
DESROCHERS

I am the dwindled son of a race of supermen,
The violent, strong, adventurous; from this strain
I take the northland homesickness which comes
With the grey days that autumn brings again.

All the fierce past of those *coureurs de bois*—
Hunters and trappers, raftsmen, lumberjacks,
Merchant-adventurers, labourers on hire—
Bids me to seek the North for half the year.

And I dream of going there as my fathers did :
I hear within me great white spaces crying
In the wastes they roamed, haloed by hurricanes;
And, as they did, I hate a master's chains.

When the tempest of disasters beat upon them,
They cursed the valley and they cursed the plain;
They cursed the wolves which robbed them of their wool :
Their maledictions dulled their pain.

But when the memory of a distant wife
Brusquely dispelled the scenes that faced these men,
They brushed their eyelids with the back of their sleeve
And their mouths chanted *A la claire fontaine.*

So well repeated to the echoing forests
This simple lay (where the wood-warbler tunes
On the highest branches his own plaintive song),
It mingles with my own most secret thoughts :

If I bend my back beneath invisible burdens
In the hubbub of bitter leavetakings,
And if, when thwarted or constrained, I feel
That urge to strike which clenched their massive fists;

If from these men, who never knew despair ALFRED
And died even while they dreamed of conquering DES ROC
   nature,
I take this sickly instinct for adventure
Beneath whose spell I sometimes fall, at night—

In this degenerate age of ours, I am like
The beech whose living sap was never drawn,
And I am leafed around by dead desires,
Dreaming of going forth as my fathers did.

But the faint words emitted by my voice
Remain : a rosebush, branches and a spring,
An oak, a warbler in a sheen of leaves;
And, as it did in my forefather's day,
In the mouth of him who was *coureur de bois*,

My joy or sorrow sings the landscape still.

Psalm

Thou has set me down, Jehovah, by the pleasant waters,
In the orchard of love, amid the fairest fruits;
Far from the frost, the blight and the wild thorn,
Thy holy word puts forth its tender shoots.
Behold me, apart, one of Thy wise virgins.

O brothers, tremble with joy to bid me welcome!
God made the blossoms burst out of the seed;
He alone heals us under the rippling steel :
He picks the kernel from the worthless husk,
And the heart quivers in its nakedness.

I had laid me down beside the Adversary,
In a cradle of flowers and of idle dreams;
With another yoke already on my neck,
I was bearing a false elixir to my lips.
And Thy regard plumbed all my infamy.

Yet who can number the ways of happiness?
For laughter and joy have passed by like a dream.
I lost my betrothed, and the children of his love;
My glories burst the bubble of their falsehood,
And all my highest hopes fell back in tears.

But all the loneliness where our sorrows feed,
And all our sobbing, swelling out of silence—
Oh, probing them, dost Thou our pilgrim father
Open the secret of our malady,
Delivering happiness from the breast of pain.

For the lying mouth, it must be stopped. The smile   SIMONE
May be the fruitage of delectable death   ROUTIER
And the least dreaded of the baits of the world :
Its charm erodes, sift in an hour-glass.
I desire, for Thee, a profile carved from eternity.

How long wilt Thou withhold Thy countenance from me,
Jehovah, my Bridegroom and my only stay ?
Look upon me, tell me what I should do.
See, am I not delivered to Thy mercy ?
What have I done, that Thou shouldst so forget me ?

Gone all astray, Thy people have been corrupted :
Of pleasant cities battlefields are made;
For Thy days of forgiveness, Lord, are past :
Bodies are heaped together in seething layers,
Where the living quiver, at times, among the dead !

Who then, O Lord, shall dwell within Thy tabernacle ?
Who but she whom Thy Son, near to her dwelling,
Made trophy of, and all her company,
Forging for her, through Thee, a soul of worship
Whose perfume pours upon the blossoming nights ?

My bliss resides no longer save in Thee,
O Divine Crucified, and only in Thy bosom.
Thou hast bent me at last unto Thy holy will.
Henceforth I'll be Thy prey and Thy delight,
And beneath Thine eyes drink myrrh from Thy chalice.

Thou visit'st me by night to search my heart,
And when my soul stifles to find itself alone,
I hear Thee draw near to me quietly,
And Thou reviv'st each of Thy mysteries for me,
Telling me like the Rosary in my fingers.

My heart, between my hands, melts like a candle   SIMONE
In Thy embracements, Eucharistic God;   ROUTIER
I hear, lapped in Thy everlasting peace,
Utterance of the word and the immortal Host
Sings a hymn of surrender in my mouth.

The Lord is my Shepherd. Which of His lost sheep,
Freed of the thorns, finding her home again,
Had ever a greener pasture, a warmer fleece?
My Shepherd bears in His hand the crook of love;
I graze upon His heart the livelong day.

Behold the flock of all those who have sought Him!
And I too flourish among this bléssed troop,
Your Prodigal Daughter and the Child of Truth,
Prostrate and happy, and before your face
Thankful at last, O Divine Crucified.

Abandon youth and all its blind revolt,
Tumult of blood and pride of spirit;
I was only a cry, tremulous and naive,
I waved in the wind, like a banner, brazen words:
Forgive this yielding to illusive things.

O Lord, how pleasant is Thy dwelling place!
The tree with all its greenery hides the sky.
Here Thou are quite denuded of all foliage.
Christ was stripped unto the last attrition:
Oh, let us break the bars of our straitened nature.

Tell me, indeed, of what should I go in fear?
Of men, of eyes, of books, of earthly praise,
Of women, money, evil, ugliness?
Lord, none of these. Thou knowest well that nothing
Can change me now. My traffic is all with Thee.

For me, Thou has turned all mourning into sounds of joy . .
From the steeple bursts of jubilation were ringing,
The church had opened up its nuptial nave
When the call passed from carillon to knell,
And Thou didst take me, a bride, into Thy arms.

In the depth of my anguish, He spoke His tenderness.
I the rebellious, lost, bereft of belief and choice,
I heard Him murmur, 'See, there is the Cross :
Wouldst not die there, to be reborn, with Me?'
And this 'with Me' redeemed me from despair.

ROBERT
CHOQUETTE

b. 1905

Prologue from *Suite Marine*

Iseult, behold the sea!

Look, from this rocky height
This coign where none but the gull dares come and cling,
This roof of winds where the wind is waltzing with the sands
Look down, Iseult, on the vast, imperishable sea,
On the sea whose breadth of utterance is like God's.

From this steep height carved out in the blue sky,   ROBERT
CHOQUETTE
Hail to the male and female element of things,
The water of five oceans, the primordial milk!
Source of all life, O Sea, and puissant cordial,
Body of fecund Night where the primal seeds
Evolved in fear their colours and their forms;
Perverse abyss where the animal is a flower,
Where the breathing plant ingurgitates the beast,
And death and love and love and death, conjoined,
Change places in one vast, eternal feast,
All hail! To the east, south, north, the births of yesterday
Give place to all that wishes to be born,
To the blind instincts hungering to know
The delight of having eyes. Glory to the sea,
Which under the soft, blue-giving lustre of this sky
Insatiably in turn creates and kills
To feed this hunger with the jaws of iron!
Glory to the sea and glory to life, and praise
To the life inexorable where the forms shift
To awaken life herself to her finest flights—
She who engenders youth out of dead things,
She who fashions hope even out of rags,
So that the dark, devouring gangs which stain
The sea with blood are turned to quickening tombs
And the very victim is reborn in joy!

But behold, in the Sea, the symbol of the heart,
Its pulse of frenzy, its pulse of tenderness :
A dizzy maelstrom over which wheels the choir
—Like screaming seagulls made hoarse even to madness—
Of the wild desires which nothing can assuage.

See, the heart's image, altering, always new,
Dial of light and dark whose outlines waver
In fleecy mists of the dream! Depths of the Sea,
Night of the Heart, which a greater dark beyond
Prolongs forever : O twin depths in torment,

God surely formed you with a single gesture—
You, shadowy holds of the monster-haunted sea,
And you, Heart where the lust for murder and incest lurks,
Yet whence arise voices of such a purity
That blasphemy expires before their utterance;
Sea, creatress of gems of such a splendour
The dreams of jewellers fade before your beauty.

And in the heart, too, brim and withdraw
Alternately, and like the moving tides,
Uncertainty and hope, and love and hatred;
And in the heart, too, ships are fitted out,
And in the heart's night foundered hulls
Slowly decay around their buried secrecies.
O Sea, where roars the hideous tidal wave,
And yet wherein such tenderness can live;
O thou the harmonious, thou the sorceress
Pre-eminent, siren that soothes and terrifies
At once, all hail! Ennobled by thy voice
And by its multiple, rolling, roaring echo,
O Sea, two lovers shall from this day forth
Offer their youth to the old words of love,
And these words shall, imposing on two hearts
The universal rhythm, re-create the world!
Welcome us, Circe : our love is newly born!
Our first kiss has the very taste of salt!
Before thy countenance we have come to know,
In the exaltation of two hearts attuned,
Felicity which makes us like the gods.

Iseult, behold the Sea! deep as your dreams :
But close at our feet, the roadstead and its birds,
Its men, its quays, its houses on the shore,
And the little boats which look from here like cradles;
And it is all crackling with sparks of joy,
The beach, the nets, the roofs, the fishing-boats,

And so many on the tide, so bright, so white,   ROBERT
So sprightly, gulls upon gulls, it seems as if   CHOQUETTE
The sea, the sea itself were beating its wings!
Iseult we will go down to this narrow village,
This harbour where sou'westered fishermen
Steep in blue light their doors' chiaroscuro;
And will not go till the season of dead leaves,
And this means never, since time is now no more.

Dear village lulled by tidal ebbs and flows,
Dear unknown village whose least winding path
Lies open to our gaze in the young morning light,
Hail! pretty village to which we are going down
To trim lightheartedly the bark of fate.

The Grotto of Neptune

The threshold is blue-green like a moon-tinted night.
Let us go in. Here is the watery resting-place,
The grotto with its laminated walls, where light
And sinuous Neptune glides, hiding his wealth from sight.
This is dream-coloured land, where the horizon's trace
Withdraws into the depths, rendering the soul strange.
Into this magic palace where the sea-weeds range
Above our heads, and bristling sea-urchins repose,
Come, follow me. Here let us sit together, close.
How many secrets, treasures and what wondrous shocks!
These four carved walls, like friezes hewn from rocks,
Blossom and bud and grow like richly-painted bowers
So that the eye can scarce distinguish beasts from flowers.

REGINA SHOOLMAN

Awakening

ROBERT
CHOQUE

Dawn in bright gules and dusk with azure shield
Struggle behind the hills in combat fierce.
Now the young sun throws down his pointed spears,
And with flanks crimson from the bloody field
Rises victorious and encased in light.
All wakes; all laughs; all waxes clear and bright.
The air is soft, sweeter than honeycomb.
The branch still trembles where a bird has flown
Skyward to hover like a star. Now nature
Quickens and pours her gloss on every creature.
Such largess and such beauty! So much splendour!
Where now is sorrow in this world of wonder?

REGINA SHOOLMAN & A. M. KLEIN

Yorick

'Make haste,' he told me, 'youth comes not again.
     That greedy sleepless vulture, Time,
Hanging in space, deceives the gaze of lovers:
It is your passion and your love that fly!
Ah well, the withering and the death of things
—The flower upon its stalk, the bird that hovers
Over the roof an instant—they are everywhere:
Summer so young, so lusty and so fair,
     It seemed eternal, and is gone.
—Voluptuous bloom of Ronsard and Hélène,
Life of a little day! The kindly ground

Feeds on their bones. Ah, see you not, my friend,   ROBERT
CHOQUETTE
    How death devours you every day,
And how your heart, tied to the very sound
Of death's own rhythm, still beats towards the end?
Death strikes at all things in his daily round,
Yet you ask Echo to repeat *Again! Again!*
    Tomorrow! See, tomorrow's end:
A wooden casket for your hopes and fears,
A mouth deprived of kisses and of breath,
    Tomorrow's flesh, the food of death,
Tomorrow's eyes, with no relief in tears.'

Nocturne

Face to face, ageless and ever renewed,
The two deeps: the Sea which was once a furnace,
The Night cerulean with its infinite arches.

Here is the eternal reign of Genesis
When Jehovah, hovering above the lonely floods,
Still kept within him the fructifying Word.

One gulf of calm, the other of horror, joined
Each to each forever in one immense embrace,
Exchanging words of darkness and words of stars.

I am the eternity which always recommences,
Which never alters and alters every moment,
And without dying re-creates itself:

The Sea! I am the Night, the abyss that quivers
But remains eternal as the Theorem is,
As the circle is, immutable, unending.

My stars, borne onwards by primordial law,   ROBERT
Are so well counterpoised I give the illusion   CHOQUET
Of being motionless in time and space.

I am the Sea, the sea illimitably rich
In flowers and animals, where each takes its way
Obedient to its own dark will's impulsion.

I body forth deformity and grace alike;
Creating these flowers and animals, I essay
Images which strike God himself with wonder.

I am the Night, the crucible where dissolve
The world's colours and forms! And the world wakes
To its dream, a dream higher than joy or tears.

I sing, but the song is not for any ear,
O you my sweet carillons sounding for the eye,
Stars of crystal in the pure inaudible!

I am the Sea, I am the stupendous organ
With a thousand inexhaustible throats whence arise
Such hymns as make the nave of heaven tremble,

Eloquent of horror and fear, of ineluctable
Violence, of murder implacable and joyous
In the gulf of an insatiable greed.

I am the Night, the Night whose impearled fingers
Bring scintillating and sombre Poetry!
I am the Sea . . . So, each with the other mingling,

The abyss of stillness and the abyss of frenzy,
Utter the words of darkness and the starry words—
The gulf of the sea, the icy crucible,

And the deep of Night with all its infinite arches,
The same today as in the time of Genesis
When Jehovah moved upon the face of the waters.

Autumn Evening

My heart is racked this autumn evening :
I have no friend left, and no compass-card,
I have no sorrow left : only the wounds
And rhythms of this deconsecrated heart.

Evening is hunkered in the forest of sandalwood;
It wakes within me at this dismal hour.
Oh, evening is dreadful ! Evening, pink and brown,
Opening before me her hyena-jaws ...

The too-short night divides the too-long days;
And now is the final spasm before the truce
When the night's laughter drinks the tears of day.

My dreams are dying, replaced by reverie.
I am like a vessel drawn up on the shore,
Bound for preposterous victory over Love.

To the Land of Quebec

O my poor country
Where nothing ever changes,
Yet to change is to be alive, O my country !
And you motionless, fixed, like an eye of glass in a
    robot's head,
You the immutable, your belly crammed with
    meats
And promises.

You whom they soil, whom they smutch with
    filthy dribble.
Oh, that mucous clot on your Titan's face!
There is indeed no life left in you.
When our fathers went forth beneath the
    untouched hair of virgin forests,
Portaging their canoes, staking their scalps,
When our fathers set out to return no more,
And their widows seized the plough with both
    hands by its shafts—
When our fathers died only once
Before oblivion . . .
The great ones, the mighty ones begat no children
    in their image.
I crumble into the void. I too am the unworthy
    son of those who wrote an epic with their blood.
They could not write their names.
And we can no longer create, even with words.
To think that perhaps I have the blood of
    Frontenac in my slender veins,
And my pale forehead could be the flesh of
    Madeleine.
When a race dries up, it breeds politicians.

All this prosing bores me to death. A drink!
See, a tricoloured vision. All the heroes.
The white robe of Jeanne Mance,
The blue coats of the Monongahela,
And the purple brow of the great defeated one,
    Montcalm, with that poppy, there, on his
    breast . . .
They are all there, as in the age of legends,
The days of History.
They raise their hands : *Seek*, they say, *pick up
    the thread once more!*
And here am I dreaming of toilsome alchemies,
    of transfusions
Of ideas.

Oh to wash our thin blood in theirs,   FRANÇOIS
HERTEL
Rich red blood of the buffalo, blood of the moose,
Blood that does not run, that clots on the hands.
In my dream there's a whole tumbling river
Of this blood of a possible reincarnation.
A river of phantoms : the blood of the men of
    1660, the blood of 1760, the blood of 1837.
I drink it, drink it. Where am I? Here's to death!

There was a plain, immense and green,
Where the sun drank the roses.
And all at once there was Cape Eternity,
The unconquerable rock, inviolate, facing the
    winds,
Winds from the north, great polar birds,
Winds which d'Iberville conquered in the *Pelican;*
Sou'westers wailing like wildcats : blasts from
    Acadia
As the dusk falls on Port-Royal.
And the old **Cape** cursed them in the storm.
Suddenly the forest bristled.   The sound came
    from the West, the death rattle,
The voice of Louis Riel.
And then it was another voice, other voices, a
    thousand voices beating upon me.
All together they spoke; and the dead said to me,
'Let them spit in our faces,
Let them forget us, let them curse us,
Let them deny us, turn from us,
But let them stand fast!'
This is what my fathers said to my sons!

And the poet came down from Sinai.
He kept only the substance,
Only the congealed metal.
The times have not yet come.

Song of the Exile

FRANÇO
HERTEL

My misery is too great to be of this world,
It must lie somewhere in eternity.
My damnation is here and now, and my crime is
    to have been born,
But I do not wish to die : sometimes I like to see
    the sun glisten on the Seine.

My heart is pierced by innumerable swords.
I have lost all my blood on roads of fire,
The ice has entered me for good and all,
My hell is an icy one. I am freezing to death.
I have lost everything that can be lost in life
And await with neither eagerness nor joy
The day when I shall sink like an iron nail
Straight to the bottom of the sea, some evening,
    soundlessly.
No longer can I even formulate
My special formula for damnation on earth.
I have lost even the rhythm
With which I could pursue my terrors
In cadences.
I sing without singing, I leave all to chance.
I am through with finery and through with
    swagger.
I was almost a poet and almost a philosopher.
I suffered from too much of being almost.
I was almost a man.
I am almost a corpse.

Mine the cadaver's twitchings
And the pangs of the dust which has been
    schooled
By contact with the worms of life !
How well I love the worms of tombs,
How clean they are, and sleek and shining,

How well they do their business,   FRANÇOIS
HERTEL
While the other ones, the ones called men and
    women,
How cravenly they bite you in the heel
When they suspect you
Of caring too little for this all too formal life,
When they see at last you had a certain gift for
    the useless,
A certain love of the absolute,
A certain thirst for the infinite—
What you were hounded for, you, weak and
    small,
Who wished for greatness.
You were chilled all your life long, and sick;
And you are the nursling with no nurse's kindly
    breast,
You are the suffering child, abandoned
On the Nile of destiny.
When you thought you had to 'play the game',
Give yourself to people, believe in them, be good,
When you learned, in thirty years,
After close study, in spite of your rashes of hatred
    and your taste for contempt,
That you had learned only how to love,
Then you set yourself to this task of loving,
A little promiscuously perhaps, without
    discernment.
You loved everyone who crossed your path.
You saw this as a duty, a great task,
A kind of grandeur.
Then, you felt well : this warmed your heart.
You loved children, who becoming old men,
    denied you.
You loved men who, becoming old men, hated
    you for your miraculously prolonged youth.
You loved women who despised you because you
    treated them like queens.

You loved old men who had still time to spew you FRANÇO
    up in the death-rattle of their agony, HERTEL
Because you persisted in remaining odiously
    young.
You loved God with despair, with horror, because
    to love God is to renounce a little of oneself,
And one day you felt God withdrawing, perhaps
    never to return.
You were humble to the point of pride, in
    self-annihilation,
You were chaste, to the point of ceasing to feel
    yourself a man,
You were compassionate, to the point of taking
    the bread from your own lips to throw it to pigs.
You were just, to the point of being loyal to your
    enemies.
You were a sublime idiot.

And now one fine morning you wake up, a pig
    among the pigs,
With all those instincts you deplored in others
And thought you had suppressed in yourself,
With all those instincts shining like licked beasts,
Loosed and ravenous.
You had thought you were blessed, and you were
    only more assuredly accursed than those others.
And what you saw above all was how happy they
    all looked,
Children, men, women and old men,
All those whom you had loved,
For whom you had chopped yourself in pieces
Like a log to be burned on the hearth of all good
    works,
All those who are glad to realize that a man is only
    a man,
And that they need blush no oftener than when
    their turn comes round.

Let us totter at last, pillar,
Wall, let us collapse,
Let us cease to be a reproach to our brothers,
And to shame them by our goodness.
Let us become that unforgiven tiger,
Let us become the pitiless whip swung by an
    aimless hand
In the ways of transgression.
Crack then, whip of my vengeance,
And score me, hair-shirt of my vengeance!
This humanity cursed so many times,
Let us curse it again a little, for form's sake,
And so God may not be alone in regretting the
    birth of man!

FRANÇOIS
HERTEL

To the Holy Martyrs of Canada

O my valorous athletes
Martyrs for Christ and France,
Your sceptre dwindles into a distaff.
See what we have become,
Observe these notaries and grocers
For whom your blood was shed.
See our pitiless stupidity
And all the fine words in which we dress it up,
Look at this shameless city
No longer called Ville-Marie,
Look at those mighty spaces where you died
And whence your beautiful tongue has been
    expelled.
See how low we have fallen

Since we ceased being French to become only
    Canadian.
See me in church, me with my eyes full of
    worldly lights,
With the immense distractions which beset me
In this country where you died for love.
Listen to my foetal squeakings rising to God,
The garbage of my prayers full of dung,
Savour the irony of having gone to your death
For a lout like me.
What is most frightful
Is that I am not the filthiest
Of my country's abortions.
Why did you not keep your precious blood?
It should have flowed full-channel
Through your blue veins and upon your foreheads
Bowed before the one God.
Alas! Alas! These things had to be,
This ignominy be accomplished,
And your scalps, staked
On so many gigantic ventures,
Be torn from your skulls with a single stroke
And hung at a red warrior's hips.
It was necessary that you be flayed
Lest we should lose our faith.
But for you indeed, but for that seed of life,
But for that pool of blood which rotted
    somewhere in Ontario,
But for the supreme sacrifice made and accepted,
You would have been anglicized after your death,
But for this engorgement of swallowed affronts,
We might all have followed Cheniqui,
That tenth-rate Panurge.

For having become no more than fleeting footmarks,
For having lost the love of God,
For voting at elections,

Pardon us, on our knees, pardon, my holy martyrs,   FRANÇOIS
Pardon us for not walking better in your ways!   HERTEL
Pardon us, Lallemand, for the red-hot coals laid
    on your eyes
Which have not unseeled our own!
For the hatchets reddened at your neck,
Brébeuf, pardon!
For your fingers lopped before your head, pardon,
    O holy Jogues!
In the name of this degenerate people,
In the name of God who cannot grow old,
In the name of our mother, Madonna of Victories,
I beseech you, mighty martyrs of my country,
Do not grant me the terrible favour of dying on
    the gridiron!

Accompaniment

I walk beside a joy
Beside a joy that is not mine
A joy of mine which I cannot take

I walk beside myself in joy
I hear my footsteps in joy marching beside me
But I cannot change places on the sidewalk
I cannot put my feet in those steps and say
  Look it is I

For the moment I am content with this company
But secretly I plot an exchange
By all sorts of devices, by alchemies
By blood transfusions
Displacement of atoms
  by balancing tricks

So that one day, transposed,
I may be carried along by the dance of those steps of joy
With the noise of my footsteps dying away beside me
With the fall of my own lost step
    fading to my left
Under the feet of a stranger
  who turns down a side street.

F. R. SCOTT

Bird Cage

SAINT-DENYS-
GARNEAU

I am a bird cage
A cage of bone
With a bird

The bird in the cage of bone
Is death building his nest

When nothing is happening
One can hear him ruffle his wings

And when one has laughed a lot
If one suddenly stops
One hears him cooing
Far down
Like a small bell

It is a bird held captive
This death in my cage of bone

Would he not like to fly away
Is it you who will hold him back
Is it I
What is it

He cannot fly away
Until he has eaten all
My heart
The source of blood
With my life inside

He will have my soul in his beak.

F. R. SCOTT

Spectacle of the Dance

SAINT-D
GARNEA

My children you dance badly
One must admit it is difficult to dance here
In this lack of air
Here without any space which is the whole of the
    dance.

You do not know how to play with space
And you play in it
Without chains
You poor children who cannot play.

How can you hope to dance   I have seen the
    walls
The city cuts off your vision at the start
Cuts off at the shoulder your maimed vision
Even before one rhythmic movement
Before its outward reach and faraway resting
Its blossoming   faraway   out of the landscape
Before the flowering of your vision   the blending
    with the sky
The marriage to the sky of the vision
A meeting of infinites   a clash
Of wonders.

The dance is a second measure and a second
    departure
It takes possession of the world
After the first victory
Of the vision

Which itself leaves no mark on space
—Less even than the bird and its furrow
Than even the song and its invisible passage
An imperceptible trembling of the air—
Which is an embrace   through the immaterial

Most near to the changeless transparency
Like a reflection on water in the landscape
That one did not see fall upon the river.

For the dance is a paraphrase of the vision
The rediscovery of the road the eyes had lost in
    the search
A statelier pace slowing to recapture
From its source an enveloping enchantment.

F. R. SCOTT

The Game

Don't bother me I'm terribly busy

A child is starting to build a village
It's a city, a county
And who knows
        Soon the universe.

He's playing

These wooden blocks are houses he moves about
    and castles
This board is the sign of a sloping roof
                not at all bad to look at
It's no small thing to know the place where the
    road of cards
                will turn
This could change completely
                the course of the river

Because of the bridge which makes so beautiful a
    reflection
            on the water of the carpet
It's easy to have a tall tree
And to put a mountain underneath
            so it'll be high up

Joy of playing! Paradise of liberties!
But above all don't put your foot in the room
One never knows what might be in this corner
Or whether you are not going to crush the
    favourite
            among the invisible flowers

This is my box of toys
Full of words for weaving marvellous patterns
For uniting separating matching
Now the unfolding of the dance
And soon a clear burst of the laughter
That one thought had been lost

A gentle flip of the finger
And the star
Which hung carelessly
At the end of too flimsy a thread of light
Falls and makes rings in the water.

Of love and tenderness who would dare to doubt
But not two cents of respect for the established
    order
Or for politeness and this precious discipline
A levity and practices fit to scandalize grown-up
    people

He arranges words for you as if they were simple
    songs
And in his eyes one can read his mischievous
    pleasure

At knowing that under the words he moves
  everything about
And plays with the mountains
As if they were his very own.
He turns the room upside down and truly we've
  lost our way
As if it was fun just to fool people.

And yet in his left eye when the right is smiling
A supernatural importance is imparted to the
  leaf of a tree
As if this could be of great significance
Had as much weight in his scales
As the war of Ethiopia
In England's.

We are not book-keepers

Everyone can see a green dollar bill
But who can see through it
              except a child
Who like him can see through it with full freedom
Without being in the least hampered by it
              or its limitations
Or by its value of exactly one dollar

For he sees through this window thousands of
  marvellous toys
And has no wish to choose between these
  treasures
Nor desire nor necessity
Not he
For his eyes are wide open to take everything.

F. R. SCOTT

A Dead Man Asks for a Drink

SAINT-DE
GARNEAU

A dead man asks for a drink
The well no longer has as much water as one
    would imagine
Who will bring the answer to the dead man
The spring says my stream is not for him.

So look now all his maids are starting off
Each with a bowl for each a spring
To slake the thirst of the master
A dead man who asks for a drink.

This one collects in the depth of the nocturnal
    garden
The soft pollen which springs up from flowers
In the warmth which lingers on at the enclosure
    of night
She enlarges this flesh in front of him

But the dead man still is thirsty and asks for a
    drink

That one collects by the silver of moolit meadows
The corollas that were closed by the coolness of
    evening
She makes of them a well-rounded bouquet
A soft heaviness cool on the mouth
And hurries to offer it to the master

But the dead man is thirsty and asks for a drink

Then the third and first of the three sisters
Hurries also into the fields
While there rises in the eastern sky
The bright menace of dawn
She gathers with the net of her golden apron

The shining drops of morning dew
Fills up a cup and offers it to the master

But still he is thirsty and asks for a drink.

Then morning breaks in its glory
And spreads like a breeze the light over the valley
And the dead man ground to dust
The dead man pierced by rays like a mist
Evaporates and dies
And even the memory of him has vanished from
    the earth.

F. R. SCOTT

Weights and Measures

It's not a question of pulling things along by the
    hair
Of tying a woman by the hair to the tail of a horse
Of piling up the dead one after another
Along the sword's edge, the edge of time.

You can have fun tying knots in parallel lines
It's quite a metaphysical entertainment
Absurdity not being reduced to the nose of
    Cyrano
But looking at this with your head upside down
You catch glimmerings of other worlds
You see cracks in our world which make holes

One can get angry at seeing holes in our world   SAINT-D
One can be scandalized by a torn stocking a vest   GARNEA
            a torn glove which shows a finger
One can insist that it all be patched up

But a hole in the world itself is already something
Provided we catch our feet in it and drop
Our head in it and drop in headfirst
This lets us wander about and even return again
This allows us to measure the world on foot,
                                    foot by foot.

F. R. SCOTT

Concerning This Child

Concerning this child who didn't want to die
And of whom we have cherished at least the like-
    ness like a portrait in a picture-frame in a living-
    room
It's possible that we could be tremendously mis-
    taken on his account.
He was perhaps not made for the high priesthood
    as we believed
He was perhaps only a child like others
And high only for our lowliness
And luminous only for our great shadow without
    anything at all
(Let's bury him, with the picture-frame and all).

He has brought us here like a squirrel which loses
    us behind him in the forest
And our care and our cunning were completely
    wasted seeking obstinately in the underbrush.

Our eyes were completely unnerved seeking his
    leap in the underbrush.

Our whole soul was lost lying in ambush for his
    passing which has lost us
We thought to discover the new world in the light
    of his eyes
We believed that he was going to return us to the
    lost paradise.

But now let's bury him, at least the picture-frame
    with the likeness
And all the tentative paths we have beaten down in
    his pursuit
And all the inviting traps we have set to catch him.

JEAN BEAUPRÉ & GAEL TURNBULL

My Eyes a River

My eyes   my seeing eyes
are wide as a sunlit river
open to all reflections
astonishing
this freshness beneath the lids
and images washed this morning
to a new lightness

as waters freshen the island
and as moving ripples
flow around
the sun-dappled girl

G. V. DOWNES

The Body of This Death

SAINT-DE
GARNEAU

We had thought that suffering
Would mould our faces to the splendid hardness
 of our bones
To the clear and resolute silence of our bones
That last unconquerable castle of our being,
Would stretch clearly over our bones the skin of
 our faces
The tired and troubled flesh of our faces
Continually crumpled and convulsed
The skin which hangs in the wind the tawdry
 flag of our faces,
A feeble flag to all the winds which betray us—
That suffering would reduce it to the fixed form of
 our clear bones.

But was suffering forestalled
Could death have made a secret nest in our very
 bones
Pierced, debased our very bones
Chosen to make its home in the very pith of our
 bones
Amidst our bones?
So that after filtering through all our flesh
Through all the layers of flesh given it to feed on
After all that gnawing at the soft and sluggish
 flesh,
Suffering itself should find no substance to lay
 hold on
Nothing of substance to be firmly seized
Nothing solid to pierce with a living sting
No living silence to heat white hot
No core of silent feeling to torture without
 destroying

But only meet with a surface in decay
A porous fabric dissolving
A phantom which crumbles and leaves nothing
     but dust.

We shades of corpses as those shades are
                    realities of corpses, bones of corpses
And what pity (and what wonder) seizes us
                    sentient shades of corpses
And what kindred terror
Facing this answer given
This proffered image
Bones of corpses.

          When we are reduced to our bones
          Resting upon our bones
          in bed with our bones
          with the night before us

We shall unjoint our limbs
                    and set them in a row for listing
To see what is lacking
To find the joint that is out of joint
For it is unthinkable to sit
                    quietly accepting
                    the body of this death,

     For always standing within us
     A man not to be beaten down
     Erect within us, turning his back
                    to where our looks are turned
     Erect in his bones, eyes fixed on the void
     In a fearful dogged facing and defiance.

Have done with the hill which you shall never
     climb
And the cloak covering the silence of the bones

And the living grape of the heart at last despairing   SAINT-DE'
Wherein this cross might now be carved in grain   GARNEAU
Instead of the acid blade of scorn
In the place where the driven knife is fixed
Whose handle probes the ever-aching wound
Whenever your hand is turned towards your
      breast,
There where the cross is carved with its iron arms
Like the iron wire nailed to the tree's bark
Cutting the surface, but this is a wound
The scarring bark soon covers and enrinds
And in time the iron thread which cut the surface
Is seen embedded in the core of the trunk—
So let the cross be planted in your heart
And your head and arms and feet stretched far
      beyond
And Christ over all and our small sufferings.

Have done with the hill which lies beyond the
      horizon
Henceforward take your place at the edge of
      things
With the whole land behind your shoulders
And nothing before you but this march to make
With the pole marked out by a measurable hope
And your heart drawn by the lodestone cross of
      iron.

My heart this heavy stone within me
Heart turned to stone by this barren fixity
And backward gazing at the fires of the city
And hunger lingering in the ashes of regret
And spent regrets for all the possible lands

Gather your cloak about you hopeless pilgrim
Gather your cloak about your bones
Fold those arms unhinged by happiness relinquished

Pull the cloak of your poverty over your bones   SAINT-DENYS-
And as for the dried grape seeded in your heart   GARNEAU
Now let its skin be softened by another

Have done with the hill unthinkable in the scheme
Of an absurd land where you yourself were only
An ambush laid for the secret learned by night,
The secret of the illusion of escape from grief.

Lamps

Old
Poor lights hung
Motionless in the smoke
Like lost silences
What are you doing here, and what,
I ask, are you looking at?
Lost dead lights

Sadness   like you of the ready-made smiles
And glances over the shoulder
Like you   hanging
On the swinging breasts of the dancing-girls
Red and green and blue
As poor as you are
As old
As dead.

World Beyond Recall

SAINT-DE
GARNEAU

In my hand
The shattered end of all the roads

When did we let the moorings slip
How did we miss the roads

Insuperable space between
Bridges broken
Roads lost

On the sky's edge a hundred faces
Impossible to see
The light cut off long since—
A great knife of shadow
Cleaves the centre of my gaze

From this place set apart
Any appeal of outstretched arms
Is lost in the insuperable air

The memory we question
Has heavy curtains at its windows
Why ask it anything at all?
The shadow of the absent ones is voiceless
Is melting now into the walls
Of the empty room.

Where are the bridges the roads the doors
The words do not come
The voice fails to carry

Am I to spring out on this tenuous wire
On a wire of make-believe strung over the gulf
Perhaps to find the faces turned away
And batter myself with a heavy hollow blow
Against their absence

The bridges broken
Roads cut
The beginning of all presence
The end of the wedge of all fellowship
Lies broken in my hand.

Perpetual Beginning

A man of undetermined age
Rather young and rather old
Wearing an absent-minded look
And spectacles of clearest glass
Is sitting at the foot of a wall
At the foot of a wall facing a wall

He says I'm going to count from one to a hundred
At a hundred I'll be through
Once for good   once for all
I start in   *One, two* and so on

But at seventy-three he is not quite sure
It's like trying to count the strokes of midnight
                    and making them only eleven
It's pitch dark   how can you tell
You try to rebuild the rhythm from the intervals
But when did it begin?

And you wait for the next hour to strike

He says come on   we've got to finish
Let's start all over   once again
Once and for all
One to a hundred
One . . .

Landscape in Two Colours on a Ground of Sky

Life and death on a pair of hills
A pair of hills and four hillsides
The wildflowers on two sides
The wild shadow on two sides.

The sun upright in the south
Lays his blessing on both peaks
Spreads it over the face of the slopes
Far as the water in the valley
(Looking at all and seeing nothing)

In the valley the sky of water
In the sky of water the water-lilies,
Long stems reach into the deeps
And the sun follows them with a finger
(Follows with a finger, feeling nothing)

On the water rocked by the lilies
On the water pricked by the lilies
On the water pierced by the lilies
Held by a hundred thousand stems
Stand the feet of the pair of hills
One foot flowered with wildflowers
One foot eaten by wild shadow.

And for him who sails in the midst of all
For the fish that leaps in the midst of all
(Seeing a fly at the very most)

Down the slope toward the deeps,
Plunge the brows of the pair of hills
One brow of flowers bright in the light
Twenty years' flowers against the sky
And one brow without face or colour

Wanting either sense or sunlight
But wholly eaten by wild shadow
Wholly made of the black the empty
Gap of oblivion, circled by still sky.

Children (I)

Children
Oh the little monsters!

They clasp you round the neck
The way they climb the aspen trees
To make them bend
And pour down over them

They lay their traps
With incredible persistence

They would not leave you alone
Until you were wholly won

Now they have left you
The traitors
                have abandoned you
Laughing as they ran away.

There were some of them who stayed
When the rest went off to play
These remained demurely seated.

There were some who went as far
As the very end of the lane
Their laughter was a thing suspended

All the time they were looking back
Just to see if you were watching

A remorse and a regret

But the laughter was not lost
It has taken up its peal
Heard now running in the air
Even though they've disappeared
Where the lane runs down the hill.

My House

I want my house with open doors
An open house for all the poor.

I'll open it to all that come
As one who can himself recall
How long he suffered out of doors,
Beset by all the dead
Refused at every door
Bitten by cold, eaten by hope

By endless weariness worn out
By dogged hope made desperate

Forever seeking after grace
Forever on the trail of sin.

Et je prierai ta grâce

SAINT-DENYS-
GARNEAU

And I will entreat thee of thy grace to crucify me
And nail my feet unto thy holy mountain
So that they may not run upon forbidden roads
The roads that lead bewilderingly away
From thee
And so my arms should also be held wide open
To love by firm-fixed nails, and that my hands
My hands drunken with flesh, burning with sin,
Should be, beneath thy gaze, washed in thy light
And I will entreat thy love, a fiery chain,
To bind me fast beside thy calvary
And keep my gaze ever upon thy face
While still above thy suffering shall shine out
The resurrection and the light eternal.

**RINA
LASNIER**

b. **1915**

Jungle of Leaves

Blurred forest choked with leaves,
luxuriance throttling the tree's armature,
fleece without head or bonework, monster of hair,
skyless foliage in the branches' arms.

Each fat leaf stuck in a grease of sweat,
a viscous tangle of soft creeping things,
flesh of flesh without echo of cries or arrows;
swamp sapping the city's pedestal.

Maze of torpor with no outlet in dream,
greenish night with no plumage of stars, no
      slabbed moon's horn.

Welter of leaves that will not wipe the feet of the
      rain,
each leaf rejecting the assault of rain and wind :
each leaf should be rain-note, wind-hymn,
each tree be skeleton of the fire to come.

Ferment without fruit, breached by sickly hunger,
empty revolving sameness with no escape in
      death.

The forest should move towards the faintest
      shudder of water,
the forest should funnel itself for one outflow of
      birds,
the forest should gather around the spark's
      danger;
warm jungle wanting the amorous glory of a body
      on fire.

Scarecrow

RINA
LASNIER

Scarecrow I lean
with gaping mouth
no hunger left for seed,
rags that softly
stir in the wind.
And yet, beyond all wings,
I can deride
the mockery of crows
jeer at your careful sheaves.

This straw is not my prison.
I have escaped the field
and my harvest
comes on the wind
gently lifting
these limp tatters.

G. V. DOWNES

Suicides

They are marked by the stars, lost sailors,
each temple a blue tattoo
where the shot went home;
love's a fine anchor for some, but these
found chain's weight galling,
slipped from the silent docks, hopeless,
spat on the sea.
Lights out,
they sailed forth under the implacable stars
answering no signals but those
in the pure cruel eyes of death their only lover.

G. V. DOWNES

The Body of Christ

RINA
LASNIER

Out of his long hairs with blood and clay clotted
the unswerving purity of stars and fire

Out of his tongue with no spittle and parables
the spices, the honeys, and the balms of silence

Out of his arms stretched out like moorings
the sheltering woods that contradict the storms

Out of his side deep blue and dead
the living waters and the plasma of the seas

Out of the thrusting and gray arches of his feet
the deep veins and inflexible metal of rock

Out of his holy eyelids at last unfolded
forgiving shadows and the clear light of justice

Out of his heart stagnant on the cross
the sun's face in the face of our wickedness

Body of Christ, sleep on in your naked slumber,
we all have pillaged your crucified paradise

FRED COGSWELL

From *La Malemer*

RINA
LASNIER

I will descend to the bed of the Undersea where night lies close by night—to the crucible where the sea shapes her own affliction,

to the amnesic night of the Undersea no longer remembering the embrace of earth,

nor the embrace of Light when the waters were born into air's meandering chaos,

when God covered the firmament with his two hands—before the contradiction of the breathing upon the waters,

before that kiss laid on the sea to disjoin sea from sea—before the Word spawned fish in the womb of the shallows,

before the division of waters by the blade of light—before the contention of waters through the restraint of light.

All swallowed spittle of silence—I will taste once more the accursed waters of my birth;

faulty water of birth encircling the blood's innocence—and you hang from life like the fruit of the tree of discord;

is there a night newer than birth—is there a day older than the soul?

mysterious motherhood of the flesh—shelter open to the doors of the first cry, and death more maternal still!

Betrothed face of the open sea poised on the RINA LASNIER breath's spiral—Undersea lodged in the sea-pits of fecundity,

open sea! eye painted with the blue of legends —moire of images and burnt-out stars;

water blithe in the deadfall of the brooks— dancer in listless fountains;

plastic flesh of your dance—daring word of your dance and phoenix of your roving spirit in the green flame of the dance;

lover surrendered to the vertigo of cataracts and the slow nuptials on river-beds—faithful to the one zodiacal union as to your primal height;

circling water with no rein but the play of your circular roads—you are the spoor of our fables and the dryness of our mouth;

reversed clouds, we have seen your metamorphoses—and your sleep of crystal, o mummy couched on the poles;

ascensional water—I have heard the murmur of your falsehood redescending the narrow ear of the sea-shell;

you play at knucklebones with the shellfish— your hands play with the dead wood of corpses on all the shores of the world;

on all the tables of sand—you take the measure of your own might and of your breaking combers;

raider of the sentinel-cliffs—I have seen the feminine shouldering of your tide abrade their stony denial;

flowing fiancée of the hard and precarious winds—how will you escape the doom of your obedience?

Purified by the farthest water—how will you cleanse yourself of the saltness of the dead?

Open sea! I reject your rose of silver strewn on the sands—and your aerial passage dispersed in foam;

I will be no longer the seamew of your mirrors —nor the erect sea-horse of your surging Parnassi;

open sea! I hail the Southern Cross spilled on your breast—and I descend bitterly to the oceanic night of the Undersea!

Undersea, sea changeless and impervious to the lightning as to the bird's wing—sea heavy with young and blind to what you bear,

carry me far from the current of remembering —and from the long drift of memories;

tow me into your tactile night—deeper into your darkness than the double blindness of eye and ear;

undersea, you that no longer climb the flowery hummock of the meadows—like a thought weary of images,

you that no longer plough the shore in a clash-
ing of pebbles—a stirring of thoughts at the whim
of vocables,

you no longer chained by the tides—nor by the
brief honour of vertical revolts,

let me become your ritual and recumbent
swimmer—like a secret hidden in the folds of
soundless cloth,

with a heedless step—may I walk your shoreless
roads,

undersea—rub out my face and drown this tear
where the clarities are recovering,

may I forget in you the wavering frontiers of
my own day—and the lucid range of the sun.

ANNE
HÉBERT
b. 1916

Manor Life

Here is an ancestral manor
Without a table or fire
Or dust or carpets.

The perverse enchantment of these rooms
Lies wholly in their polished mirrors.

The only possible thing to do here
Is to look at oneself in the mirror day and night.

Cast your image into these brittle fountains
Your brittler image without shadow or colour.

See, these mirrors are deep
Like cupboards
There is always someone dead behind the quick-
   silver
Who soon covers your reflection
And clings to you like seaweed

Shapes himself to you, naked and thin,
And imitates love in a long bitter shiver.

F. R. SCOTT

The Lean Girl

ANNE
HÉBERT

I am a lean girl
And I have beautiful bones.

I tend them with great care
And feel strange pity for them.

I continually polish them
As though they were old metal.

Now jewels and flowers
Are out of season.

One day I shall clasp my lover
And make of him a silver shrine.

I shall hang myself
In the place of his absent heart.

O well-filled space,
Who is this cold guest suddenly in you?

You walk,
You move;
Each one of your gestures
Adorns with fear the enclosed death.

I receive your trembling
As a gift.

And sometimes
Fastened in your breast
I half open
My liquid eyes

As strange and childish dreams
Swirl
Like green water.

ANNE
HÉBERT

F. R. SCOTT

The Two Hands

These two hands that one has
The right closed
Or open;

The left open
Or closed.

And the two
Not waiting
For each other.

Two hands that are not joined,
Two hands that cannot join.

One that we give
And one that we keep;

One that we know
And the other, the unknown.

This hand of a child,
This hand of a woman.
And sometimes this working hand,
Simple as the hand of a man.

Then this makes three!
And I discover
In myself
An infinite number
Of hands that reach
Toward me,
Like strangers
Of whom one is afraid.

Oh! who will give back to me
My two hands as one?
And the shore
That we touch
With both hands,
Preparing for the same journey,
Having discarded on the way
All these useless hands . . .

F. R. SCOTT

The Closed Room

Who then brought me here?
There was certainly someone
Who prompted my steps.
But when did that happen?
With the complicity of what quiet friend?
The deep approval of what long night?

Who was it laid out the room?
In what calm moment
Was the low ceiling thought of
The small green table and the tiny knife
The bed of black wood
And all the bloom of the fire
With its red billowing skirts

Around its core enclosed and held fast
Under the orange and blue flames?

ANNE
HÉBERT

Who then took the exact measure
Of the trembling cross of my outstretched arms?
The four cardinal points
Start at my fingertips
If I turn myself round
Four times
For as long as will last the memory
Of day and of night.

When my heart was placed on the table
Who then laid the cover so carefully
Sharpened the little knife
Without any torment
Or hurry?

My flesh is bewildered and wastes away
Without this familiar guest
Torn from between its ribs.
The bright colour of blood
Seals the hollow vault
And my hands folded
Over this devastated space
Grow cold and fascinated with emptiness.

F. R. SCOTT

The Tomb of the Kings

ANNE
HÉBERT

I carry my heart on my fist
Like a blind falcon.

The taciturn bird gripping my fingers
A swollen lamp of wine and blood
I go down
Toward the tombs of the kings
Astonished
Scarcely born.

What Ariadne-thread leads me
Along the muted labyrinths?
The echo of my steps fades away as they fall.

(In what dream
Was this child tied by her ankle
Like a fascinated slave?)

The maker of the dream
Presses on the cord
Drawing the naked steps
One by one
Like the first drops of rain
At the bottom of the well.

Already the odour stirs in swollen storms
Seeps under the edges of the doors
Of chambers secret and round
Where the closed beds are laid out.

The motionless desire of the recumbent dead lures
    me.
I behold with astonishment
Encrusted upon the black bones
The blue stones gleaming.

A few tragedies patiently wrought   ANNE
Lying on the breast of kings   HÉBERT
As if they were jewels
Are offered me
Without tears or regrets.

In single rank arrayed :
The smoke of incense, the cake of dried rice,
And my flesh which trembles :
A ceremonial and submissive offering.

A gold mask on my absent face
Violet flowers for eyes,
The shade of love paints me in small sharp strokes,
And this bird I have breathes
And complains strangely.

A long tremor
Like a wind sweeping from tree to tree,
Shakes the seven tall ebony Pharaohs
In their stately and ornate cases.

It is only the profundity of death which persists,
Simulating the ultimate torment
Seeking its appeasement
And its eternity
In a faint tinkle of bracelets
Vain rings, alien games
Around the sacrificed flesh.

Greedy for the fraternal source of evil in me
They lay me down and drink me;
Seven times I know the tight grip of the bones
And the dry hand seeking my heart to break it.

Livid and satiated with the horrible dream
My limbs freed
And the dead thrust out of me, assassinated,

What glimmer of dawn strays in here?
Wherefore does this bird quiver
And turn toward morning
Its blinded eyes?

ANNE
HÉBERT

F. R. SCOTT

Snow

Snow puts us in a dream on vast plains without
    track or colour
Beware, my heart, snow puts us in the saddle on
    steeds of foam
Ring out for a crowned childhood, snow consecrates
    us on high seas, dreams fulfilled, all sails set
Snow puts us in a trance, a widespread whiteness,
    flaring plumes pierced by the red eye of this bird
My heart; a point of fire under palms of frost flows
    the marvelling blood.

F. R. SCOTT

There Is Certainly Someone

ANNE
HÉBERT

There is certainly someone
Who once killed me
And then walked away
On the tip of his toes
Without breaking his perfect dance

Who forgot to put me to bed
And left me standing
All tightly bound
On the road
My heart sealed up as before
My two eyes like
Their own pure image of water

Who forgot to erase the beauty of the world
Around me
Forgot to close my hungry eyes
And permitted their wasted passion.

F. R. SCOTT

A Little Dead Girl

ANNE
HÉBERT

A little dead girl
        is lying across our doorstep
We found her in the morning, curled on the sill
Like bracken touched by frost.

Now that she is there
We do not dare go out,
This pale child in her frothy skirts, shedding
A strange milky darkness.

We try to go on living inside
Without making any noise
Sweeping the room
Organizing boredom
Letting gestures fall as they will
At the end of the invisible thread
Touching our open veins.

We are scarcely alive at all, so quiet
That not one of our slow movements
Reaches to the back of the limpid mirror
Where a sister swims
In faint blue moonlight
As her heady odour grows.

G. V. DOWNES

The Planting of Hands

ANNE
HÉBERT

We had this notion
Of planting our hands in the garden

Branches of ten fingers,
Little trees of bone,
a sweet border

All day long
We have waited for the russet bird
And the fresh leaves
On our polished nails

Neither bird
Nor spring
Has been caught in the snare of our severed hands

For a single flower
A single tiny star of clear colour

A swoop of a calm wing
A single pure note
Uttered three times

We shall have to wait for the new season
And our hands melting like water.

G. V. DOWNES

A Touch of Despair

ANNE
HÉBERT

The river has taken back
islands I loved
and I have lost
the keys to silence
the scented memory of hollyhocks
has deceived me,
the false promise
of the singing waters

my tired heart no longer
moves with the stream

G. V. DOWNES

Cities in Sail

Cities in sail, provinces of salt, lilies of stone
Isles descending the slopes of the sea, headwind, sun
    at the prow
Bitter blossom spun on the wave, geranium sun-
    combs of greencocks flung
Plunging of oceans, turmoil of sun, back-brusque-
    tumbled mantles of brine, night, deep night
Movement of sea-heave, the port as a star, roadbed
    tasting the rind of the lemon of dulse
Harbourings had, balancing, day furled, heart
    spread among loose of the wrack
Palms open, strange ibis of sapphire come in silence
    to drink
All sweetness breathing largesse of air. Tigers of
    that country tractable.

RALPH GUSTAFSON

The Little Towns

ANNE
HÉBERT

I shall give you the little towns
The poor sad little towns,

The little towns cupped in our palms
More exigent than toys
As easy to the hand.

I play with the little towns,
I turn them over
Never a man escapes them
No flower, no child.

The little towns are empty—
Given into our hands.

I listen, my ear to the doors
I lean to the doors, one by one,
With my ear . . .

O the houses are dumb sea-shells—
No longer in the frozen spiral
Any sound of the wind
Any sound of water.

Dead, the parks and the gardens
The games are all put to sleep
In a dead museum.

I cannot tell where they have put
The deathstill bodies of the birds.

The streets resound with silence
The echo of their silence is a weight of lead
More leaden
Than any words of menace or of love.

And here am I too, in my turn
Forsaking the little towns of my childhood . . .
I offer them to you
In all the infinite depth
Of their loneliness.

ANNE
HÉBERT

Now do you grasp the dangerous gift?
I have given you the strange sad little towns
For your own imagining.

Under the Rain

Oh may the rain come down
Small and cool
On the huddled world
Passive and soft.

Rain rain descend
Slowly gentle rain
On her who is sleeping
Pulling upon herself transparent sleep
Like a thin coverlet of water

All the raindrops of the day
Poured upon this sleeping one.

We shall see her heart
Only through the break of day

The day she draws
Over her grief
Like a veil of water.

GILLES
HÉNAULT
b. 1920

The Prodigal Son

The child who used to play see him now thin and
    bowed
The child who used to weep see now his burned-
    out eyes
The child who danced a round see him running
    after a streetcar
The child who longed for the moon see him satis-
    fied with a mouthful of bread
The wild and rebellious child, the child at the end
    of the town
In the remote streets
The child of adventures
Of the ice of the river
The child perched on fences
See him now in the narrow road of his daily
    routine
The child free and lightly clothed, see him now
Disguised as a bill-board, a sandwich-man
Dressed up in cardboard laws, a prisoner of petty
    taboos
Subdued and trussed, see him hunted in the name
    of justice
The child of lovely red blood and of good blood
See him now the ghost of a tragic opera

The prodigal son
The child prodigy, look at him now as a man
The man of 'time is money' and the man of *bel
    canto*
The man riveted to his work which is to rivet all
    day

The man of the Sunday afternoons in slippers   GILLES
And the interminable bridge parties   HÉNAUL
The numberless man of the sports of the few men
And the man of the small bank account
To pay for the burial of a childhood that died
Towards its fifteenth year

F. R. SCOTT

Hail to Thee

I

Redskins
Tribes consumed
in the conflagration of fire-water and tuberculosis
Hunted down by the pallor of death and the
    Palefaces
Carrying off your dreams of old spirits and the
    manitous
Dreams shattered by the fire of the arquebuses
You have left us your totemic hopes
And our sky now has the colour
of the smoke of your pipes of peace.

II

We have no limits
And abundance is our mother
Land girdled with steel
With great lake eyes
And rustling resinous beard
I salute you and I salute your laughter of waterfalls

Land helmeted with polar ice
Haloed with northern lights
And offering to future generations
The sparkling sheaf of your uranium fires.
We hurl against those who pillage and waste you
Against those who fatten upon your great body of
    humus and snow
The thunderous imprecations
That roar from the throats of storms.

GILLES
HÉNAULT

III

I already hear the song of those who sing :

Hail to thee, life, full of grace
the sower is with thee
blessed art thou by all women
and the child radiant with discovery
holds thee in his hand
like the multicoloured pebble of reality.

Beautiful life, mother of our eyes
clothed in rain and sunny days
may thy kingdom come
on the roads and on the fields
Beautiful life
Praise be to love and spring.

F. R. SCOTT

Times of the Dawn of Time

GILLES
HÉNAUL

Paleolithic times
are you then so far from my ear
that I no longer hear the burst of laughter from
   the caves!
Times of the dawn of time
Times of fossil pleasure
in a calcareous world.
The flint of memories whistles over my head.
Times of tomahawks, of tom-toms and of drums
muffling the shrill source of silence
times of needles, ferocious times of hammers
abolished in the sands of solitude.
May the sphinx more human than love arise.
The eyes can then rediscover the roads of peace
amid the forest of mirrors
where despair is a lie with a thousand masks.

The little girl stood barefoot in the melting ice
Her heart like a lantern.

PETER MILLER

Childhood

GILLES
HÉNAULT

Snowlight is shining in my head
And wolves are tracking down early Christmases.
Out of the bells and knells beaten by snow
I summon a childhood of castles in Spain
Vitriol of blue years
Softness of firelight and its flaxen fingers
Candles and toy trumpets out of tune
In the canticle of olden times :
Hurdy-gurdy of crumbling civilizations.

The world ebbs like the tide, further
And further, as we think more and see less.

Genesis Abridged (Apocryphal)

TO ROLAND GIGUÉRE

I

Adam and Eve
are only shades
in the springs of Time.

II

Eve with teeth
virginal
Eve and Adam
discover the seed.
Adam and Eve with virginal lips
plant the tree of the human race.

149

Headless woman
Fecund Venus
Where man takes root
Breasts, belly, vagina
Cycle of love and clay
Woman, half of darkness
With two feet on the earth
And arms in the sky
Thou art the horizon of our childhood
Flaming in the sun
Of our fleshly love.

IV

A life cut short
At the tip of its stem
A fine tree pruned of life
Droops the fruit of its breasts
Over the ever-growing generations
So that its slavery
May quietly overshadow
All who survive.

V

An Eden of bread-fruit trees and flowing time
Was mingling with the sand
The netted stars
Played hide and seek
This was the time of thornless love
Of youth in flower
Of women without make-up
And men without memory.

VI

That very day
God appeared in all his splendour :

In a violet robe
with white buttons
his beard rinsed in blue
and his hair waved in lightnings
He lit a seven-branched candlestick
And there was Light!
Adam astride the horizon
Between the oceans of Good and Evil
Was awaiting the signal to dive.
Satan was taking a nap
On the beach of time.

VII

The horse was inventing his breed
out of manes and gallopings
Inventing the pace and the leap
But dreaming already of strange roots
Of whips and work and war
because man . . .
Had eaten the apple.

VIII

God put on his policeman's suit
His peaked-cap with three stars
Into the scabbard he pushed his sword
Under his tunic a heart of stone
And took his way towards Earth
Followed by his sergeant, the archangel
The Father was going to chastise his sons
Because of a sour apple
Which Adam had eaten
God was watching over his orchard
For though he is full of love
for his children, men,
Still he prefers
Good apple jam.

Then we knew
Days of savage beasts
We fought
Against monsters almost human
We invented
glittering Reason
We discovered
The cock and his song
We bestrode
The wild ox and the buffalo
We lit
the fire of hope
in the depths of our hearts.
And one fine day the sun rose
at cock-crow!

X

Man left the prehistoric night
The Stone Age and the door-stopper
At the entrance of the cave
He planted the totem-pole of his fate
The camels invented the caravan
And man was fooled by mirages
age after age
In a desert of thirst, of sand
and of unquenchable desires.

XI

But the oases
Reflect a prospect of palm trees
in the inward sky of every man
who sees, in men, brothers
and in peace the quenching spring.

GILLES
HÉNAULT

Totem, thy shadow
declines at noon
The earth is swaying
her teeming loins
The rivers are rocking
in their bed's hollow
The harvests are swooning
combed by the wind
The child opens eyes
as big as hands
he begins the game
of loving love, life, bread
And the compass-card
predicts fine weather.

ÉLOI DE
GRANDMONT

b. 1921

The Hunter

Grand-dad here's a jolly sporting type.
The old boy's absolutely mad about hunting.
He'd take his gun (a regular Foxy Grandpa,
This one) and off he'd go. Alley-oop!
And the gun'd go off too.

He's killed a moose,
A deer and a dozen kildeer
As well as a lovely gazelle,
Four rabbits in his own coppice,
Three goose and any number of *quack-quacks*.

He'd say I've killed myself
Working: now I'm resting.
I kill to kill time.

Well, when he got home one evening
He killed Grandmamma, his wife.
Absent-mindedly; without thinking
—Force of habit, see?
Heh! heh! they hanged him anyway.
A good job too! That'll learn him.

A. J. M. SMITH

Parade

The trumpets sound.
The drums rebound.
Only, no cannon shakes the ground.
So then, we still have peace?
Not only peace
But jollity.
It's holiday,
A raree-show.
It's the operetta of the rank and file,
Of the Brothers of the Christian Schools
And of the Sacred Heart of Jesus,
All together,
These worthies
Stepping like turkeys
To the rhythm of patriotic nonsense,
And the plaudits of a delirious crowd
Tipsy with national pride
And Coca-Cola.

The wares of patriotism,
Nationalism and religion
Blaze
On floats loaded with allegories
More mysterious
And more sublime than parables.
Then come the Cadillacs
Stuffed with nationalist embalmers
Who are nonetheless patriotic or religious
Or both.
The parade dribbles along
For hours and hours . . .
The crowd goes mad.
To quiet them down, now come
Just in time
The drum-majorettes
From Saint-Sacrement
Or from Shawinigan,
Riding upon their skittish thighs
And with posteriors quivering
From the impact of their energetic heels.
This is the finest moment of the play—
Except perhaps
The eventual and concluding lamb,
Mammal ruminating
Some undefined old dream,
Hailed by the flock
Of Panurge and of Jean-Baptiste,
Lapped in the ecstasy of the general bleat.
A child made up like a precocious fairy
For queers worried about the nation's future,
Leads the lamb
Leads the sheep
Guides our steps,
For he is the patron saint . . .
The mothers of large families
Cannot restrain their tears.

ÉLOI DE
GRANDMONT

Model Parents

ÉLOI DE
GRANDMO

There are parents who punish their children.
Others who scold them
Bother them
Badger them
Lecture them
Sicken them
Break them in
Cut them off
Keep them under and
Pull their ears.

Others who reason with them
Jaw them
Worry them
Confine them, bore
Them to death, chide

Them, chivy
Them, crush
Them, curse
Them and disinherit them.

There are also parents who chastise them.
Parents who pinch them
Strike them
Slap them
Spank them
Torment them
Knock them around
Smash them to bits
Hand them over to the Social Welfare and then
Go to bed and make others.

Then there are the ones who
Take away their dessert, keep them
From sleeping, forbid

Them to go out, cut off
Their pocket money, tell them to
Shut up.

Finally, there are those who give them
A good swift kick in the pants and a
Father's blessing on New Year's Day.

Christmas

The church in its Sunday best
In the dead of night, the deep;
Icicles hang
From the nostrils of the horses
Standing asleep.

Christmas! when we are young,
Ready to roam the world
(Tyrol and Spanish beaches!)
And when we fall asleep
While the preacher preaches.

The organ tones
Pursue the passerby
In the village street;
And the husband promises
Whatever the wife demands.

A day when the mothers weep
For the girls who ran away
With gay deceivers,
And for the penniless boys
Who went to the town to stay.

For the children, what a day!

Seven O'Clock

Gone from the tarnished beach the memory of
   light
The trampled sand, wet lump
chill to my wilful feet
This is the end of the party
Pédalos, pédalos, mesdemoiselles?
What do you have to offer?
A sea where one cannot be lost?
Sea dogsea at dusk
Hideous with small quiverings
Sea of wily picnickers
Sea of shysters

The Watcher

Prolonged by the whole of summer
my desires reaching high as hollyhocks
I want the rain, I want the wind
for every morning, a stationary world,
to make my inventory
The grayblue gravel path is seething
Wipe it out! It is almost noon
I want a sky levelled at the dolphin

Time Corrected

So I retraced my steps
I retreated to my birth
And rolled back to their beginnings
My family and all my ancestors

I said a mass in reverse
That blood might taste of wine
That flesh might taste of bread
That I might return to the name of the Father
And never again say Amen

I returned everything I possessed
My faith to the King of Heaven my tongue to the
    King of France
I gave back to Rome its hills
I dismissed the twelve Apostles
I sent home the shepherds and the Magi
I tore down Babel storey by storey
And returned the stone to the mountain
I sent back the dove to Noah
And drank all the waters of the Flood
I rehung the forbidden fruit on the tree
And handed to Satan the sin of knowledge
I took the first Eve again into my side
And restored sex to unity

And then,
Nothing remained for me
But to give up the first sigh
In order to blow out the light
And everything returned to darkness

F. R. SCOTT

A la Claire Fontaine

PIERRE
TROTTIER

Let me take you to the *Claire Fontaine*
Let me sing you an old refrain

For a long time I have loved you
And never shall I forget you

Let me console your Cinderella-people
Who cannot forget their Prince
And whose memories are but poor sketches
Of a dream gone astray and a hope too slight

For a long time I have loved you
And never shall I forget you

Let me console your poor schoolboys
Whose prizes were only for memory
And who feel themselves prisoners of time
When they should take their place in history

For a long time I have loved you
And never shall I forget you

Let me sing you an old refrain
Let me take you to the *Claire Fontaine*

F. R. SCOTT

State of Siege

PIERRE
TROTTIER

FOR GÉRARD PELLETIER

Fear of the police
Fear of arrests
Made me afraid of permissions
But even more of the unknown
And of the freedom that led to it

Fear of God
Fear of priests
Fear of men
And of the woman who gave them birth

Fear of my sins
Fear of confessing them
Made me afraid to receive grace
And the holiness that came with it

Fear of war
Fear of the enemy
Made me afraid of friends
And of the peace they heralded

Fear of words
Fear of thought
Made me afraid of magic formulas
And of the sorcerers who recited them

Sign of the cross or cry of race
Magic of amulet or mask
Oh the fear primitive the Indian fear
Which impelled me to work on the canoe of
    suicide

I had already carved a paddle of the folksongs

The one that leads up there as high perhaps as the
   land
Where I might rejoin the Chasse-Galerie

But the minute I was ready
Authority had surrounded me
Had beamed on me its searchlights
Which relentlessly pinned me against the wall
Of the priestless prison of my conscience

PIERRE
TROTTIE

F. R. SCOTT

Anti-Credo

I do not believe in myself,
a feeble son,
failure in all things visible and invisible,
losing Heaven from too much dreaming
earth from too much seeking.

I no longer believe
in anything but the word
the word that I put into verse
very shadow of very shadows
words of the earth

I believe in the word   PIERRE
conceived by the tormented spirit   TROTTIER
born of the mad and virgin image
who was made skeleton
who suffered under the foreign tongue
and was crucified on Mount Royal
who died in the fall of the poem
and descended into memory
on the third day he rose again
he ascended onto the untouched page
and lieth in the margin
from whence he shall come to judge
both sounds and silence

And I believe in the tormented spirit
born of the quarrels of the father and the son
and still imprisoned with the father and the son
in a poor provincial church
I look for the punishment of good intentions
the falling back of the poem
the breaking up of words
the sterilization of lost time
whose weight
threatens my survival.

So be it not.

G. V. DOWNES

The Lesson

PIERRE
TROTTI

Let us learn to travel light
With this thought

Let us learn silence
Learn to live by ear
Making only enough noise
To know our dying

Let us learn silence
Give the ear a chance
To hear, among pure echoes
The crumbling bones

Let us learn to travel light
In this freedom.

G. V. DOWNES

The Star of the Great Lakes

The moon was on holiday
The stars were on holiday
And in the school of night
Before the blackboard of the sky
We were alone without teachers

The pure sky of your forehead the sky of my
    country
Came down so low it laid its head
On my shoulder and I felt its breath
A breathless wind of love on my neck

Alone we learned to count on our fingers PIERRE
TROTTIER
To count ten kisses and ten provinces
And we have even learned from our errors
So that on the blackboard we erase with a caress
To join our ten fingers to unite ten provinces

Then I cried out your name that of my country
Alas the echo which returned was broken
Into ten different names of provinces
To write your name I ran to the blackboard
But in a sudden storm the lightning sundered it
In ten pieces of the sky and I received its tears

The moon was on holiday
The stars were on holiday
And in the school of night
Before the blackboard of the sky
I was alone without you

To write of our history I have no more
Than pieces of chalk where breaks the sweet
Burst of the arms of the star of the Great Lakes
Where the heart of the country swells in tides
Of useless uncontrolled sobbing
The tablet of love the tablet of the earth

R. A. D. FORD

The Unknown Soldier

PIERRE
TROTTIER

I thought it would be enough to raise my arms
On the public square like the two hands of a clock
To tell the people the hour I was alive
But everyone had a watch of his own

I thought it would be enough to join my hands
Over my head to make an arch of triumph
But nobody came
To light the flame on the tomb
Of the unknown soldier I shall always be

I thought a good warm bed would be enough
For me to draw all women to my breast
And wake up rocking children in my arms
Alas the nights were never long enough
To keep the women from running away
And the children from being born far from me

I thought an open door would be enough
To let my bread gladden a host of friends
But the bread was stolen and eaten somewhere
    else
And I was left alone with crumbs for the rats

O my little hour my arch of triumph
My solitary loves my lonely bread
Will there be nothing faithful to you but my
    death?

Of all that I am and of my death itself
Will nothing remain that wakens any wish
For the unknown soldier whom nobody knows
And all they know of him is that he is dead?

The Word Is Bleeding

The word bleeds in the throat of fog
Blowing on men from lewdness of their night
The sun softly strokes the word that mates
With the wind of damp thoughts and fiery limits

While heaven-granted gladness
And the blight beneath the mummy
                                        Breathe their last
The plinth and corpses of your songs
Number and rend the silences to come

The Hinge of the Sea

The hinge of the sea points to the brain

The theatre of the world is raised
And spewing its mechanical elves
Endlessly violates and soils
The feeling thinking skull

No more flowers   no more
The calm void of fire and water
Neither asks nor replies

The sea unceasingly dies
Speak
And you too will die

What Matter the Silt

FERNAN●
DUMON

What matter the silt that clogged our pleasure
The vision of swarms of everlasting thirst
And debased crawling corpses of the dead
Since I have longed for the traces of your blood

The hours will slip away as the lamp of waiting
    burns
Day will mix with the waters of my prayer
I do not know if you will come
Like the primeval sun to the death of night

But in the tall grass mirroring the shadows
Like the raucous bird led onward by his grief
I will still seek the old forgotten path
Strewn at times by the thunder of your love

GASTON
MIRON

b. 1928

Héritage de la tristesse

Sad and confused among the fallen stars
pale, silent, nowhere and afraid, a vast phantom
here is this land alone with winds and rocks
a land forever lost to its natal sun
a beautiful body drowned in mindless sleep
like water lost in a barren thirst of gravel

I see it bridled by chances and tomorrows
showing its face in the dreams of anguished men
whenever it breathes in wastes and undergrowth
    of bracken

whenever it burns, in poplars old in years and
  neglect,
the useless leaf-green of its abortive love
or whenever a will to being sleeps in the sail of its
  heart

bowed down, it awaits it knows not what redemp-
  tion
among these landscapes walking through its stillness
among these rags of silence with eyes of the
  dying
and always this ruined smile of a poor degraded
  future
always this hacking at the stands of darkness
and horizons fading in a drift of promises

despoiled, its only hope is a vacant lot's
cold of cane talking with cold of bone
unease of the rust, the quick, the nerves, the nude
and in its livid back the blows of heated knives
it looks at you, worked out, from the depth of its
  quarries
and out of the tunnels of its abstraction where one
  day
it surrendered and lost forever the memory of
  man

winds that shuffle the lots of precedence by night
winds of concourse, winds with solar eyes
telluric winds, winds of the soul, universal winds
come couple, o winds, and with your river arms
embrace this face of a ruined people, give it the
  warmth
and the abundant light that rings the wake of
  swallows

FRED COGSWELL

October

GASTON
MIRON

The man of our time has a face of flagellation
and you, Land of Quebec, Mother Courage
you are big
with our sooty sorrowful dreams
and an endless drain of bodies and souls

I was born your son
in your worn-out mountains of the north
I ache and suffer
bitten by that birth
yet in my arms my youth is glowing

here are my knees
may our world forgive us
we have allowed our fathers to be humbled in spirit
we have allowed the light of the word to be debased
to the shame and self-contempt of our brothers
we could not bind the roots of our suffering
into the universal sorrow of each degraded man

I go to join the burning company
whose struggle shares and breaks the bread of the
    common lot
in the quicksands of a common grief

we will make you, Land of Quebec
a bed of resurrections
and in the myriad lightnings of our transformations
in this leaven of ours from which the future is rising
in our uncompromising will
men will hear your pulse beating in history
this is ourselves rippling in the autumn of October
this is the russet sound of deer in the light
the future free and easy

FRED COGSWELL

The Reign of Winter

GASTON
MIRON

Grey land and furious, brown and savage
split in the ghostly beauty of the cold
in tides of birch, in brotherhoods
of spruce and pine, and in your similars
of hidden rocks, of enmities

bare ancestral land, our land
over your infinite patient miles you are flowing
into a landscape maddened by loneliness
into the towns where famine chars your face
into our empty and unfurnished loves
and into us stiffened by restoration to your earth,
    our death

and you are helpless in this captive wealth of ours
you shiver
in this slow fire that is burning in our backs

GILLES
NEAULT

b. 1928

If All the Ships . . .

If all the ships that we have built together
Take to the sea before I shall return
Clew up your sail, and also mine
Try to pretend . . . try to pretend
That we are still the captains sailing them
That we are still the captains sailing them

171

Deep as the open water off the island
Soft as the wing of a starling
As far away as England
I shall love you
I shall love you

If the treasures to which we had the key
The plan the map and the lovely adventure
Should only prove a dream and imposture
Think of them still . . . think of them still
By adding more flags to sail at the mast-head
By adding more flags to sail at the mast-head

Deep as the open water off the island
Soft as the wing of a starling
As far away as England
I shall love you
I shall love you

If I should become an agent or gardener
Don't come to tell me of forbidden traffic
But if you should want me to hang myself
From the great topsail . . . from the great topsail
Tell me that you have sailed and seen Ireland
Tell me that you have sailed and seen Ireland

Deep as the open water off the island
Soft as the wing of a starling
As far away as England
I shall love you
I shall love you

LOUIS DUDEK

To the Birds from Afar . . .

GILLES
VIGNEAULT

To the birds from afar and the roses new-blown
My love, go tell with your fingers and lips
What my songs are, what my native speech is
When my talk is of you while time wears us
    down

It is time your hands and your voice should show
To the roses afar and the wood-birds about
The caress of my hands and the songs of my
    throat
Before rumour or wind are mingled with those

Tell them you love, and if that does not much
To make the flowers fade somewhat less
Or the birds to come down to your shoulder to
    rest

Tell them the secret of souls that can touch
Then the birds will join in the morning hours
To praise the new rose and the autumn flowers

LOUIS DUDEK

Song

GILLES
VIGNEAU

I have made my sky from a cloud
And my forest from a reed.
I have made my longest journey
On a blade of grass in a stream.

From a little plaster, the city;
From a puddle of water, the sea.
From a pebble I made my island
And from an icicle, winter.

Each one of your silences
Is a parting without return
And a moment of indifference
The whole sorrow of love.

Thus it is when I dare
Offer your beauty
A rose, in this rose
Are all the gardens of summer.

A. J. M. SMITH

Looking Is Enough

Whose is the dark body
crying in pain
under the fingers of the wind?

who walks in a mask of tears
close as your hand
from shadowy places?

what secret
hangs over the pond
as the blood withdraws?

there is nothing
in these uneasy pools of memory
but a reflection   pitted with holes
and sickened eyes

G. V. DOWNES

Polar Seasons

No flame. No warmth.
It was a cold life, the heart gripped in a ring of ice.

The sun had withdrawn its rays and finally left the humans who had insulted it for so long. They had spat in its face, in broad daylight; they had desecrated love like a whore, right on the street; they had dragged liberty through the mud and barbed wire. The noblest reasons for living torn to shreds under our windows and thrown to the four winds.

In autumn, we watched the dead leaves fall and, mentally, counted them among the green ones that we should not forget the colour of our hope. In our deepest selves, secretly and timidly, there still wavered the idea of the dignity of man.

But the centre of the earth was growing colder and colder . . .

No flame. No warmth.
It was a cold life, the heart gripped in a ring of ice.

The eyes drained away, pierced by needles of cold. We that were brands became icicles, and everything froze in a terrible transparency.

White dominated, a cold white. A white that hid more than one festering wound of black, thick blood. But on the surface, to the eye, it was white . . .

And the eye-sockets grew still, the flutter of eyelashes grew still, the beat of the wing grew still in a sky crystallized red and low while the other, the beating of the heart, still kept on but now reached

us deadened, muffled as though from far away, as though it moved farther and farther from the breast.

Those who continued to believe in something, no matter what, remained haggard. They were as lost as children in a railway station. They raved, adrift.

No flame. No warmth.
It was a cold life, the heart gripped in a ring of ice.

After death we would not rot but it would have been better to rot—to leave well-washed skeletons, clean remains, without a speck of flesh or blood, bones bleached and like new as the carcasses of horses that one finds on desert sands with skulls as beautiful as sculptures.

No, we would not rot but it would have been better to rot, for what was waiting for us was even worse: we were to be mummified at the foulest and most revolting moment of our lives and the image of our suffering preserved unchanged for ages and ages, reflected and magnified on the sky in humiliating auroras.

At any cost some other traces of ourselves had to be left, or none at all. None.

And we were caught there, caught in the ice, longing for a scorching summer.

No flame. No warmth.
It was a cold life, the heart gripped in a ring of ice.

And yet, a single night of universal love could save everything. A single white night of love and the earth is lighter; the sea withdraws into its bed

taking with it the rags with which we are covered. Everything is washed clean. Man can sleep in white sheets without fear that his slumber may be murdered.

But at this time from which I speak to you, one saw even in the eyes of man a longing for man and it is in the eyes of animals that one found again the gentleness that causes you to be torn from the ground and to soar in the pure air, caught up in the ectstasy of the dream lived in flesh and bone. The flower, too, in spite of everything, clung to its petals, and after their migration the swallows came back to us as though there had always been a spring.

Silently, we sought a new horizon on which to find a foothold for a new life, to start all over again, to re-invent everything beginning with ourselves.

F. R. SCOTT

Landscape Estranged

ROLAND
GIGUÈRE

The storm raged about
and the snow blew into our breast
right in the breast
crowned with pain-sharp ice
crowned with thorns
love words driven into the brow

great storm before our eyes in a world estranged
every night tore a cry from us
and we grew up in agony
slowly we were aging
and the landscape aged with us—against us

the landscape was no longer the same
the landscape was sombre
the landscape no longer fitted us like a glove
no longer had the colours of our youth
the landscape the beautiful landscape was no
    longer beautiful
there were no more streams
no more ferns no water
there was nothing left

the landscape had to be remade.

F. R. SCOTT

A Protracted Affair

ROLAND
GIGUÈRE

Above the lintels where I live
I set your name in majuscule
girl of my joy girl of my grief
my being twined and steeped in yours
under a new moon sleepless hours
between the ordinary sheets
girl of love's opening gesture girl
naked in the panting lists
girl of one time and of all

FRANCIS SPARSHOTT

The Age of Speech

There's an old wind understage blowing the
    boards away
on a fretwork plain the aurochs is back
life sacramental dons once more
iron accoutrements grey blade gold cuirass
to fight in fealty

the flint waits in the rock
we have no words any more
the sun bleeds in the sky
we cannot name it

tomorrow we find the serpent's head in our dish
swallow his poison gulp down his forked tongue
and where shall we find then
new songs to beguile us?

FRANCIS SPARSHOTT

The Future Rose

ROLAND
GIGUÈRE

I

At the quarter-moon or at hollyhock bloom
on clubs or on hearts
the Wheel of Fortune will fall
and the sword in the midst of the emerald table
will divide the blood of the earth

the black pearl will fix on the day to come
the hour of fulfilment or the moment of pain
and the tiger will leap all-fours into Reality
the tiger or the sacred snake
all claws bared or its poison pure
for the return to transparent origins

II

No gleam of light on the lagoon but the waiting
crash
under the hood the whip of steel waits for the
flesh
and the trophies lie in their thousands
on the marly roads

the time of lightning past
we shall take our place at the windows of exile
the shadow of the sentinel is his own enemy
and the shadows will be beaten down like shadows

III

In the eye's crook the great forests beheaded shall
pass
from behind the rock pyramids of wood bedsteads
rise
then the wood-rose and the rosewood
and the rose of the wooden bed for a love without
defeat

forgot shall be the knot of red veins in the blond
    wood
the flame return to the centre of the hearth
where its ashes were dispersed and will take up
    its task

IV
In the murmurous night the voracious one ever
    hovers
his wings wide open above the fortunate prey
crouched at the side of the well.

LOUIS DUDEK

From *Adorable Femme des Neiges*

We are far from here
on the roads of snow
we are far
from the vigil without a morn
we are alone
and silence readies the perfect flame
in the very shadow of our wish

we belong to futures of every kind
because your reality is possible
because you are real
at the heart of eternal snows
I leave my last look
on the borders of your beauty

LOUIS DUDEK

The Wave-Words

ROLAND
GIGUÈRE

The wave-words come beating on the white beach
where I write that water is no longer water
without the lips to drink it

the wave-words wreathing the ultimate desert
   island
the bed where I see you swim at night
and your eyelid covering you like a sheet
on the steep slope of morning
when the world comes splintering in at the
   window

the wave-words which give the brooks
the whispering voice we know
the dappled voice
See how I see you   I who close my eyes
to the tiniest hair of your head
I who close my eyes to everything
so I can see it all balanced
on the microscopic point of the heart
the point studded with the diamonds of haunted
   Sundays
Speak for my enchantment and till I drown
some of those long ribbons of wave-words
which you unroll at evening between your breasts
as if a whole river were crawling at your feet
as if the leaves had no other wind to rock them
but the wind of your eyelashes of milky silk

the wave-words always the wave-words
on the sand the naked bride
waits for the great salty hand of the tide
and a single grain of sand misplaced reveals in a
   moment
the mountain of life
with its snowy peaks its throbbing crests

its unconquered heights its fine-drawn summits   ROLAND
                                                                  GIGUÈRE

only a grain of sand and suddenly
thousands of dunes appearing
then deserts without mirages
an ebony sphinx
and three hundred human pyramids dead of thirst

only a grain of sand and the bride is herself no longer
no longer mistress of herself
becomes a mother and lies down smiling
as an overturned tumbler spills its water
and the wave-words pour in upon the table
the house the field
the tumbler is multiplied by being shattered
and disaster becomes transparent
like the morning entering
by the thinnest edge of an unsilvered mirror.

PAUL-MARIE
LAPOINTE

b. 1929

Poem #28

kisses   poppies at the end of the stalks of legs
the pin twists your two mouths so tight   shat-
ters your pleasure   bits of windowpane   great
nose of remorse   brown snout belly-prober belly-
sniffer   river of women drowned in the rocks and
the branches to pluck a breast an eye a hip I
make love with my teeth

JEAN BEAUPRÉ & GAEL TURNBULL

Poem #102

PAUL-MARIE
LAPOINTE

They are words from blue chests
decapitated sayings
in the anthems without eyes
the family lice in the bathtub
they are the future
roots torn from justice
while shooting empty hearts

They are the stars of the beardless prophet
he who looks behind
but who looks forward behind
the same eyes in the stellar nape

So many walls to demolish in the past
to rebuild tomorrow
plugged like a mouth
confronting corals of anchors in the forehead
facing the contradictory skulls of stones

each step closer to the preceding
until it precedes the instant of perceiving
electric rage of its rock
each step eternity
but the course of the nocturnal sun
the yellow reflections
the wells of flowering brains   the seeds
of mauve lemons in the dead brows of oracles

JEAN BEAUPRÉ & GAEL TURNBULL

Poem for Winter

PAUL-MARIE
LAPOINTE

I am releasing white birds
                              in your heart
white birds are rare, except for doves
and those who have lived out the winter
hanging against the sky like crosses,
a sweep of wings, shivering in the dry cold,
birds strange as this snow
relentlessly driving, landing
                              on villages, cages,
between stones, and small branches shaped by the
    wind

the dead do not take flight
except in our secret selves
                         like children we engender
who make new roads through the heart's
    landscape
white birds   aery fragments of bone

G. V. DOWNES

Time is Falling

PAUL-MARIE
LAPOINTE

> (the earth threatens us
> at the streetcorner, every noon,
>   the same sated face
> brass of parades
> brass bands
> and the hole in the heart
>   of all the dead . . .)

time is falling

> peoples   cloudbursts   sparrows

time is falling

> a lost tribe re-emerges
> children of the pyramids   of the
>   sun
> amphoras of dust   corn and furs
> and a mountain wall of the dead
> (wall like a hive whence fly out
>   the gorged souls of the necro-
>   phagous the whites)
> a people petrified

time is falling

> Abenaki   Maya   Birmingham
> Negro
> citizens   souls of my savage dead
>
> and anger buried in the droppings
>   of wild horses
> in the knowledge of soldiers and
>   saints
> in the armoured frigates
> all for the swoon of an infanta
>   and the bombast of a tribute to
>   the unknown soldier

time is falling

in the Month of the Salmon the
    villages and councils are set up
the fishermen
the capitals polished by the hand
    of death

time is falling

ships of the slavers
Atahualpa
savages there
annihilated
(cinderella quivers in silk   her
    three meals   her prince
O quiet sleep
round planet where the uniform
    houses hug themselves
day after day may rest eternal
    come)

time is falling

the little prehistoric men are
    moving around
between the buildings
in the rain charged with missiles

time is falling

glutted species

The Stranger Hereabouts

He came from a country of devout pirates
Where indifference was taken for dogma
The idiot for master
The sick man for the seer

It was a country of useless struggles
And magnificent ruins
A country eaten out by vermin

When he wished to shout out his rage
They would not allow it

They hardly allowed him to die

F. R. SCOTT

Hope That Triumphs

Down below, in the most mysterious depths of space, the hand and its fingers emerge from the vast upheavals of the earth. Then the whole body sways upward on its twisted roots and calls to other bodies above the wreckage.

Suddenly, as the colour softens, the faces grow larger and lift up, and the eyes too and the hands and the men who take their place in this morning of too white a sun.

From that moment, man resumes his true stature above all things. He is king by his proud glance and lofty brow on which the beginnings of evil, like waves, roll in to die. Authority in order to live, and the patient strength of intelligence.

If one day you wander lost in these unfamiliar regions, and on the edge of the country where rocks crash together in the fury of the lightning you see a hand appear and thrust itself upward, you will be in the land of giants who are your brothers in the utmost way.

F. R. SCOTT

Inventory

I shall establish for you the inventory of my tenderness, the seasons which model my body and the whirling winds which hammer space.

What does it matter if the trumpets are shattered at the tolling from the ramparts, if encounters redden our earthen bed which we must acknowledge every night? No one shall share the secret of our abode.

Rings of thorn bushes may well overlie the roads that lead us into the city! We shall learn patience. Humbly. Our first steps will be sure and the footbridges that swayed yesterday will link the strangers and the besieged.

Because you will have placed between my latent cowardice and the triumph of our blood your profile of so few words, I shall know the strategy of beasts and the deep-laid plans of the wholly free tree.

F. R. SCOTT

The Room

JEAN-GU
PILON

I say your name
twice over, slowly,
I say your name
and melting space
no more divides
our towns of different colours,
merges to a room
where sliding walls
unfold your thighs
imperious as earth
and all high heaven

A world is born in light
intensified
by fingers' every movement
wordless we have
only our arms
only our hurrying hands
only the blood's calling
and our bodies' new humility
as mouths destroy their walls

And so she appears again
the goddess, the Merciful,
delivers us for a little space
into her many-splendoured glory

G. V. DOWNES

The Burning

JEAN-GUY
PILON

In hurrying waters I fished
for rare woods, drifting down centuries
from forgotten lands

In a deserted garden I plucked
through blood-stained briars
a single delicate flower, made of dust

In a mirror's centre I hollowed out
a secret hole
for a drop of perfume mixed with woman's milk

I grew too rich
I set my house afire, without even
looking at the blaze

On these cold ashes
we will rebuild
on what new image?

G. V. DOWNES

Shadows

JEAN-GUY
PILON

Because one day
I wished to make her part of my destiny
My dreams recreate her patiently
In a thousand mysteries
She is plant bird or woman
Her name trembles with the same syllables
If she becomes water-lily
Seagull or mistress

R. A. D. FORD

The Daily Agony

One instant among the others
And I forget my name
An instant which I would retain
And I have crossed secular distances
An instant of life and death
And I mock what I shall become
An instant and you are all the women in the
    world

After having been you
And I forget who I am who you are

An instant
A drop of blood on your lips
And everything becomes difficult again

R. A. D. FORD

The Pure Presence

JEAN-GUY
PILON

Stark plains where we shall raise up mountains
Dressed in colour
Faces of silence, boundary stones—
O rediscovery of our body's roots
And trial of new roads!

Our only skill in the world's way
Is a coward flight:
This is an age of draughtsmanship
And the blood's crushing weight.

Only the tree, the tree is a pure presence
A speechless strength

A re-weaving of the daedal arms
To deck once more denuded love
And trace deep furrows in the ground
Like an inconstancy in the mind

For day is always pitiless to the blind.

The Dry Season

JEAN-GUY
PILON

When summer shall have sung her strength
Above this heavy sleep of ours,
We'll have forgotten how to walk abroad
To reach out our hands
To look on the shaken shoulders of women
To comfort the lost, the forsaken
To hide all innocence pursued
By what rejoices in the name of justice.

Unreconciled to starve
We'll not have bowed our spirit's head
Down to the burning level of the field
Where the corn yellows to its goal . . .

We're at the soul's dead-centre, a strengthless
   place
Of ultimate defections :
Awaiting the pardon that shall set us free
We lift no finger to unlatch the door

And when, some day, the tree
Protestant of her purity
Displays her naked limbs,
We shall know shame, if any shame is left.

J'ai posé ma main

I put
My closed hand
In the water

I made an island
With a dark
Tunnel
At its heart

I opened
Its smiling lips of flesh

I would have drunk the sea
With the thirst of my five fingers
Given every frailty
The permanence of a shaft of rock

I gave my hand
The water's hand stayed open

I dream of a glove of sand
And a bench of white fleece

Cathedral

CÉCILE
CLOUTIER

To be
The first
Man

To be
The circling
Horizon
Of the first morning
And from it form
The first
Roman arch

To take the wind
In both hands
And give it
All the fervour
Of joined fingers
And create
From this gesture of warm marble
The first
Column

I have had a dream

CÉCILE
CLOUTIER

I have had a dream
Soft as the wave
Which never dies
Finding no beach
To rest its heavy liquid arms
When they can no longer bear the swell
And have at the heart of all their liquid drops
An infinite thirst of sand
That cup of water granted to the ocean
When earth is not too unkind

I have had a dream
Sad
As an empty
Shell

It is a boat
Far away
On the sea

Poor François

I walk, with the city wind against my cheeks
—Lover of black cats and old parts of town—
Along the pavements, hearing for three weeks
The knock-knock of my heels as they come down.
In other days I loved the leafy vine,
Sweet milk, the village green, haying again.
And I had friends. Jeanne was a friend of mine.
Laughing Jeanne and sometimes crying Jeanne.
Ah, for the village girls of times gone by
My wine, my food, everything seemed a lark.
Now it is on the pavement that I lie,
For there's wet paint on the benches in the park.

In the old parts of town the windows gleam,
And gazing through the railings at the moon
The couples on the stairways love and dream,
And sing themselves some half-forgotten tune.
I think of evenings Françoise came with me
Along the river bank, and we would do
Our loving under a feathery linden tree.
They were short evenings, we would sleep right
    through
Into next day. Such times are at an end,
I am hungry, Françoise, sweating, in the dark,
And walking, walking, my pretty village friend,
For there's wet paint on the benches in the park.

And as for you, my silly friend, Countess,
Among your ruins, scared of black cats, rich,
Where do you think I've been? China, no less,
And brought back four magnificent buckles which
Were meant for you. I have just sold them. See

Two linen ropes I bought for us instead :
One to strangle you, one to hang me.
Tomorrow I shall be dangling overhead
From the lamp-post, like a fruit too ripe to keep.
But tonight, afraid and hungry, I embark
On a stone doorstep, Françoise, into sleep,
For there's wet paint on the benches in the park.

SYLVAIN
GARNEAU

GEORGE JOHNSTON

White and Black

Two o'clock. So I loved her, didn't I?
At three, I know, loving is shut for the night.
The girl with the comma scar begins to cry.
Nice calves she had, but hairy in the light.

Her green eyes swim forever in the sea
Of bed—three starry weeks. Dawn makes its blur.
Lucky for us the fire that burned through me
Missed my heart's wicker palace, where I keep her.

How ugly she was, ugly, an ugly frown!
And beautiful, poor little cavalier.
And drunk, oh drunk, o flesh, keep my gorge down!
And her child's laughter made my heart go queer.

Suicide, she thought, was the only way.
'Four slugs I need, I'll do the job with four.'
The big black laughed an accomplice's hurrah
Over his empty glass. God, what a bore!

That comma mark on your forehead, never mind,   SYLVAIN
Your gritty powder makes it look okay,   GARNEAU
And the stuff around your eyes turns us all blind.
Let's follow the mocking crowd is what I say,

Look at them through the window, how they run!
On the floor upstairs—you were fifteen years old then,
Now fifteen minutes later you look done.
Should we try again? Come on, sweet, let's try again.

It's not your eyes, whatever the drums may play,
That we praise you for, but the whiteness of your thigh.
Keep those slugs for a week from Sunday, eh?
But why did you thank me? I keep wondering why.

GEORGE JOHNSTON

My School

SYLVAIN
GARNEAU

I have four good friends, they are four do-nothing
   kings.
Their brows are bucklers masking a thousand roles.
They sleep the sleep of giants after the noon-bell
   rings,
On the sidewalks, in the shadow of the schools.

Like the restless cats that prowl the yards and
   lanes,
The bushes are their timeless jungle; with their
   hands
And sharpened nails they sound the tambourines,
And the message rings among the garbage-cans.

Their castles are of broken tiles; and in each fount
Behind the homes of people of slender means
The water-lilies lengthen as the sun's rays mount
In the summer, when the cops go walking with
   the queens.

Then, light as bubbles upon the air, one sees
The kids of the quarter dancing on the sidewalk.
But tomorrow it will rain; in the too-black eyes
Under their brows, stubborn yet smooth and soft
   as silk,

Castles and princes, giants and all ancient things
Will come back, dancing to the tune of barcarolles.
—These cats of the quarter are do-nothing kings,
Who sleep stretched out on the benches of the
   schools.

FRED COGSWELL

My Friend Pierre

SYLVAIN
GARNEAU

My friend Pierre has infants three,
Three babies plump and point-device.
His wife adores him too, and she
Is oh so pretty. Oh so nice.
My friend Pierre has everything.
He knows he's lucky, and should be,
For he's as happy as a king
With his big babbling bratlings three.
He dwells upon the water-side,
He has a little castle there
Beside the water : close beside.
A lucky man, my friend Pierre!

I went to visit him one day
To tell him of my hapless lot,
Of living homeless and alone
And hungry oftener than not.
I told him of a love unkind
And how my suit went all astray.
But ah, Pierre has settled down . . .
He sings no longer in the wind,
He talks no longer to the tide.
He has his little castle there,
His little nest at the water-side.
A lucky man, my friend Pierre!

He thought himself the king of kings
Within his pretty maisonnette.
He told me, as it were in joke,
'I have no use for wretched folk!'
My friend Pierre, he laughed at me.
But then I robbed him of Pierrette.
We took the highway on the wings
Of love one morning, she and I.
He threw himself from the water-side.
He'll have a pretty castle there
Within the water : well inside.
A lucky man, my friend Pierre!

'My friend Pierre, where are you now?'
'Down within the river-bed.'
'Speak to me, Pierre my friend.
Pierrette was fickle. She has fled.
She ran off with a vagabond . . .
I loved her better far than you.
My love was true as true, I vow.'
'The fellow found her pretty, too.'
So black, so black the water-side,
I dare not leap and join him there.
I fear those castles in the tide.
A lucky man, my friend Pierre!

From *Kings and Castles*

SYLVAIN
GARNEAU

You were the merry fool of ten do-nothing kings.
You dyed your hair. At dinnertime you were found
Dreaming, you troubadour, of gentle giants,
While the delicious wines went round and round.
But the giants were sleeping in their Spanish castles,
Giving no thought at all to the King's poor fool.
The giants went on snoring beside their lemans,
Happy and proud, the lordlings of misrule.
Why do they never come, these cowardly heroes,
To free the princess or the fool from the tower,
Open the cage and let the bird fly out,
Or loosen the collar from the bear?
—Oh, like the riotous children of my quarter
After they've crossed the rivers and the rocks,
They sleep the sleep eternal and serene
Of an immaculate, happy golden calf.
And you'll be the fool of ten kings big and fat,
A minstrel, poet, ballet-master ... Laugh!
Some day your grandson will read on your tomb,
Here lies the King's poor fool: your epitaph.

ERNAND
ELLETTE

b. 1930

Aubade

Close your eyes
          as lightning
seeds the dark

Exile from space, a star
          falls out of the sadness
the silent depths
          into your dream

Our dull bodies
          catch fire in its light
as a country of birdsong
          lying along the dawn

What a forest of sounds
          over your silence
as long flower-flames
          purge rosy heel
the moons of knee and thigh

An absolute of song
          this love, our tears
lilac and glowing coals

Heavy with fruits
          fragments of infinite light
our body slips
          into the day's starvation

G. V. DOWNES

Psalms for Shelter

FERNAND
OUELLET

I

The gods were sleeping, loins shadowed in
   darkness
       the word
              brooding over the earth

Came the woman of dark lashes, death-bearer

And the echo of the falling star wounded
       the solitary ones
              the lamentation of the lightning
              burned their throats

Since then doubt has attacked the ivy
       the lilac is blind
       the sun unreadable

In the depths
             a stirring of the bone people
And the earth
       slowly
          tires

II

On this last day for man
           no sky at all, no gulls
reflected on the river . . .

O make your way
back to the heart of being with your star

In this time of falling sickness
hair, violet-sweet,
           rots on the shoulders
little breasts
       made for song
       melt into ashes

One evening, hope being quite dead
bodies turned into stones, hurled themselves
               into their nightmare

The heart no longer illuminated the seekers

And the soul of man, the dead soul
like a cloud of insects
ravaged the infinite

In the darkness of his head
who shall suffer a nest of light?

The sun, cold in his very depths
is breaking up

Who shall die in space
as falling snow
              from a megabomb?

FERNAND
OUELLETTE

G. V. DOWNES

50 Megatons

FERNAND
OUELLET

All things coming to an end
Easter
in vain tames the cold.

Oh the cantata of wheat.
where a day breaks
of black words!

Bearlike the angel
paws the dawn
it wheels round.

Aflame,
the spirit
faces
the mirror.

Run, o tightrope-walker,
your tinsel of frost.

The sun
espouses
      silence,
the atom
      death.

Eternity
     severs itself
          from man.

JOHN REEVES

Communion

FERNAND
OUELLETTE

Naked, she wove herself into the ferns
her hair a glad welcome for butterflies.
I was her rich mould, her hidden nutriment
the musician of her strings.
I set her apart from the gold the green the
    transparency.
My life in her shone out from her very eyes.

F. R. SCOTT

Angel

The angel impregnated the stone.

A long thread of silvery blood
flowed through the hardness of the landscape.
How the flowers all around
like elms wondered at growing.

And space, the impenetrable,
where the bird crashed
where the eye turned to stone,
in a shudder of the sky
split to its very soul.

F. R. SCOTT

Towards Dawn

FERNAND
OUELLET

My body speaks to you takes you
burying itself in the moments of your flesh.
So worn so bloodless is your dream
so leprous my infinite agony
of the exhausted beast.

For I never stop dying
preying on the beautiful jade in your soul.

The more you give yourself
the more I graze my flocks on peak after peak
but the valleys drag me down.

How terrified I am when I hear the dawn
that prowls and attracts me wanting me changed.

But I block my ears.

I never stop wanting to die.

F. R. SCOTT

GATIEN
LAPOINTE

b. 1931

The First Word

I say tree, but cannot grasp the word
Nor name the time which carries it;

I carry the world upon my shoulders,
A wing's touch makes me stagger.

Within me there's a suffering land,
In my mouth a word of blood;

I say blood, to challenge every death,
And to believe in the strength of man;

I carry man within my breath, my cry
Grows tall into the sky.

I carry in me a living cathedral
And all the sins of God;

My eyes look through the rifle's O :
My childhood is effaced in snow.

I do not know what I am,
But there's a quivering in me
Which will not go.

Upright, I shall be born within a word.

JOHN GLASSCO & DUGALD STEWART

Your Country

GATIEN
LAPOINTE

If you will open your eyes
And if you will lay your hands
On the snow, the birds, the trees, the beasts,
Patiently, softly,
With all the weight of your heart;

If you will take time by the hand
And look upon the land
Patiently, softly;

If you will recognize your people
And if you recognize the pain
Trembling upon the background of their eyes;

If you will write the words love and loneliness
Patiently, gently,
On every season, every house;

If you will name bread, blood, day, night
And that wild unalterable desire
Burning at the heart of all things;

If you will take every death of your childhood
Patiently, softly, in your arms,
With all the strength of your despair :

Then your country can be born.

Down to Earth

GATIEN
LAPOINTE

Enough of the sky, the sand, the faultless words
Enough of the panoply that dimmed my eyes!

Show me the violent and lovely world
Show me man learning his suffering
Learning the cold of the night that covers him
And the sun's yoke upon his neck
And homely hope and justice in excelsis
And all the dumb allegiance of the earth

Show me man generous and awkward too
Building his face up word by word
Mixing his pains and pleasures, dreams and
    memories
Flowers of his love and the accolade of dawn

Show me man building up his heart
Dew upon desert rest upon fatigue
With all the taste of roots within his mouth
And all the sap of the tree within his veins
And all the seasons and all the forests
Galloping through his flesh and blood

Show me man on the door-sill of his house
Making the tender and powerful music of the
    earth
The green and supple star on the left hand of
    woman
Rise at the gentle pressure of his hand

Show me man baptized in water
Lighting his household fire upon the hill
Show me man sharing oil and bread
The light of dawn and the tools of every day

Show me man also in the toils of doubt
Made in the beating of his blood
Seeking his double heart in the divided tree

Show me the image of juvescent man
Planting his body in all space and time
Giving the landscape his own face
Show me *this* man in my own land

I'll rise to the destiny which dwells within me
   then.

Le Chevalier de Neige (I)

We return by two and two from the heart of the
   land
We carry the newborn day upon our hands
My country is this fire burning beneath the snow
My country is this word in the hand of a child

Here we will draw the primal plan.

I have read the oracles in the eye of time
Mine is the natural gesture of the beasts

The primal dress to be remade
The primal need to overcome
The first horizon to overleap!

Our destiny's here among our countrymen
Out of my exile I have dreamed the way

The stirrings of the land within me
And the first song of the flesh
To make the prairie beautiful and the river serve
This immense space between the houses
Between the men
Towards what quarter shall we turn our hands
Shall fix our eyes upon what bleeding wound?

We stand upright in our dreams
Our tools shine in the dark

We'll lay our burning bodies on the snow
We'll breathe into the frozen heart of the springs
We'll take the fallen tree in our arms
We will compel the birth of spring

Shall we reach the seasons' end before we die?

Each evening at the horizon's base
Our bodies like two heaps of earth
Rediscover the primal love.

The first house to be warmed again
The first face to be named
And all this land to mould from dreams and blood!

Our faces burn in the living air of winter
And summer is a sun in haste to die

My country is all too much too far away
And our mouths are formless forests
And man is a road without plan or pattern
How should men be saved?

Our hope is a patient and inviolate tree
Our hands can bear the weight of the world

We will utter this country which our bodies know GATIEN
LAPOINTE
Utter the river's tameless flood
And the vast wind out of three oceans
We will utter the grief of every evening
And the weight of the march that man makes in
    the snow
And the cry of an animal in the lonely woods
Will be the cry we make while any breath is in us.

Each morning at the horizon's height
Our bodies like two living springs
Remould the primal landscape.

We have kindled fire in a drift of snow
A song is born in the hollow of our hands

Warmth of swelling seeds
Furrows like trembling lips
Day holding night in the arms of love!

Something will grow upon our naked faces
Images will blossom in the pupils of our eyes
Suffering will give us every word we need
We'll throw a deathless word into the world!

Our hands are the wings of birds
Our spring is a hard and blazing path
Shall we the living keep our despair alive?

How shall we name this day we enter?

I can see gardens in the eyes of women
And a great river where horses dream
I can see autumns longer than eternity

And springs more beautiful than heaven
I see the snow abolished by the hand of a child
As he writes his country's name upon the ground
I see a whole country rising from his hand!

GATIEN
LAPOINTE

Here we shall plant the primal word.

Homeland you my childhood's hands and eyes
You are rising now out of the heart of earth
The sun is touching your first bough
The sun is striking on your upturned face

And all your body already a tree in leaf!

Rue Saint-Denis

The bells ring out on sullen Saint-Denis
    where I drag in the new year the thirtieth of
    my life
The bells ring out on sullen Saint-Denis
    and I am alone and naked like a little man-
    child in his bare skin
The bells ring out on sullen Saint-Denis
    and ruffle the pale surface of the sleeping
    griefs
The bells ring out on sullen Saint-Denis
    and quietly my tired memory covers
    itself with the linen shroud of the snow

I know that the shadows under the staircases
    laugh at my dreams
It will come soon that thing which happened
    only to another
It will come soon that thing which happens only
    to me
The cold light at the end of the street raises an
    arm and signals me

I think of this street of my childhood I think of
    winter among the grey houses
I hear the sound of another world in this street
    where my steps are ending
It was yesterday it is now the same cramped
    despair that limps along on the ice
The same clumsy and threadbare story at Julie's
    the forgetting days afterwards

I think of those faceless loves forgotten I don't
    know where

JACQUES
BRAULT

The bells ring out on sullen Saint-Denis
Their cracked voices repeat my sordid hours
The fumbling hand like a brute at the lap of the
    little girl
The jaundiced grass on the lawns the splash of
    shit on the sidewalk
The damp stale cigarette the six o'clock sun on the
    shoulder
The street that makes a noise like old black
    pennies
And in every show-case a chrome print of my
    pain

Beggar of my loves swindler of my own days
I'm going away yes I'm going away for good
I'm going away with one hand feeling the warmth
    of the other

The bells ring out on sullen Saint-Denis
And their dissonance wakens in me an old and a
    new gentleness
That thing at the end of the street is not so
    terrible
That thing that's come there to call me with its
    unseeing eye

F. R. SCOTT

Knowing

I have in my mouth the honey of your mouth and
  of my body in your body
O unknown country my beautiful stranger of this
  love I do not know the name of your arms
around my neck like a night full of regal women in
  this unknown country
No do not speak let the breath of your breath
  breathe on my lips
Do not speak stay with your moans wholly my spar-
  row my captive
and my silence is in your eyes as a strange body I
  am absorbed in the water of your eyes
I am lost and search and roam in the kernel of your
  hair
I disappear in you O sleep of man O house of love
I die in you I have no face but your face and look
  you are grieving to die in me
You no longer exist I no longer exist   we are
  come and as one to our newness

F. R. SCOTT

JACQUES
GODBOUT

b. 1933

Et frotte et frotte

And rub and rub
and shine your shoes
till the leather gleams
like the tip of your nose
and sweat and sweat
and brush and buff
till the dust in the streets
disappears like a monkey
and search and search
under the worn-thin sole
where perhaps is stuck
a little truth
and take and keep
this searched-for stone
this immense medallion
an old shoe steps on

JOHN ROBERT COLOMBO

Enfant

JACQUES
GODBOUT

child
listen to father and mother
child
listen to brother and sister
child
cry not
break not
child
shout not
it's not nice
listen to what they say
listen to them they say
child
no one listens to you
it's best that way

JOHN ROBERT COLOMBO

Homme

Man
a sow
dirty and black mired in mud
a sow

sixteen children in her belly
man

pretty bad
dirty and black mired in mud
pretty bad
poor and alone upon the pavement

man
you knew once how it was to weep

JACQUES
GODBOUT

today you do not even want
to look her
in the eyes
the sow of truth

JOHN ROBERT COLOMBO

Elle est née

She was born
hand in hand
with a flower
she was born
flower of the desert
lonely as the pope
no azure lipped her door
she feared the water
as the child the father
or the werewolf
She was born beautiful
just as she was
without sap
without sap without pulse
until a gardener
only a little while ago
let loose the flood
a new flood
Now a new ark is needed
for this tiny flower
that I have placed
under glass

JOHN ROBERT COLOMBO

It's all a Matter of Décor

How does one say: Indonesia? How does one
    write:
Polynesia?
What does one drink in Korea?
What does China say? What does Japan sing?

It's all a matter of memory:
How do you kill memory?
With *papier-mâché* or water-colours?

She was wearing a beautiful crinoline, made
    entirely of rustling paper

In a wicker basket I dropped the passions
And flowers she had laced together.

How do you kill a name, your name?
And memory?

She never stopped smiling because she was talking
    another language
And because it was no use us trying to sleep in the
    sun! Memory!

Here's to your whims! Even when I wash my toes!
Indeed! When was the last time I took a bath
In such ice-cold water?
At the source of rivers? At Nathalie's?
In the Swiss snows of the mountain passes?

She nudges me, nudges me in the back
We have to know so much to die old
To exhaust the smile of hopeless waiting

It's all a matter of décor :   JACQUES
But it's fading like a hat.   GODBOUT
Who wants to kill memory ?

She burned the castles one by one;
She ate violets
(Whatever were her kisses? Colours of plums or
    scents of autumn?
Swedish perhaps, or Sudanese?)

Let me not forget!
The smell of the croaking man,
The look of the cobbler's shop,
A finger in the strawberry jam, a laugh
A joy
Tell me
How do you write : Memory? or Africa?
How do you say : Canada, Holland?
How do you say : I will not forget?

How does one know : We were in love?
How does one sing : I do not wish to die?

JOHN ROBERT COLOMBO

Trees

JACQUES
GODBOU

Trees we have given you a thousand names

In the hollow of a tree I've hidden a piece of
    money
When they're sixteen they'll find it

In the tree's flesh under the torn bark
I also cut Love liberty friendship fancy
Dignity disrespect
I would like to have written peace
But there was no room left.
Then I turned my head
The forest had lain down and under the sleeping
    treetrunks
Ready for the paper-mill the box-factory
The CIL plant and a hundred industries
I slipped your name   You   your name

I hid in a hollow tree
Watchful as a bobcat for the wind of footsteps.
When they're twenty they will find me
With my head between my knees
And my bones whitened from waiting for you
What will they make of my bones?
Toys perhaps
Or drawings on the sand

When the forest rises, as in a Shakespearean movie,
And walks
When the trees split the asphalt
In spurts of freedom
When the sequoias smother the buildings of steel
    (with vines and parasite moss on the switches
    and levers)
What will they make of my piece of money?

A goddess perhaps
Or a charm against ennui

JACQUES
GODBOUT

They'll see an army of blacks with brazen trumpets
Squatting over the fuse's end
To blow it up
To be borne off by sound borne off by the flesh

In the hollows of the trees they will find
An old homesickness for vines and drums

Trees we have given you a thousand names
And streets as well
The streets we love

In the tree's hollow in the street's shadow
In the stony gardens and the moss of courtyards
We have hidden a piece of money
And friendship so dear and love itself
While others were planning prisons
And forging the iron of their angelic hatred

Almond-trees   tender trees   bougainvilleas
We made love in your shadow

Today at noon perhaps you will whisper to us
The secret of light

MICHÈLE
LALONDE

b. 1937

Le jour halluciné

the hallucinated day disintegrates about my head
I am become a boat
my eyes are trout
I have slugs instead of hands
rusty crustaceans
in my seaweed hair

but I am a dead girl

I graze the edge of a deceiving coral
filled with gall and locked
like an oyster

I win to no watery clearing
under the hysterical eyeball of the sky

I kneel at the edge of the feverish beach
nothing now confirms the pristine illusion
of my supplication

the pernicious and mineral gesture of the sea
consummates on me its faithful erosion

I have no more to fear
but my own appeal
the cry of this other who is still asleep
perhaps
within the mirror

A. J. M. SMITH

MICHÈLE
LALONDE

O Long Slow Deliverance

O long slow deliverance

who will break our hempen bonds
we are weary slaves
and bands of steel surround our ivory foreheads
we were captured at dawn
like diaphanous prey

the inconstant circle of our broken arms
closes over the highest column of black marble
we are powerless
to loose ourselves from the chains
that clasp our bruised bodies
the paralysing wait exhausts us
solitude weighs on us
a heavy jar on the broken shoulder of the hours

and we founder
like flotsam
in the eddies of a sly sleep

with only our fatigue
for a shore

PETER MILLER

The Fiancée

And suddenly there was a massive tearing as if the
    landscape itself were splitting in two,
and then in a rush the world capsized before my
    eyes;
one moment and you were gone.

And I called to you, called to you, called and called
    with my piercing metallic cry which slashed the
    night with sonorous strokes.

But already you were distant and fading ahead,
    while I clung to your lonely and fugitive sil-
    houette still impressed in a fluorescent wake of
    sound,

Your lofty image moved by the magnetized larks,
    shoulders arched elbows stiff and pressed to your
    sides under the massive cloak of the mist . . .

Ah tell me again the name of the beloved that I may
    summon him, that I may call him by name and
    by his unique designation
for alone the intimate plea of my cry bereft of
    words is not enough! And the deaf appeal of my
    pounding heart (ah my heart provoking itself,
    exhausting itself like a too-ripe fruit on the
    arteries' stem!) the stifled speech of my straining
    heart no longer casts its spell.
What is the name of the fiancé that I may speak to
    him?

Ah if he turns to me but once I'll make him great
    despairing signs, my arms outspread and unsure!
The arched retreat of my arms awaits him and re-
    claims him!

Tell me his name again for I had forgotten it, having
    lost the habit of speaking in words to him, but
    only with the syllables of my violent heart . . .
Reveal to me the name of the fiancé that I may
    string it like an arrow to the straining bow of my
    cry!

ELDON GRIER

We Have Slept

we have slept a dreamless sleep
among the stalks
at the budding heart of the world

our hands woven like a tapestry
our gaze seeking the topless skies
our lips locked
on the endless mystery of our desires

o tender prayer
with a wordless throbbing of the heart
as of a mollusc
and in our veins
not blood
but ichor

and sea water
for tears

SUZANNE
PARADIS

b. 1937

The Rings

Under the trees we exchanged our rings : rings made
So large their circles would know how
To drop from our tired fingers into the grass or sand.
We wear no rings upon our fingers now.

We solemnized in a mysterious wedding-rite
Our passion freed like some mad criminal,
Blindly we ratified a cruel pact
Never to find our former jewels at all.

I can no longer accuse our broken vows :
We thought to leave no record of their demands.
Now the new graces of our parted fingers
Blaze in the night on our revalued hands.

Let the tide or the sand or the meadow-grasses take
Our abandoned rings and ancient enmities !
Our hands in the meadow are its only harvest,
We'll only gather it on our knees.

We scorned the righteous circlets and their golden
Bite on our torn fingers : these are things
We'll not appear with on the public squares
Where love shows hands covered with golden rings.

We exchanged the meek flesh of our naked hands,
Let slip the odious money of the world,
And learned to run on fenceless fields
In the radiance of unknown stars.

Shall we be forgiven our deceit of men,
The falsehood uttered all too willingly,
Oh in the name of perfect bonds, forgiven the lie
As if we'd told impossible truths of you and me?

Our rings will rust away in the nameless grass
Or perhaps, carried away by the meadow-brooks,
Perhaps they will go, as the partners of our crime,
To swell those treasures rusting in the sea.

And softly our hands will make their claim on the future,
On the faceless happiness of wordless promises,
Those eternal dreams which no explicit ring
Could ever hold upon our submissive hands.

Lest we should find again, even in memory,
The sands or the pebbles or the doubtful springs
Wherein these storyless jewels are forever sleeping,
We exchanged invisible rings.

b. 1937

They Shine

They shine like wet jewels
the high flaming trees
O the trees shed leaves
around and about

like lost jewels
the trees

O the flaming trees all around the water
where your face
turns to ice
where your lost fingers and their gestures
crack and crumble and fade
with your inexhaustible body
and the exhausted leaves.

O   the trees like huge cries
redder than a million autumns
O   the leaves will slowly rot
even to the black spots
unmoving   .

And you my own dead love
even more dear in death
among these springs that slowly turn to ice

Tell me will the snow-drops pierce
through maples that bleed, these rotting leaves?
Will they find their voices again, these lakes,
                    these needles

Under the frozen trees?

YVES
PRÉFONTAINE

Without tears eyes are in agony

and then winter
winter where your death
lies in my veins
colder than snow

G. V. DOWNES

An Enormous Anguish

An enormous anguish is bleeding in the fall's
    shadow
Fruits shrivel as soon as ripe

This woman has no words but of live coals in
    the hearth
While man takes on alone the cold's hostility
And all wounds made across the face of his earth
He persists in sowing

This woman only babbles words
While man withers where he stands
Defenceless hands and breast
His entire body welcoming
The huge fissure of a country with no language.

G. V. DOWNES

Country to Let

I live in a land where cold has conquered green things, reigns grey and heavy over phantom trees.

I am a silent part of a race that shivers in its sleep under frost-bound words, whose frail quick speech is fading.

I am part of a cry all around me
stone with no language
steep cliff
bare blade in my winter heart

My country is quietly strangling under a snow of fatigue.

Yet I go on dreaming dreams,
persist in speaking,
but the wound has no echo,
for the daily bread of a race is its speech
and no light comes from rotting grain.

I am rooted in a people that has lost its roots,

And fields that would smile in the sun are shrinking under so many dry seasons, so many ungarnered sheaves.

I am part of an exhausted cry, weary of beating, banging, hammering against these walls, these masks that spit disdain.

I walk with the ghost of a race brushed off like an uncomplaining whore.

Round and round I go in this wilderness,
ringed by a cloud of white and furious faces.

I live in a land that is a statue sheathed in
ice.

Like a woman, it stirs my blood, but no fire
touches the lips of its men,

And so, teeth clenched, I rage against poverty
of spirit with words whose brief light flares up only
to die.

G. V. DOWNES

The River's Blood and Sap . . .

Rising in the River's blood and sap I hear the
song of tomorrow, of my country tall as a red pine,
blazing in a fire of pride on cold American sands.

Louder and louder at the headwaters grows
the murmur of the gagged men; soon torrents will
thunder from our feverish throats.

And I shall not be a single red pine consumed
in vain, but a living flame whirled by the winds
from tree to tree, until along the shores of the River
of Speech a whole forest is burning.

G. V. DOWNES

The Harsh Country

YVES
PRÉFONT

Harsh

too many stones on the horizon
too much dark water in pitted lakes

Harsh

for water and stones do not slake man's longing for earth

Man stands upright, planted firmly in the
soil, his legs like trunks of forest trees reseeding
after fire. Even though he drives the tainted breath
of his cities into hostile ground, no speech is left to
him.

Words die on his lips like melting snow.

Harsh
for victory, so that across this sky with its
eternal dark stain of priests and masters may flash,
triumphant, the taut lightning from a man's hand.

Harsh
like hard ice, before wild April awakens the
seeds of life, even in the veins of corpses.

G. V. DOWNES

Ends (I)

Something is missing
in the mirror
perhaps the blue hangings
in the salon perhaps a priest
perhaps the crucifix

to flee to flee
to search
the head in this mass of rotting
leaves to seek an odour
the autumn one has never seen
a known face
one had thought forgotten

to read in the intricacies of the carpet
the flaking plaster from the wall
a tale   the life of a dead man
say nothing
for fear of being unjust
think nothing even
read and reread
but always alas barely
I am afraid to leave
this skin dying at the end of my
fingers near the nails
this dead skin falling
these yellow spots on the shins
we live so little
we must go so far
and the time we need
and the heart

R. A. D. FORD

For Maria

GÉRALD
GODIN

There's a plaster star on the ceiling of our white
    room
'when I die I want the smell of whisky all over the
    place
and I wanna sit on the knees of the finest female-
    angel of them all'
I'm longing for french speak french to me maria
in central park an old man with white hair
is he dreaming like me maria as I'll dream of you
    in a thousand years
of a girl he loved once
maria
I'll drop the anchor of my lips in you
forever drunk forever motionless   my arms like
    roots
rusty anchor of my ancient loves
I'll haul it up when my dead and gutted sea
    needs nothing
but the cold lightnings of the absent sun maria
my arms remembering better than I do the ragged
    beach
and the new ship that I was and come a long way
like a cry out of the storm and the rubble of wind
remembering the surf of love breaking
on the joint of the cross that we are   we'll go on
    forever joined
maria
my girl of the breastlets
breastlets maria that's the breasts of a young girl
yes it's a new word I was the one who found it
it was in your blouse
maria my starched
bride

spindle of my marvellous days
o one and only spindle   crossroads

of our four wishes
my dread voyage
my night my heart
o my mythology
maria my sweet my dark one
o my lies
o the keys to my dreams   my church of grey
    images
my far-off island my locust-tree my package tour
maria in the dark night
maria my composite bride
made up of all my loves
draw the curtain over our hearts
my finger walks on your arm   you take my hand
a spatter of spent desire runs through our veins
maria my soul I'll forget you my dark one
you'll draw the curtain over your memory
leaving me at the door   I'll forget you
as I take these clouds my memories by the neck
in their inverted image
before I drown in them
no one will see maria no one will see anything till
    the end of time
except my laughter glinting in the sun
but the words untied in my throat
the words maria
even spoken without me the words will call you

A. J. M. SMITH & JOHN GLASSCO

Cantos (I)

GÉRALD
GODIN

Where do we get pleasantly drunk
chpréchen zie frantsozich?
they don't think much of me
when I want to think
they talk to me they never stop
talking to me

I'll have it all set up the day before
you got eyes like a shroud
she'll say to me
pouring the milk with a swish
into my coffee

chomebody chtole my gal
qui c'est qu'a pris ma gale
de menteur deux fois prévenu
who's this
you look a-like chomebody I knew
mon âme perhaps

he's so young maria
maybe we shouldn't tell him
tell him everything
qu'ils ont l'âme propre
such a lovely sexless
girl

they've got the souls of boy scouts

GÉRALD
GODIN

the carriage of monsieur baudelaire is ready
    steady
that bloody coachman who is always plastered
to hell with the boy-scout types!
der tee ist gütt
dear lady I put off my soul
to put you off your guard

in what drawing-room and how
to undertake to overtake your heart
god if I weren't so fed with
the run of the mill
I'd tell you things, words
to make you leave your cup of tea

another drink for the gentleman
he's so nice
the carriage is ready steady
auf wiedersehen
my lovely lady
oh! to uncover your soul
fold by fold
like a girl doing her ironing

A. J. M. SMITH & JOHN GLASSCO

PAUL
CHAMBERLAND

b. 1939

The Time of Hatred

FOR ANDRÉ MAJOR
FOR JEAN-MARC PIOTTE
FOR PIERRE MAHEU

I

bullets some morning through the stained-glass
    window
the heart stops beating
beautiful rhythms twirl through the plundered
    vestry of images

goodbye I've had my say   deconsecrated now the
    pure poem's moonstruck carrousel
the beautiful soul's lorgnette rusts in a puddle
    where I drank the dawn of cities
goodbye goodbye to the day of a princess in a
    white castle . . .
here I am naked now as the roadside grass
already at home on the streets of every day

II

I've broken the mirror of poetry shattered that
    image on the wall
I'm casting my eyes my forehead and my bare
    fists in the mould of a naked wind howling
    through chinks of anger
and nothing nothing can shield me ever again
    from the anguish of my people

naked I walk   remote in a bloodless silence
    where the fusillade-poem is arming itself to the
    teeth

already from the broken toy the hum of the image PAUL
CHAMBERLAND
   is dying and merging in the shrapnel-bark of
   the future
poetry is helved and quivering in the same wood
   as the knife

a man of dirt I walk the common way
I am silent and under my skull I hear the crackling
   hailstorm of footsteps in the cannon of the
   streets
I am the poster from which your blood has
   spurted my comrades spattering the night of
   the traitors
and revenge's peep of day

ELDON GRIER

The Land Between Us (II)

'Parce que je suis en danger de moi-même à toi et tous
deux le sommes de nous-mêmes aux autres.'—GASTON
MIRON

sweet were the springtimes yes
brackish-sweet the springs of my land
a slow malaise of coal would pass between our
   bodies yes
I'd love you I'd suffer   the suns were all
   imprisoned
a slow ashen sickness would slake the dawn
   between our teeth remember
I would go to your lips as to the spring

247

and always on the speechless path would fall the PAUL CHAMBERI
   mortally wounded shadow
of the one landscape of our love
o you and I riverbanks forever apart on the
   infinite mourning of docks
and the exile of the long-drawn bird-cry drowned
   in daybreak's pool

ELDON GRIER

Between Flesh and Silence

I

The world   only a movement
the world   or something
a movement of tables or maybe of lips

I draw you out of the shadows to which I
   bequeathed you
once again out of that prison of finely wrought
   hours
where I hid like a useless insect

the soft pressure of the mountains in the
   approaches of your hand
the soft strong presence of the hills gliding in your
   loins
I map my repose in the darkness of your thighs

look at me
some day you will be a host
and we will plot on squared paper the curve of
  our accord

look at me
never has day so looked at night
now you are the free instant of all yesterdays and
  tomorrows
twenty years I have paced the dark corridors of
  waiting
you are the city of our whole future   the movement of my body was always only a single leap
  towards you
an ice-floe melts in the mirror of your palms

I am born
an insect sanctified in the pollen and sun's arrows
I take you and hold you in a city which turns to a
  rose around you
Infinite woman   under a robe of caresses suddenly
  you flame in the heart of opposed destinies
you are the bridge where the jets of childhood are
  abolished
you are the X-ray of my stupor
I hear my own revolt in you   I am the source of
  the rainbow which rises from your thigh and
  crowns tomorrow with a thousand lily-of-the-
  valley-tipped cries of laughter

Legend of the Morning

PAUL
CHAMBERL

Today,

you will forget to be afraid

fear may whiten the prisoner's temples, you will
   not be afraid
you will see that memory has
   become an endless surface, a depth of the resins
   the atoms and the salts crying out under the
   tread of Noon

Today,

on the children's fingers are spinning

                 magnetic Sundays
                 holidays of sugar
                 light itself

Today,

the horizon is table of meals and marvels
bed of amorous delay
lawn with the blue depths of childhood
pert little miracles

                 daffodils
                 glittering mica
                 snakes
                 catbirds
                 whitethroats

the scaffoldings of dawn perfume the future

wood is good
water is pure

the garden of cool hands revolves   PAUL
CHAMBERLAND
young mothers in a tizzy
rings of nylon
sunflowers
silken hysteria

we hear the rivers brawl
the barrage resound

the hormone spawns its miracles

                    rainbow trouts
                    golden globes
                    cloudbursts of crystal

hidden salt quivers at the joyous quick
symphonic altitudes
stairs of odours
and the oil of winter games

we dream the lovely sea
with its cabins of softest moss

we dream

                    of the chords lips make in the
                        forests
                    the twinkling of winds
                    the merry-go-rounds of noon
                    the runways into space

we dream

Open Shutters

PAUL
CHAMBE

I would live for a moment in this music
like a child I would lick the windowpane
whence the sun leads his gardens out to pasture
and the night her gardens into sleep

on the way

I would pass through the season the fruit
the lucky sentinel and the bread
my steps barely heard
in the burning meadow of your laughter
like stars quivering above your sleep

I would return without memory
to the black bellies of the fountains
where night sleeps in the womb of day
and would be a god against my will

in the climate of your summer

in the ring-star soft on your finger
I see the season   the city   the season turning
time lowering its eyelid over your eye
and the flower's violet heart reddening your flesh
    setting your mouth ablaze
where I drink the wounded healed world

I love you and the earth is silent at your feet like
    a ewe asleep
I love you and the sky reflects its mirrors in your
    cloudy smile
comes the rain   and your body a sun through the
    rain
the world a flower which quivers at your breasts

the things which are born in the pathway of your
    fingers

never will I remake their design
save in the splendour of the lamps paired
above your sleep beneath my kiss

my cupped hands framing the light of your face
I a hunter on the trail of the nights turned pale
reforging on our lips the ring of our seasons

PAUL
CHAMBERLAND

ANDRÉ
ROCHU
b. 1942

The Chalice, the Egg, and the Knife

FOR GILLES MARCOTTE

He walked with his head between his knees
And heaven around his waist
Like a balletdancer's skirt
His bum on view his eyes softboiled

He juggled with a chalice
A boiled egg and a knife

The knife broke the eggshell
The egg dropped in the chalice

And ever since then Catholics
When you meet them in the street
Or at the theatre
Clap their hats over their bum

A Child of my Country (I)

ANDRÉ
BROCHU

I'm through with songs

And until yesterday I'd sing—from daybreak on—
    from mother to poem that's not too far
In fact it's hardly the width of a dust-speck hardly
    the clawing of a kiss
On the blue-shot window
Joy splintering like rain

But false was my joy
False the poem rooted in wordless clods of
This land without a landscape
False was that mother with the grooved talons
And my joy tied to the fingers of a thousand
    absent things

Mother you handed me naked into the thorns
Broken from my seasons
You poured your kerosene and neglect on the
    faggots of my destiny
You left my soul a gaping wound defenceless
I was riveted to the terror of my rabbit-warren
Evilly walled away in the cages of frost

I'm through with songs with enchantment too

Why should I sing the harvests which are denied
    me
The love and moonlight-coloured paradises
Love can never be mine I know I'm earth-coloured
I've an ash-coloured ass and my heart
Is brimming with curses against you God
No love will ever be waiting on the curve of my
    years
My country's sold her honour and her bread

I haven't a soul to lose and heaven's just too tough   **ANDRÉ**
   a climb   BROCHU
I've only the terror of being too useless
Each cry disfigures my image
Each silence
I've only my hope to throw to the dogs
I murdered my mother one spring night
I've only my country to love   to renounce

My homeland O my shame

But also   now   and still
There's heritage rising in revolt
But also   now   and still
There's the thundering threat of the children's
   bombs

ELDON **GRIER**

Daybreak

When dawn takes fire
In a wind of curdled grass
In a silence of water and stones
Woman puts her nature off
To frolic with the birds of air
Thrushes nest within her lap
Her hair is matter of dispute
For chickadees for orioles
And warblers ring her finger-ends

But soon as man appears
With his two hands full of desire
She sheds her feathers one by one
And lies before him bare as stone

My Word is Green

in our sickness we would say
'it is the sea which moulds the profile of the
    shore
and if winter comes we'll live in its season
    quietly'

—like slaves we would not see our chains—

this country's sickness wrenched the greenness
    out of me
(I speak of a land so cold it feeds the frosts
I speak for the poor who curse her
I speak for the simple who pass through the
    machine and are squeezed dry)

without pride or fear
the blood freed of its solitude
fears not the failure of all the winds

my country lonelier than our pangs
ravaged by cold by cross by silence
we have outlived the retreat of the ice
we have outlived death

(I delight in greenery again
in the winds on beaches
in kisses)

I am the song and the broken sweep of the week
the egg in the morning and the coffee

I rejoice only in the pleasure of being loved by the
     sun
this is the kind of man I am
when not knocked down by my brothers'
     breathing

I am as open as a tornado
as a wounded bird
at the same time I am a bull among the bugs
when free as fire I love the passer-by
—my eyes dimmed with dreams
I break my heart in a kiss—

you my dear who live in the meek laugh of the
     maple tree
   my hands give you more light than daybreak
   summer the vigour of fir-trees the perfume of
     your smile
   you commit my love to the noon's heat and I am
     renewed
this is the weather of breasts
froth to suckle our kisses
this is the weather of places where murmurs of
     caresses burn

the cruel landscape lives within me
and green is my word green
—a wound I give my country—

JOHN ROBERT COLOMBO

Words

ANDRÉ
MAJOR

When we lie together as leaves enfolded
our words are sharply beautiful,
wounding as memory,
holding us, shaken,
in an amazing dream

no longer together
our words
lie like tears

and your hand
passes like a comet
touching my dark with its radiance

Such leafing space between your eye and mine!

G. V. DOWNES

After Nightfall

leafy hands
hands   her heart's wealth
the woman shares
in her island's overthrow
when I fall like a storm
like a bird of prey

and the snow coming upon us
limb to limb
and the cold sheltering us
each in the other
like grass in the dew
fire in the log

such am I
o idolized world of your arms
of your lap
such am I
in the halcyon
of a perfect night
the sorrow of being man
is dust blown away in the burning
of my breath
my boundless desire
swelling to a single touch of yours

your island is my lair
what joy to return
after the fall of night
when midnight howls
in my veins

you know that nothing is as true
as pleasure
as the bird quivering
in the sullen country of your island

so by our own magic
we escape from winter
and its terrible loneliness
to dwell within this night
this shell of tawny summer

    I am lulled upon your thigh
and your tender wrist beats like a heart
against my throat

ANDRÉ
MAJOR

Index of Poets

262

Index of Translators

268